Making The Most Of It

Making The Most Of It

An Odyssey During the Pandemic

Jim LeMay

CITIOFBOOKS, INC.
3736 Eubank NE Suite A1
Albuquerque, NM 87111-3579
www.citiofbooks.com
Hotline: 1 (877) 389-2759
Fax: 1 (505) 930-7244

Ordering Information:

Quantity sales. Special discounts are available on quantity purchases by corporations, associations, and others. For details, contact the publisher at the address above.

Printed in the United States of America.

ISBN-13:   Softcover   979-8-89391-116-9
                  Ebook   979-8-89391-117-6

Library of Congress Control Number: 2024909686

Table of Contents

Making the Most of It: An Odyssey during the Pandemic by Jim LeMay is a story about a guy named Conrad Colby. He is a 25-year-old man who has lost everything because of a deadly bacteria and the only survivor of his family lineage. His story is an adventure to claiming back life and making it meaningful and purposeful. Leaving the past behind but never forgetting it, he ventures on the road toward his future.

~ P.G.

This was one of those reads that you find yourself relishing the next day's happening in the lives of its characters. I was pleasantly surprised at times to find that my anticipation of the outcome of one event or another turned out totally different than I had imagined…. I would recommend this book to anyone who enjoys good writing, interesting outcomes, and a hint into what the world will (more than likely) someday experience.

~ M. G.

Author's Note on the Rise of Antibiotic-resistant Bacteria

I first became aware of the advent of antibiotic-resistant bacteria some time in the mid-'90s. I read a newspaper article about a teenager in Mozambique with bubonic plague. Fortunately, the boy recovered. I thought that disease had been wiped out by antibiotics decades before. But perhaps it appeared in developing countries because of inadequate medical care or unhygienic conditions. The article made me curious enough to watch for related ones. By the turn of the new century, I saw that the rise of antimicrobial-resistant bacteria, even in developed countries, could no longer be denied. According to the <u>US Centers for Disease Control and Prevention (CDC)</u>, over 2.8 million Americans become infected with these pathogens every year and more than 35,000 of them die. Many others die of conditions complicated by these infections. I know some of the casualties; the epidemic has passed beyond the realm of science fiction.

The unicellular ancestors of bacteria, the first life forms on Earth, appeared about 4 billion years ago. For over 3 billion years practically all organisms were microscopic. Bacteria and archaea remained the dominant life forms. Today, they live everywhere, in the soil, water, rocks, in hydrothermal vents and cold seeps, under the deepest part of the ocean. They live in symbiotic and parasitic relationships with plants and animals and aid in the decomposition of our bodies after we die. Their biomass exceeds that of all plants and animals on Earth. In one of his articles, paleontologist Stephen Jay Gould said that referring to different periods of life as the Age of Reptiles, the Age of Mammals, etc. was wrong. Earth had had only one Age: That of Bacteria.

The first multicellular creatures finally made their appearance about 600 million years ago. The first hominids lived in Africa less than 6 million years ago. Man in his present form has been here for around 200,000 years.

During all their time on Earth, bacteria have evolved new means of adapting to changing conditions. They could write the book on evolution. Antibiotics have been around for less than a hundred years. They don't evolve at all. Who do you think is best equipped to win?

So, bacteria's victory over antibiotics seems inevitable. Yet, if a worldwide pandemic results, it probably won't prove dystopian in the long run. We will most likely return to the way we lived in the pre-antibiotic times of less than a hundred years ago. That will seem horrific enough for a generation or two. The mortality rate among mothers giving birth will rise. Few people will choose to have elective surgery because of the danger of infection. But we'll adapt. After all, we lived that way for our first couple hundred thousand years as Homo sapiens.

Yet, the appearance of a superbug that kills 80% to 90% of mankind is not out of the question. It has happened before. Just ask the pre-Columbian Americans. This future history explores the way at least some survivors might learn to live with their sense of loss and despair.

Despite the book's grim-sounding theme, I hope the reader finds it not without a measure of optimism and a dollop of humor.

One – Doc's Feast-Wagon

Gloria holds out her arms to him, looks at him with longing. He asks, Why did you leave? Will you stay with me now? She smiles sadly, shakes her head and seems to say, You must come find me. You promised. He reaches for her but she moves away, arms still extended. She grows pale, no, begins to fade away. Somehow, he knows she's desperately trying to stay. I have to leave now, Con. Her figure attenuates to translucence. When it's time, come find me. Promise me. He can scarcely see her. She smiles wanly. Then I'll always be with you. And then disappears.

Con awoke suddenly, haunted by Gloria's sad, slowly fading smile.

Yes, love, he thought. You bet I'll come find you.

He sat up. The ghostly pre-dawn light gave shape to the dark, slumbering forms around him. He heard a few snores and the quiet snap of the tarpaulin overhead in a slight breeze. He usually slept until they woke him but knew the dream wouldn't let him sleep. Still tired and already sweaty, he scooted on his butt between the bodies, afraid of stepping on somebody in the dark if he stood.

He finished in the latrine but didn't return to the "dormitory," too noisome from unwashed bodies, his and theirs. They would have a little water that evening, though. Every third day, they got enough to wash themselves and their clothes. A few, like him, used some to shave, the last bit of civilization he clung to.

After the usual breakfast of unidentifiable gruel, he and the others spent a long morning excavating the ditch and wheelbarrowing the sand away. They mounded some against the stockade enclosing the settlement and wasted some in the desert.

Then, siesta: a brief lunch and sleep, this time without dreaming, from noon until the bosses awakened them. More digging and soil-moving followed.

The dream stayed with him, reminding him of jocular talks about love and death with Gloria. She would say, "I love you, love you, love you. And then some more. If we're still around somewhere after we die, you have to come find me." He would answer, laughing, "Of course, Babe." "Promise me." "I promise." Of course, the two twenty-somethings saw death as an abstraction. In those pre-pandemic days, their lives stretched into a distant, misty future.

Keeping track of everything around him had kept Con alive since the pandemic ended, over three months since August. Like watching the rifle-bearing guards on the ramshackle tower just inside the stockade wall. The bosses assured the ditch diggers they weren't there to spy on them but to protect them from wandering, starving foragers. Con knew the guards had both missions as well as keeping the digging men and villagers apart. Twenty-some single men could cause trouble inside the walls of such a small community.

Of course, they couldn't tell how many lived in Hardy Town because of its stockade. People came and went from a gate on the south side, invisible to the ditch diggers working on the west side. Some, mostly women, came out to weed the gardens and corn field. Others, usually youths, wheeled a fifty-five-gallon drum down to the creek on a contraption slapped together from wood and plastic scraps mounted on bicycle wheels. They filled it and watered the gardens' sickly-looking vegetables and the corn field's anemic stalks or sometimes took it into the village.

That afternoon, a sandstorm hid the sky for a while but didn't affect them so deep in the ditch. It did the dormitory, though. After work ended a little before dark, they found their quarters covered in dun-colored grit. Most of them felt too tired to even cuss the storm, so they only took their pallets outside to shake the sand out.

Then they lined up in front of the paymaster to accept the day's chits: round bits of leather with a "$" stamped into them. Each earned twelve chits a day, less eight for meals. That day, two more came out for water. With only a few minutes under the shower, they remained dressed to scrub bodies and clothes at the same time, and Con and some others to shave. The water put them all in a better mood. Then supper, the only meal with a scrap of meat.

Temporary structures for the workers, including a dormitory, dining room and tavern, consisted of patched tarpaulin roofs held up by poles. Only their ditch latrine had flimsy board and plywood walls. Mayor John Hardy had hired the men to construct a ditch from the creek to the gardens and cornfield. Con had arrived and started work about halfway through the job. He knew it would only last a few more weeks. Hardy and the sub-bosses had assured them of more future projects, but Con distrusted such vague promises. He planned to leave soon in any case. He had worked six days, saving every chit left after paying for food and water, a total of twenty. He needed enough to buy food for the next leg of his journey, which would ultimately take him to Tin Cup, Colorado, high in the Rocky Mountains. Those workers who were not too tired went to the tavern every evening to blow their remaining chits. Each one bought two beers. Con decided to sacrifice the two he had left from that day's pay at the tavern.

Full dark had fallen by the time he and the others reached the tavern. On the way, to his surprise, he saw a vehicle's headlights approaching along the dirt road from Interstate 15 to the west. Powered by an electric motor or fuel cells like most modern vehicles, it made no sound. He wondered where the driver had found a power station to charge it or fuel cells.

A guy named Wade walking beside Con saw his surprise. "That's Doc Drennan. Brings most of our food from California. The gardens here don't grow enough for everybody yet."

The vehicle drew near enough for the gibbous moon and the stars to reveal it as a dune buggy pulling a cart. It moved in fits and starts until finally grinding to a halt. The driver got out with some tools, jacked the left side of the front end up and messed around with the wheel. A couple of everlight-bearing men came out from the town to help him.

Entering the tavern for the first time, Con saw a bar in the rear with a keg sitting on one end and the bartender perched on a high stool behind it. A few benches and rickety chairs completed the furnishings. When Con's turn came in the line of thirsty workers, the bartender, Wiley, extracted a glass pint canning jar from beneath the bar. He filled it from the keg and exchanged it for Con's chit. Seeing Con's expression at the beer's skunky smell, he said in a flat voice, "It smells better than the lot of you."

"Yeah, Con," said Wade. "But drink it fast before it starts to smell as bad as Wiley."

Con sipped tentatively. The warm beer tasted like wet cardboard with an underlying sourness. Con didn't know much about brewing but assumed producing a decent beer in a hot climate without refrigeration verged on the impossible. Sensing Wade, Wiley and the others watching him with half-smiles and smirks, he drank a healthy slug and let out a satisfied sigh.

"Best beer I've had in months," he said.

The drinkers hooted.

"Then it's the only beer you've had in months," said a big guy named Ed, slapping him on the back.

"True."

"But hey, guys," said a little man named Howard. "Did you know about the man from Vegas?"

No one had.

"What about him?" said Wade. "It's been forever since we heard any news from up there."

"And how the hell did you hear about somebody from Las Vegas?" asked Ed.

Howard said, "I saw him when I was wheelin sand around to the front of the stockade. By the gate, tryin to get the guard to let him inside. The guard's sayin they don't let nobody in, specially from a city. Says he might be boss. The man's sayin, nobody up there's infected. The infected ones is all dead. The man's sayin he's dyin a thirst, he has to have some water, and he's starvin. He looked it, too. The guard finally gave him his own canteen to drink out of. The man woulda swallowed it all in one gulp, but the guard made him take it easy. Else he'd a puked it all up.

"Then Boss Phelps came out of the gate and chewed the guard out for givin the man a drink. Says he could get infected drinkin after the guy. They stood there arguin for a while with the poor man watchin em. Finally, somebody came out and gave the man a bottle of water and a loaf of bread and told him to go on his way.

"Then Boss Phelps came over and hollered at me, said what the hell was I doin standin around with my thumb up my ass and suchlike. So I got out."

The group began to speculate on whether Chou's Disease could still spread. Con didn't join in but he doubted it. The majority of people who got the Disease had died. Those who survived seldom got it again, though a few who did, like Con, suffered a milder version the second time. It seemed to Con that if a pathogen ran out of victims it would perish.

"What about the children?" said Wade, his mouth drawn in a tight line. "Them and the old people went first. If there's any kids left up in Vegas, they're dyin' right now." He slammed his half-finished beer down on the bar so hard a little slopped out and stormed out of the tavern.

Ed shook his head. "Wade watched his little'ns die, then his wife. You shouldn't've brought the Disease up, Howard. You know we don't mention it. Now, let's all shut up about it."

But a pall of gloom had settled over the assemblage. Almost all of them had lost family. Conversation flagged. Con sat apart, surrounded by his own ghosts. He blamed the slight buzz he felt after finishing the beer on unavoidable abstinence over the last few months and weariness from the long days of hard work. While nursing a second beer, he happened to look out back toward the dirt road. The dune buggy had gone. The driver had apparently got it working again and taken it and its precious cargo into the village.

As he sipped his third beer, a short, white-haired middle-aged man he hadn't seen before swept into the tavern, a guy with a fair, round face, flushed pink by the heat. The others verified Con's guess at his identity by hailing him as "Doc." His appearance dispelled much of the drinkers' melancholy. He waved and smiled on his way to the bar. Wiley had a beer ready for him. Doc gulped a third of it down, grimaced and shook his head.

He said, "My God, Wiley, what do you put in this shit, dead skunks?"

In his monotone, Wiley said, "Secret recipe. Includes eye of newt and dick of salamander."

"If it did," said Doc. "It'd taste better." Seeing Con, he grinned. "Hey, here's a new guy."

Shaking Doc's outthrust hand, Con said, "Conrad Colby. Call me Con."

"I'm Doc Drennan."

Ed said, "I see you're still having trouble with your Feast-wagon, Doc."

Doc winced. "It's this damned sand. It gets in everything and it's hard to clean out. I gotta work on it all day tomorrow so I can head out the next day. I don't know how to keep the sand from getting in."

Ed said, "Ain't you scared of hungry vagrants if it breaks down on the road?"

"Who'll leave you bleedin out in the ditch?" said someone else.

Doc laughed. "That's why I tried to hire one of you candy-asses to ride shotgun with me."

"We had enough scrapes before we got here," said Howard. "This ain't no good life but we are alive."

"Then you'd better hope I make it back here with the food every time or you guys'll get mighty hungry." He finished his beer, belched and said, "That 'n didn't kill me, Wiley. Let's see if another one will." He handed Wiley his jar.

"I'd be glad to look at your buggy," Con said, "If you have a steady light."

"My everlights are burnt out. It'll take a day in the sun to bring them back to life. I haven't found a competent mechanic to look at it. Are you a mechanic?"

"Sort of. I used to work on small appliances, mostly those that ran on solar power."

"Well, it wouldn't hurt having you look at it. How bout doing that tomorrow?"

"I think Messrs. Phelps and Catlin have other plans for me."

Doc waved a hand dismissively. "They're just straw bosses. They'll let you off for me. There's enough guys digging the ditch. Meet me here at the tavern in the morning, a little later than you go to work. Wiley doesn't open till the digging stops. He doesn't have any customers till then, so he lets me work under the shade of his tarp. I guess that's still okay, Wiley?"

The bartender nodded. "As long as you don't drip disgusting fluids on the floor."

"Speaking of disgusting fluids, Wiley," said Howard. "How 'bout another beer?"

Con asked Doc, "How do you wrangle getting me off work?"

"I bring Hardy Town free food. John Hardy won't ruin a deal like that. He tells everybody to let me do whatever I want, have everything I need. And I'll pay you twice what John does.

"Hey, Wiley, give all these guys a beer on me, will you? I don't think one more round of your acid'll kill us."

✳ ✳ ✳

Con got up with the other ditch diggers for breakfast, then dozed under the shade of the tavern's tarp. The faint hum of electric motors and the crunch of heavy tires on sand awakened him. He sat up to see Doc smiling through the vehicle's windshield. He stood, walked over to it and greeted Doc.

Doc nodded. "Morning, young fellow. What do you think of my rig?"

Someone had built the buggy from scratch using formed and welded steel tubing. The open sides revealed a sturdy-looking roll cage with two bucket seats in the front and a bench seat in a cage-like structure in the back. Behind the roll cage was a long trunk lid. Solar panels covered the roof. Con assumed the small compartment in the front held the motor. The vehicle's large wheels with wide tires looked like they would fit a Mars rover. Its nose sported a sturdy winch.

"Built it myself," said Doc. "Look it over." He got out and joined Con in a walk around the buggy and cart. He had emblazoned "A Moveable Feast" in red on both sides of the cart. Hence, Ed's comment about Doc's "Feast-wagon."

Doc said, "I left the doors off so you could get a better view." He raised the trunk lid to reveal two spare tires, a jack and several metal boxes Con assumed contained tools, all held in place by steel straps. Doc tugged on a couple of straps to show how tightly they fit. "I do some pretty rugged off-roading." He opened the hood over what Con had guessed held the motor to reveal an empty compartment. "I stow my personal crap in here when I travel."

Con put hands on hips and said, "Okay, I give up. How do you power this thing?"

Doc smirked, proud of himself. "I figured the system out myself, though I'm sure others have too. Look inside the steel cage behind the front seats. I fill it mostly with medicines and breakables I pick up in California to keep em more secure. See that steel box welded to the floor?"

"Yeah?" The box sat in front of the narrow, barely two-person bench seat.

"That's the battery pack. The solar panels," He pointed to the roof, "charge it."

"And then?"

"And then, by means of wiring that runs through the body's steel tubing, the batteries power these electric motors." He knelt beside the driver's side front wheel. He had parked with the wheel skewed to show the area behind and expose a motor in a steel-mesh basket next to the wheel.

Doc stood, panting slightly, his fair face reddening from the heat. "Those motors are the weakest part of the system. The sand gets inside em and I have to change em out on the road and clean them when I get a chance. I carry a half-dozen spares in the trunk."

So, at least some of the steel boxes in the trunk held spare motors.

"What would happen if things got too hot on the road to change them?" Con was thinking of the hungry vagrants Ed had mentioned.

Doc shrugged. "Happens sometimes. Then I cripple along on three wheels as best I can."

"What would happen if you lost two wheels?"

Doc grinned. "Boss Hardy's folks'd get mighty hungry."

Con shook his head. "Seems like depending on solar power causes a lot of problems. Like limited range and speed, accessories draining the battery, weather problems. You can't drive at night. What do you do on cloudy days? What if a bunch of starving maniacs attack you when it's raining?"

"Taking the latter first, you're familiar with McClain batteries, right? The ones that power everlights?"

"Sure."

"My battery is a larger version of them that stores more power. It lets me run on cloudy days. Even through rain. I could keep going all night too, but I don't because the light would attract the crazies. And accessories? It doesn't have any. I can live without air conditioning. Besides, I wouldn't know how to hook one up to my system. As far as speed goes, I only need to outrun people on foot."

"What about headlights? They're accessories. You must need them sometimes."

"I use everlights mounted in the grill. And, of course, they use their own power."

"Doc, you take a pretty cavalier view of what could happen to you. That Chou's Disease didn't leave many people alive and most of us are starving. That's why I'm digging this damn ditch. That makes your cargo a mighty tempting target."

Doc chuckled. "Yeah. They're dying to get hold of what I carry." Then he turned serious. "You're a youngster. What, twenty-something?"

"Twenty-five."

"Well, I just turned fifty-five. I was chained to a desk all my working years. Adventure scared my wife, even the mild type I wanted – God bless her – and we had kids to put through college. I built this crate as a hobby but never got much chance to run it. Whatever sadistic trickster that runs the universe took away all I loved. But he gave me a chance at adventure. Without those loved ones, young Con, all I have left is this game against the fates.

"My dad always said, 'Make the most of all that comes and the least of all that goes.' I survived Chou's, as you obviously also did, so I'm making the most of that. When I finally look death in the eye, I'll make the least of that. Now.…

"How are you going to fix this fucking thing for me?"

Two – Chewing Sand

Doc explained the problem: The motors' proximity to the ground and their attachments to the wheels allowed dust into the housings.

Though Con had worked at repairing small electric motors, he didn't know much about the mechanical things related to them. He had volunteered to look at the motors primarily to get out of back-breaking ditch digging but sincerely hoped he could find a solution to the problem. He removed the motors, took them apart and cleaned them. After replacing them, he checked and tightened all the connections and made sure they worked, but he couldn't figure out how to keep the sand from getting in the wheels. He went to the trunk, opened it and began to loosen an iron strap holding one of the spare motors, intending to check and clean it.

Doc stood over him and cleared his throat. Con looked up at his glare.

Doc said, "I could've done that. You don't know any more about this problem than I do."

"Oh, I know what the problem is. I just don't know how to fix it."

Doc grunted, "You're as flummoxed as I am and a smartass to boot."

Con felt his day's pay slip away. He should at least have withheld his remark. "Sorry, Doc. I honestly did hope I could fix it."

"Oh, well," said Doc. "At least I won't have to clean those motors myself."

"It's almost lunchtime," said Con. "I'll head over to the eatery and then go back to the ditch."

"Are you nuts? I got you off for the whole day. And you can have lunch with me. It won't be much but it's better than Hardy Town's slop. C'mon."

He inclined his head toward the front of the buggy and went to sit in the driver's seat. Con took the passenger seat. He found the bucket seat far more comfortable than the one in his old Ford. Doc opened a door between the seats that accessed the cage behind them. He produced a wooden box, opened its lid and pulled out two leaf-wrapped bundles.

"Hope you like dried fish," he said. He handed Con one of the bundles and a packet of crackers. He filled two chipped mugs with water from a canteen and handed one to Con.

Con unwrapped the grape leaves and nibbled a flake of the fish. It was moister than he had expected, a bit salty and delicious. He resisted gobbling the next bite.

Doc watched him, amused. "Beats the grub here, huh?"

"For sure. But I won't have to put up with it long. I'm working just enough to get a couple weeks' store of food. Then I'm gone."

"You sound like a man with a goal."

Con said around a mouthful of food, "I am. I don't know how long this little burg will make it and I don't figure this 'free food' from California will last forever." He looked sharply at Doc. "Will it?"

Doc took in a breath. "I don't know how long. But it's only intended to last until people learn how to live on their own. Hardy's gardens and fields –"

"Won't be big enough to feed all these people for a long time. The ditch won't bring enough water from the creek."

"Why not?"

"It slopes too flat and runs through sand. Once it's open, most of the water'll soak into the ground before it gets to the gardens. Some of the digging guys figured that out but told us to keep our mouths shut. Hardy might stop the job if he finds out. Others think that once he sees how little water the ditch carries, he'll set us to digging another one. I think the first ones are right."

Doc nodded. "Yeah, Hardy wouldn't know about ditches and water. He was a bureaucrat, a city manager, I think."

"The straw bosses promised us more jobs and said Hardy'd let us move into town but that'll never happen."

"You're right."

"I figure after the ditch project's done, whether it works or not, he'll run the guys off. And when the California food runs out, Hardy Town won't be so hearty. I need to get outta here before all that happens."

They continued eating.

Finally, Doc said, "You sound like a pretty seasoned traveler."

Con scoffed. "You shoulda seen me three months ago when I left home. Naïve, soft. Didn't know from nothin."

"Where was home?"

"Tres Robles."

"In California? I'm from California too but never heard of Tres Robles."

"It's a little burg. Too far from the ocean, too far from the mountains, too close to the desert." And after downing a little fish-and-cracker sandwich, "Tell me, Doc, where does this free food come from?"

Doc ate his last bite of fish. "Why don't you come with me and find out."

"What?" Con hadn't expected that. "And risk getting my ass shot off? I heard what the diggers said about your chances on the road."

"And I heard you say you want to get out of here before it hits the fan. And with enough food to get you a ways down the road."

"Yeah, but –"

"Do I look like an idiot to you, Con?"

"'Course not, but what's that got to do with –?"

"I've made six food runs. They're no fun. I've had bad weather and my share of assholes to deal with. But they've made it possible for me to squirrel away enough food and supplies to make it after all this comes to an end." He swept a hand to take in Hardy Town, its gardens and the surrounding desert. "These diggers, good sorts though they be, come from around here. They haven't seen the desolation you did on the way from Tres Robles nor what I saw in San Diego. They think Hardy Town will save them, at least till the government's restored –"

"Yes, some of them say that."

"I ain't got much faith in Hardy Town or new County, State or Federal governments."

Con agreed about Hardy Town but believed in the revival of government, though he said nothing.

"Here." Doc held out his canteen and filled Con's empty cup. He took Con's lunch detritus and stowed it in the box.

"Why do you want someone to ride along?"

"Two armed people look more formidable than one."

"I don't have a gun."

"And you made it this far from home? Don't worry. I have an extra one. Even more important, two can change out one of those damned motors quicker than one. And I'll pay not two, but three times what they pay here. Not in worthless chits but food and equipment."

"Another problem," said Con, "is the agreement I signed with Mayor John Hardy. If I leave with you, I'd better not show up on your return trip."

Doc waved a dismissive hand. "Hardy'll let you go if I talk to him. Hardy Town depends too much on me to bring them food."

A vulture circled slowly far to the west. They sat for a time, shrouded in sweat and silence, without a hint of breeze. Con watched a lizard scurry from behind a clump of prickly pear cactus and disappear over a low rise. His ultimate goal remained to reach Tin Cup because his nurse Chloë had gone there to meet her boyfriend. Not for romantic reasons – Gloria still claimed his heart – but because she had been the only survivor of the pandemic he knew and felt close to. Of course, they both knew the slender odds of the boyfriend, Carl, surviving Chou's. And Chloë may not have lived through the dangers on the way there. But he could put the trip off long enough to go with Doc at least once. The extra food Doc offered made it worthwhile.

Con asked, "How long does one of these food runs take you?"

"Eight to ten days. Depends on the weather, sand in the motors and just plain dumb luck."

Two vultures joined the first. They descended. Some creature's plain dumb luck had just run out.

✳ ✳ ✳

He and Gloria watch the news. Chou's Disease has stricken the cities. The news anchors tell them the pandemic of 2072 is just another bacterial infection, only a little more virulent than usual. They smile confidently at each other and reassure the watchers that it won't last long now. In the background, figures run in the streets shouting, carrying torches.

Then he's running with them. They don't notice him. Somehow, he knows if any of them do, they'll kill him. He ducks into a dark room. His mother takes his hand, squeezes it and lets it go. Smiling, she says, "Goodbye. I'm going to see your father." She dwindles into the distance. He calls, "No, stay!" But she pops out of existence. He reaches for Gloria but she's no longer there…

He sat up in the dark, smacked away the hand on his shoulder. "What the hell?"

"Whoa, kid." Doc's voice. "We gotta get outta here while it's still cool."

Oh, yeah. Wiley had let Doc and him sleep in the tavern last night so they could get an early start. He wiped the sweat from his forehead with his shirttail. "Cool" just meant sweating less.

Soon, they bumped down the rugged dirt road in the buggy away from Hardy Town. The cloud of sand accompanying them infiltrated the buggy. The empty cart rattled, banged and leaped behind them. The night before, Doc had reattached the buggy doors but left the windows down. A faint glow tinged the sky behind them in the east.

Doc said, "Gloria must've been somebody pretty important, huh?"

"Yeah." Which meant Con had spoken her name aloud in his sleep. But he wouldn't share her with Doc or anyone else.

The dream stayed with him. He pretended to doze to keep Doc from asking him about it, though actual sleep would have been impossible on that rugged road.

Real-life television news anchors usually consisted of two guys bookending a stereotypically attractive blond woman. They discussed the spread of Chou's Disease almost cheerfully, reminding watchers that pharmaceutical companies had always come up with antibiotics to end bacterial infections. And this time, university research centers and Federal agencies like the NIH and the CDC had joined forces with them. So, how bad could it be?

In August, during the second week of the epidemic, rumors spread by social media claimed that most infected people died. The authority-approved news outlets denied the claim but admitted that the government now declared Chou's Disease a pandemic.

The epidemic had started in China, named after a physician-scientist named Chou, who had isolated and described the bacterium. In the United States, it struck California first – the San Francisco Bay cities, Sacramento, Los Angeles, San Diego – and then connecting population centers along the coast. It soon spread quickly throughout the US and Canada, then Mexico and the rest of Latin America. It simultaneously spread west from China along the so-called New Silk Road across Central Asia into the Middle East, Europe and Africa. And through Southeast

Asia to Australia and the Pacific world. Except for rural or isolated areas, it encompassed the whole world by the end of the fourth week. Distance had once caused epidemics to spread sluggishly. This one moved by the speed of air travel.

No one knew how it spread. The media cautioned everyone to cover sneezes and avoid physical contact. People bought masks to cover their noses and mouths. No one shook hands. Large cities began to quarantine infected people. The news anchors started looking at each other nervously when reporting on overflowing hospitals, riots and food shortages. "But remain calm," they said with forced smiles. "The cure is right around the corner."

Still, though with increased trepidation, Con and Gloria kept going to work.

Then Chou's came to Tres Robles. Com's mom numbered among the first victims. She chose to remain at home with pictures and memories of his Dad. She wanted Con to move out to avoid the infection but he stayed to care for her. A lot of people at his shop had quit coming to work for fear of infection. He finally did too. She went after three days.

It's only now, he tells Gloria, that I can say thank God she went quickly. Some suffered for weeks. Then your parents' turn came, and your brother's. Then my turn, though I recovered. Then yours. I stayed with you in that gloomy warehouse-turned-clinic for a whole week.

Death wasn't the worst thing the Disease did to people. Ask some of us who survived…

A sudden lurch of the vehicle threw him forward against the seatbelt. He had somehow fallen asleep.

"I swear," said Doc with a grin. "You must be tired as hell to sleep on this damned road."

Con didn't say anything. He didn't want to encourage Doc's cheerful banter. When Doc struck ruts made invisible by the wind-blown sand, only the seatbelts held them in their seats. Con would find bruises where restrained by them. Doc seemed not to notice the sand's invasion of the buggy, so Con pretended not to. Closed windows would have made the heat unbearable even at this early hour and probably would not have completely discouraged the sand.

He didn't look forward to chewing sand for eight to ten days.

What seemed much later, but from the sun's height, Con knew scarcely an hour had passed, they reached Interstate 15. They passed through a gap in the right-of-way fence the Hardy Towners had made for access and bumped across a shallow ditch, the northbound lane and the median to turn south on the southbound lane. The smoother surface allowed Doc to put the accelerator to the floor. Yet Con could tell by passing off-road objects that their speed scarcely exceeded 50 mph. On the return trip, the loaded cart would slow them down even more. Seeing Doc watch all about them, Con did too, though he didn't know for what. They couldn't have heard each other well enough to speak while jouncing across the desert. Now Doc seemed too preoccupied to talk.

When the sun approached its zenith, and Con felt faint from the heat, Doc left the freeway. Not by means of a paved exit but across the shoulder, down an embankment and, for a short distance, over uneven ground parallel with the freeway. Finally, Doc turned to the right toward a thicket of tamarisks. He drove into a gap between the low trees, which hid them from the freeway. Con recognized the tracks leading into it as those made previously by Doc's buggy.

Like Doc, Con got out of the vehicle and stretched.

Doc grinned through his dust mask. "Bet you thought I'd gone nuts running alongside the interstate, huh?"

Con grinned back. "Yeah. I thought the heat had got to you. Then I saw, it was because you leave the freeway at a different place every time to keep from making a permanent trail."

"Smart kid. You might survive this shit yet." After a light lunch, Doc said, "So you don't have a weapon. Do you know how to fire a pistol?"

"Nope." He mentally winced at the memory of trying and failing to fire a revolver because he didn't know to flip the safety off.

"Okay, I got just the thing for you." He went to the buggy and returned with something wrapped in a chamois-colored cloth, which he opened. "This Smith & Wesson .22mm target pistol is easy to fire and to take apart for cleaning." He handed it to Con. "It's loaded so leave the safety on. It's not a powerhouse but if you shoot somebody, you'll get their attention. When it cools down this evening, I'll show you how to fire it."

Con withdrew his knapsack from the front compartment where he had put it with Doc's belongings and put the pistol in a pocket on its side. Con had brought all his gear, of course. Otherwise, it would have disappeared before he had gotten out of sight.

Then Doc lay down in a little trough in the sand, apparently formed by previous naps and said, "Get some sleep if you can. You can drive when we take off again."

Con selected a spot and lay down but napped fitfully in the heat.

Con drove in the afternoon. The air above the paving shimmered in the heat. Doc sat beside him with a rifle across his knees. When Con asked if he expected trouble, Doc said he had never seen anyone in the area but, "starving people move around. Never let your guard down."

The freeway crossed the unrelentingly flat desert. Late in the afternoon, it began to undulate gently. As Con topped a mild rise he saw a barricade of junk cars across the front of a bridge at its bottom. He stopped.

"Friends of yours?" he asked Doc.

"No." Doc studied it for a long moment. "Clever. That'd stop most vehicles, but we can detour it. Better let me drive from here." Then, "No. Too late. Roll your window up. Quick!"

Aware of someone approaching from his side of the car, Con did as he was told.

Doc said, "Now. Hurry. Reverse."

Con shifted and floored the accelerator. The buggy's tires screeched as it leaped back. A man to his left with a shotgun stepped in front of the buggy. He sensed another approaching Doc's side.

Doc said, "Now you're gonna learn how to do some fancy driving."

Three – A Moveable Feast Crosses the Desert

Panicked, Con shouted, "What do I do!?"

The man raised his shotgun.

"Run over the son-of-a-bitch!"

"But –"

"Now, if you wanna live!"

The man aimed directly at Con through the windshield. Frantically, Con shifted into first gear and floored the accelerator. The man's eyes widened. He threw the shotgun aside and leaped away. In the wrong direction. The buggy struck him and bucked as it crunched over his body.

Con heard a spang! against the back window. Shit! He had forgotten about the guy slipping up on Doc's side. The buggy now faced the median.

Its tangled wetland grasses probably hid a water-filled ditch, potentially a deep one. He braked.

"Go, goddammit, go!" Doc shouted as another bullet hit the back window. Unbelievably, Doc unbuckled his seatbelt, opened his door and poked his head far enough out to look behind them.

Con went, crashing into the overgrown median at top speed, trying to hit the ditch at a right angle to keep the buggy upright, with the cart banging behind,. Not daring to look away from the median, he started when Doc fired the rifle. They hit the ditch in a spray of water and a bounce that thrust Con's bruised shoulders up against the seatbelt. A glance showed him Doc's empty seat. But just before he stopped to look for him, Doc's hand grabbed the door frame to push the buggy forward

Doc shouted, "Don't stop those wheels turning now or we'll be stuck. Go, go, go!"

Con stomped the gas again, but the vehicle barely crept up from the ditch. He hoped the water hadn't stalled a front wheel motor. From outside the buggy, Doc kept pushing on the door frame. When the rear wheels cleared the ditch and caught solid ground, the buggy spurted forward. Doc's hand disappeared but he hollered, "Keep going till you cross the road, then stop!"

The vehicle sped across the smooth pavement and Con stopped on the shoulder. Doc appeared in the open door, wet and muddy, breathing hard, but grinning. He put his rifle inside, pulled himself in and plopped into his seat.

"Well, that was exciting," he said.

"Too exciting for me." Con whipped around to look for the man who had come up on Doc's side of the buggy.

Doc waved a hand. "Don't worry about him. I got the bastard. But we need to get outta here. Make a wide detour around that roadblock. Others'll come up here to find out what happened to their buddies." He gestured toward the open desert.

Con shifted through the gears. At full speed, the buggy moved only at walking pace up a long but gentle slope away from the interstate. After the land flattened it ran a little faster.

He said, "Is this what it's like to drive with a motor out?"

"No. You asked if it would go with two out. Well, we're finding out it will. Feels like the front two."

Con said, "At least we're moving faster than a man can run." Though not as fast as a bullet, he did not say.

"Yeah. Let's just hope they don't have a vehicle of their own."

"Damn, I hadn't thought of that." Con looked back. Doc didn't, which probably meant he didn't think that likely since the two men who attacked them had been on foot.

Doc lay back and, surprisingly, given the recent attempt on their lives and their bouncing over rugged terrain with the empty cart rattling annoyingly behind, fell asleep. Though thirty years Doc's junior, Con hadn't jumped out of the vehicle, shot a man, helped push the buggy out of a ditch and clambered back in. Yet Con felt wrung out. He wondered how Doc had done it.

He thought about the man he had just run over and the one he had killed in Tres Robles. Both had deserved it, so he felt no guilt, just surprise that homicide came to him so easily.

Con looked about him as he drove. As a kid unfamiliar with the desert, he had considered it a desolate wasteland of creosote bushes and rattlesnakes. But hiking across it on the way from Tres Robles to Hardy Town had proved him wrong. Now, driving through it, he marveled at its many colors, varieties of rock formations and diverse plant life. The myriad wildflowers surprised him most of all. He had learned the names of many cacti from his father: cholla, prickly pear and barrel or mound cactus. Along with the creosote bushes, he recognized yucca, manzanita and juniper. A thicket he saw in a low-lying area might have been arrowweed. Still, they passed a lot of cacti and shrubs that he couldn't name. He wished to hell he had paid more attention to his father!

The wind, seldom absent from the desert, blew sand into the windshield and through the open windows. He worried about fouling another wheel. Hoping they had gone far enough to outrun pursuit, he turned right to drive parallel with the interstate. The western mountains began to point longer shadow fingers toward them. Con knew they should change out the wheel motors and clean the defective ones while enough light remained but wanted to get as far from the barricade as possible. He needed advice but Doc needed his sleep more. Con drove on.

The Feast Wagon's wheels decided the matter. A grating sound came from the left rear one. Doc woke up as they ground to a halt. He sat up and looked around.

"This doesn't look like much of a camping site," he said.

"We lost another wheel."

"Okay then," said Doc. "Time to change the damn things." He got out and stretched.

Since Doc had more experience replacing the motors, Con held the cart's tarp over the windward side of each wheel as Doc changed them. Then Doc, much refreshed by his nap, took over driving. They returned to the freeway and drove until after dark. Doc didn't risk attracting attention by using the everlights. The light of a gibbous moon and the stars illuminated the pavement as far ahead as they needed to see.

At last, Doc pulled off the road and down a slope into a culvert that ran under it.

"This is why I kept driving after dark," he told Con. "If we spend our first night here, we have a good chance at making it to the food depot in four days."

"After today's little surprise," said Con, "the shorter the trip the better."

"Few days pass that we don't learn something new, my boy."

"What I learned today was that I shouldn't've come along."

Doc tsk-tsked. "You young'ns. No spirit. We learned something from the guy on my side before I shot him."

Con said nothing, annoyed by Doc's revelation of a mysterious little epiphany.

"I bought these windows because they advertised them as bulletproof. I wasn't sure of it until that asshole's shots bounced off the back window."

"What if he'd been closer? Like, would the other guy's shotgun blast have broken through the windshield?"

"I don't know. It would've been an interesting test."

"One I'm glad I missed," grumbled Con.

As they ate supper, Con asked, "Did you hear about the guy who came to Hardy Town from Las Vegas?"

"Yes, the guys who helped unload the cart told me about him."

"They wouldn't let him stay because they said he might be infected but that's bullshit, right? I mean, those who survived it so far won't get it, right?"

Doc shrugged. "There are rumors about new outbreaks of stronger strains but I've never met anybody who witnessed them. Not enough scientists lasted long enough to figure out how it spread. Some people might be carriers. Remember how kids and old people died first when it hit? If this guy was a carrier and caught it from a baby born in Las Vegas before it died –"

"Wait a minute." Con didn't like to think about children dying. "The parents of any baby born now would be immune. Doesn't that mean the babies would be too?"

"Not always. Over half of the babies born in Hardy Town since the pandemic have died. Most seemed to have symptoms similar to Chou's."

"Jesus, Doc."

"Remember, Dr. Chou Liang, the Chinese scientist who isolated and described the bacteria, showed that it didn't respond to any existing antibiotics. Scientists all over the world verified that. They claim an 80 to 90% mortality rate. A lot of the survivors died from other illnesses, starvation, violence. I had read about the coming of superbugs for decades. Scientists predicted that eventually, bacteria would win the arms race against antibiotics. The Chou's bacteria did. Others will follow."

"Arms race?"

"Sure. Bacteria have been on Earth for billions of years, antibiotics for less than two hundred. Bacteria could write the book on evolving to overcome new enemies. Antibiotics don't evolve at all. Who do you think would win?"

Con said no more, hoping Doc would shut up about the subject. And he did. Con didn't want to think about the dying babies. He pretended to sleep after eating and shortly, did fall asleep.

But he woke up deep in the night with a disturbing thought.

No more babies meant no new generation of humanity.

They started in the morning's first light, Doc driving. The sky remained overcast, reducing the heat to an almost bearable level. The interstate turned from its mostly southerly course to southwesterly and then almost due west. The wind blasted the windshield but, on the paving, contributed less to the buggy's interior grit. A splatter of rain struck the windshield just long enough to turn its dust to mud and then stopped. As always, Doc watched their surroundings carefully and spoke little. That suited Con, still haunted by the specter of dying children.

In late morning, Doc said, "Shall we forego our siesta and keep going?"

"You bet." Con wiped muddy sweat from his face with a grimy red handkerchief that he had begun to wear around his neck to soak up sweat and daydreamed of a shower.

The highway gradually climbed in gentle undulations.

Sometime in the early afternoon, Con asked, "Want me to take over, Doc?"

"No, some parts of the freeway are dangerous. This is one of em. I'd better keep the wheel."

The stretch didn't look any more dangerous than the ones Con had driven on before, and certainly not as bad as the desert he had negotiated while Doc slept. About mid-afternoon, Doc pointed to a copse of California junipers some distance off the roadway and said, "That's where I usually spend my second night." They passed it.

Con nodded. They were ahead of schedule. Good.

At dark, they found a culvert big enough to drive the buggy and cart into. The metal structure's length hid them from anyone not looking directly into its opening. A landslide blocked the other end.

"We're lucky to find this culvert," said Doc. "After we eat, we can risk using the everlights to clean the motors."

After supper, they draped the cart's tarp over the culvert's open end to hide the everlight's glow. Con climbed the slope above it to secure the tarp's upper edge with rocks. Doc had kept a large cloth dust-free by storing it in a strongbox behind the battery and under the bench seat, so well-hidden Con hadn't seen it. They disassembled the motors and spread the parts out on the cloth.

"By the way, Con," Doc said as they worked, "Last night, I didn't mean to imply the world would come to an end because of antibiotic-resistant bacteria. We human beings have lived almost all our time on Earth without antibiotics. We'll adapt to a world without them again." Then, looking at a disemboweled motor, he shook his head. "This is why I bring six spare motors. The brushes on this one'll have to be replaced before it'll work again. We can get them at Orlando's."

"Orlando's?"

Doc nodded. "The food bank."

Con asked, "So if we get along without antibiotics, how long do you think this shit's gonna last?"

"Which shit?"

"You know, people starving, criminals running around loose, no government."

"Taking the last item first, just like nature abhors a vacuum, society abhors anarchy. We still have governments. Surely you haven't forgotten Hardy Town."

Con said, "No, you know what I mean…."

"I know what you mean but you don't. You mean more than government; you mean civilization: returning to the rule of law, to businesses manufacturing and selling things and people working at those businesses and buying things. I hate to be the bearer of bad news, Con, but all that'll be gone for a long time."

"Surely not. There are still people who know how to do all the necessary stuff."

"True. There are still electricians and electrical engineers and half-assed amateurs like me who know a little bit about motors." Doc held up a rotor from among the parts. "But it's tough to fabricate even the machinery needed to make this rotor, let alone the motor it goes in. And forget about geniuses in their basements figuring out how to save civilization. They're too busy just feeding themselves and their families and keeping them alive. Most knowledge like this will die with this generation. If people save the right books, maybe future generations can rebuild. Of course, cyberland books don't count. You can't turn on computers without electricity and the power companies have all shut down or soon will. But civilizations have collapsed and arisen before. We'll probably reestablish ours someday."

"What do you mean 'probably'?

"Civilization is fragile. It took the Europeans a thousand years to recover from their Dark Age. The Mayan civilization never did. The verdict on our renaissance is still out."

Con frowned. "You sure know how to give people hope, Doc."

"Remember, Con, make the most of all that comes…"

"Yeah, yeah, I know." Anger flared in Con. "Well, I fucking forgot to make the most of all that came before this goddamn disease. Now I have a hard time making the least of all the people I've lost." He felt on the verge of tears, from anger or grief, he didn't know which.

Doc reached over to put a hand on his shoulder. Con shrugged it off and went back to polishing a rotor with a cloth.

That night, all those Con had lost to Chou's walked through his dreams: Gloria, his mother, drinking buddy Henry and all the others.

✳ ✳ ✳

The next morning opened steaming hot in the culvert. They ate their dry breakfast cereal outside, sitting on the embankment beside the culvert.

Con looked at Doc and said, "Sorry I was an asshole last night. I didn't mean to blame all this death and mayhem on you."

"Maybe I was the asshole, Con. We all face our grief in different ways."

They shared grim smiles.

The accustomed heat fully returned that day, exacerbated by the afternoon's hot wind. When they stopped for their siesta Doc showed Con how to hold and aim the target pistol, though without firing it. Bullets were too scarce to waste on practice. Afterward, Con could hardly sleep for the heat.

That night, they chose a spot hidden behind boulders north of the interstate for their camp. They had to wrest it from its sole occupant first: a six-foot-long rattlesnake. After its demise, Doc surprised Con by knowing how to butcher and grill it over an open fire. The rattlesnake also surprised him by being delicious. Of course, he reminded himself, he had had nothing but cold, dry food for three days.

∗ ∗ ∗

The next morning, the fourth of their trip, opened still, as if the world held its breath. Con's trek through the desert had taught him that could bode ill. They left, as always, before full light. A vague, dark band crossed the western horizon. They recognized its threat immediately.

Doc said, "Shit!' and raced the buggy across the desert, the cart leaping and clanging madly behind, to the interstate. Upon reaching it, to Con's dismay, he took them west, directly toward the darkness. The burgeoning dawn light changed its shadowy form into an all-too-substantial dun-colored wall. After a few miles, Doc crossed the median's barren hump and the interstate's eastbound lane to race south jarringly across the sands. Con realized Doc knew where to hide from this. Sure enough, a house lay not far ahead.

And indeed, just before the first blast of wind-born sand struck them, Doc pulled buggy and cart into a sagging carport on the lee side of the abandoned adobe shack. He and Con closed the windows, unfastened their seatbelts and leaped out. The shrieking wind blew eddies of sand around the only corner of the house visible from the carport. Some of it entered the carport but with anemic force. If it blew past the cart, it would harm only the buggy's rear wheel motors. He hoped. Two steps took Con to the house's door. He found it unlocked, thank God, and barreled through. Doc followed him and slammed it shut.

They had entered the central room of a shotgun house. Doc raced into the kitchen and returned with curtains, dishtowels and unidentifiable rags. He began stuffing them in the cracks around the west-facing window. The howling gale precluded conversation but Con understood. He went into the room in the other direction and ripped curtains from windows and yanked a throw rug from the floor, all he could find to plug cracks. Soon, they had sealed the room as much as possible, even doors to the other interior rooms.

They took seats in the room's two chairs. The wind howled and buffeted the house like a vengeful desert spirit. The stuffing in the cracks kept most of the larger grains of sand out but insidious small particles gradually filled the room with a false gloaming. Doc had grabbed an everlight from the buggy's back seat. Its light relieved the gloom for a while but eventually dimmed to an angry red eye that limned the furniture and men as insubstantial wraiths. Time passed slowly. They didn't bother trying to speak over the shrieking wind. Despite handkerchiefs over their noses and mouths, Con's mouth felt gritty. They hadn't brought any food inside, but the sand and dust would have fouled it. Not that Con felt the least bit hungry.

Finally, the wind began to quiet. The sand and grit's invasion slowed. The air slowly cleared. When at last they saw each other's features, they removed their bandannas, relieved that they could breathe unmasked without choking.

Doc grinned. A white band crossed his lower face. "You look like shit."

Con grinned back. "So do you."

They went outside into a dun-colored world. House, desert shrubs and flowers, dune buggy and cart all looked molded from the same desert dune. After brushing sand off their own and each other's clothes, they walked around to the west side of the house. The wind had blasted grit deeply into the windward sides of the decorative tamarisks and shrubs and shredded their leaves. It had sand-blasted the house's adobe brick walls and front door and pitted its windows.

They returned to the house's rear, where everything merely looked filthy. Doc slapped the cart's rear; the sand fell away like a crumpled sheet. He grinned. "If our chariot had been on the other side of the house, it would've needed a new paint job. Let's see if the buggy'll start."

It did; the sand hadn't gotten into the wheels' motors. They left and soon reached the freeway.

The next day, the fifth since leaving Hardy Town, they pulled off the highway onto the pocked paving of a California State route that led into a welter of barren mountains. That, Doc said, would take them to Orlando's food bank.

Four – The Food Bank

Con drove after their siesta. A short distance down the road, Doc said, "Remember me telling you to keep one set of clothes clean?"

"Of course."

"Well, here's where we'll need em. Pull off at this next road."

So Con did and drove toward a clutch of sagging buildings.

"Used to be a tiny town," Doc explained. "Too small to have a post office or even a school. The only businesses were an automated convenience store and a bar. Had about a dozen houses."

"What did people do for a living around here?"

"I don't know. Some were probably on the government dole and couldn't afford to live in cities. Others might've worked on local solar farms. And with a computer, you could live and work just about anywhere."

"But here?"

Doc shrugged. "I know. Go figure. Every house has been looted. I checked when I first found the place. Though in the bar I found a fifth of rum that had rolled under a booth. But our goal is up ahead." He pointed to a large house surrounded by trees at the far end of the main street. "That big water tank on the hill yonder apparently supplied the town's water. With the electricity gone, the pumping system no longer works so the tank's worthless. This house musta belonged to a high whoop-de-fuck, though. It has its own cistern, most likely fed by a spring."

At the house, Doc told Con to take a driveway that led down to a basement three-door garage and park next to the garage doors. They took their clean clothes out of the forward compartment. Con followed Doc through a door next to the garage. Someone, either Doc or looters before him, had forced its lock open. The huge room they entered had once been an expensive entertainment center. Looters had ripped apart stuffed sofas and chairs, torn doors off cabinets and strewn their contents around and wrecked the wet bar. The carpeting had been ripped, stained and then soaked by rain leaking through broken windows.

Seeing Con's appalled expression, Doc said, "I know you've seen worse than this on your way from Tres Robles."

"Yes, but I'll never get used to it."

"We won't be here long enough for you to learn to like this one either. C'mon."

Con followed him into a small maintenance room behind the wet bar. He saw two tubs against the far wall, each large enough for a bather if he sat up. A small table sat between them. Doc reached above the table, opened a hand-sized door and pulled out a flexible metal tube with a spigot on its end. He held the tube over one of the tubs and opened the valve. Water sprayed into the tub.

He raised and flourished his free hand melodramatically. "Voila!" he said with a grin. "I searched this place assiduously and checked the computer log upstairs, which still worked when I first came by, learned about the cistern and how to tap it. I found these little tubs in the kids' bathrooms. Unfortunately, there's no way to heat the water but it's not all that cold for a bath." He handed the hose to Con and said, "If you'll fill the tubs for us, I'll fetch something I'm certain you haven't seen for a long time." And left the room.

He returned a few minutes later carrying two fluffy towels and washcloths and a fist-sized white lozenge.

"Soap!" said Con.

"Yep," Doc said proudly. He placed it and the towels and wash cloths on the table.

"Where did you find that?"

"I found bars in all four bathrooms. Apparently, the looters were looking for things other than soap. I took some with me and hid others here in case future looters realize how rank they smell. I'll show you where they are before we leave." And indicating the towels, "We'll wash these before we leave too."

"Sure. But why two tubs? You couldn't have known I'd come with you." Con continued filling them.

"Of course not, you dumb shit. I didn't even know you."

"You had somebody else in mind, didn't you?"

Doc didn't answer but frowned, grabbed the tube from Con and continued spraying water into the tubs.

Con found his response strange but didn't push it. Since the pandemic, he had learned to leave people alone with their demons as he wished to be left with his.

An hour later they emerged refreshed and went on their way.

* * *

In mid-afternoon, the State route sloped uphill onto a desiccated plateau. The air lay still and sultry, but wind whined through a copse of pinyon pines on a rise on their right. They hadn't seen a sign of human occupation since the barricade so after Con rounded a scarp of rock he stopped, stunned.

"Whoa," he said. "What's that?"

A large compound sat some two hundred yards off the highway. A ten-foot-high wall topped with concertina wire surrounded it and a guard tower stood just behind the wall to one side of its gate. The roof of a large building rose above the wall. Dozens of makeshift tents and shacks crowded both sides of the gravel lane leading to the gate.

Doc said, "That, my friend, is Orlando's food bank."

"Where does the food come from?" asked Con. "I figured they grew it or something but not in this wasteland. They gotta truck it in from somewhere."

"Some used to get delivered from California but now they seldom get a truckload. So they grow most of it right here."

"Not unless the land is a helluva lot more fertile on the other side of that fence and they got a lot of fields and gardens."

"Well, it's not and they don't."

Annoyed by Doc's little secrets, Con wouldn't give him the satisfaction of questioning further. Besides, the gaunt, ragged people beginning to appear amidst the slovenly village outside the wall made him nervous. He wanted to devote his full attention to getting past them. He turned onto the gravel drive.

"By the way," said Doc. "Roll up your window and lock your door before we get to that crowd."

Which didn't relieve Con's fears even after he did as Doc said. Sand-coated cars and pickups, serving as homes now, sat along the road. People had pitched tents between and behind them. The more imaginative had cobbled shacks together from branches of desert shrubs, rocks and building materials they had scrounged somewhere, maybe from the ghost town they had just left.

The people gathered along the road, singly and in family groups, well over a hundred. Con felt relief at seeing a few children, ragged and dirty though they were. The people had a hungry, haunted look. Most stared bleakly at them but some glared. A few men sauntered in front of them to make Con drive around them. Something struck the back window. A thrown rock? Neither turned to look.

"They don't seem to like us," Con noted.

"A most astute observation," said Doc. "They think I'm taking food away from them. As I suppose I am. The food bank gives them a little food but can't provide all they need. Orlando's told them they'll cut off all of it if they don't let visitors through."

"The food bank has visitors?"

"Yes. People who take food to places in California and Arizona and Nevada. And Hardy Town."

As they neared the wall, a guard in the tower signaled to someone on the ground behind it. A man pushed the gate open only far enough to admit them, waved them inside and shut it behind them. They passed between small one-story houses. A man wearing a white apron sat outside a larger building peeling potatoes: apparently a kitchen and dining room. Con saw no gardens nor enough land to accommodate them. Then the big building's purpose struck him. Of course. They produced vegetables hydroponically, something he had heard of but knew almost nothing about. And there had to be pens somewhere to raise the poultry for the meat they sent to Hardy Town.

The warehouse dwarfed a small building facing it across the driveway. Though a cross above the door and arched windows identified it as a church, it bore no identification showing its denomination.

Doc indicated a space by the warehouse's front door. Con parked and they got out. A sign over the door said ORLANDO SUSTAINABLE INDUSTRIES. Except for the door and heavily curtained windows on each side of it, the three-story building looked nearly featureless. Con followed Doc into a room large enough for eight or ten people at desks though only three tapped away at computers. Desk lamps provided the only light. Smaller enclosed offices ringed the open room, all dark except one…

Wait a minute! Lights and computers meant electricity. Con had been right after all. If these people could keep civilization afloat in this desert, cities must be coming back to life too. He could hardly wait to challenge Doc with this evidence.

A dark-haired woman looked up from a desk near the opening door and abruptly stood. "Doc, you're late," she said with a smile but also a worried look. She hurried over to them.

"Bad weather, Lucille. Took an extra two days getting to Hardy Town and an extra one coming back."

She took his hand and held it a trifle longer than one would that of just a friend. They briefly looked into each other's eyes. Then she looked curiously at Con.

Doc said, "This is Con, my new sidekick. Con, Lucille."

Con and Lucille exchanged greetings.

Then she said urgently to Doc, "Mrs. Orlando needs to see you right away. She says for you to go right into her office."

"Sounds serious. While I do that can you show this young guy around, or if you're too busy find somebody who can?"

"Of course, Doc."

"Good. I leave you in good hands, Con. I won't keep Lady Orlando waiting." And he started toward the lighted office in back.

Lucille said to Con, "Like to see our operation?" An attractive, middle-aged woman, she spoke as though she liked showing it and undoubtedly had few visitors.

"Why sure."

She waved a hand over the office. "As you can see, we don't have much office work anymore. We just keep track of production, inventory, growth projections, stuff like that."

Con asked, "You used to be busier?"

"Oh my, yes. When I started here twenty-five years ago, we had departments for admin, accounting and finance control, financial risk management and so many others. Regulatory compliance was a biggie because we were non-profit."

She opened the door into a huge room that covered the rest of the ground floor. Rows of metal racks holding troughs reached to the twelve-foot-high ceiling and extended to the far wall. Greenery poked up over the top of the troughs. Raised walkways gave access to higher levels of the racks.

"This is the growhouse," she said, leading him over to look into one of the lower troughs.

Con said, "So you grow all this food using hydroponics."

"It's similar to hydroponics except there's no soil. It's called aeroponics." She touched one of the troughs. "See, the plants are suspended over air chambers. The roots hang free. They're sprayed with an aerosol…" and seeing his blank expression, "a mist of a nutrient solution. It allows excellent aeration and the plants get all the oxygen and nitrogen they need. Aeroponics uses a lot less water than hydroponic systems. And far less than plants grown in irrigated soil. An important consideration in a desert."

Lucille sounded like his high school science teacher. He asked, "Where do you get the water?"

"Wells here in the compound. That's one reason Mr. Orlando picked this for a plant location."

"Orlando. Isn't that the guy who… He was some kind of activist, wasn't he?"

"That's right. Ruben C. Orlando. He pushed aeroponics. He got backing to build his first warehouse in New York City thirty-some years ago. In a poor neighborhood with no grocery store within walking distance. He wanted to build them all over the country so he put every penny over cost toward building others. The big industrial farms used too much water and topsoil. They fought him but lost. They couldn't match his prices even with their government subsidies. And his system produced fresh, clean vegetables all year long. He built this plant to prove he could raise crops in the desert. Or any place else. NASA's interested in using his system for a Mars colony."

"How can you afford to give all this food away for free? And why?"

"From the first, Mr. Orlando gave food to the homeless, orphanages, other needy people. When Chou's struck, he immediately recognized how disastrous it would become. He wanted to make each facility self-sufficient and produce food for the survivors. He said people couldn't rebuild the world if they didn't have enough to eat. When communications began to fail, he made each facility autonomous. We seldom hear from the others, so we don't know which ones have survived.

"Chou's claimed him and their children but not Mrs. Orlando. After he died, she chose this place to run because it was the most vulnerable and Mr. Orlando had wanted them all to survive. We built the houses you saw coming to the growhouse and moved the employees and their families here. We have a kind of farm on the other side of the growhouse for poultry and rabbits for food.

"As to how we afford it, we produce almost everything we need. We get wool from our angora rabbits, fiber from plants like hemp that we grow in the growhouse. Early on, we scrounged for tools, scrap metal and other stuff from the ruins, though they're pretty meager around here. The rare trucks from our San Diego and LA facilities bring medicines and other things we can't find here."

"But aren't you limited as to what kind of plants you can grow?"

"Not with this system. In this row, we have green leafy vegetables: lettuce, kale, spinach, mustard greens. Over there, we grow dozens of herbs. Here, let me give you a tour." She led him through the first and second floors. They passed troughs bearing artichokes, asparagus, peppers and chilis; cabbages and all its relatives: cauliflowers, broccoli and Brussel sprouts; then onions, garlic and leeks; other troughs with many varieties of beans; and beets, parsnips, peas, cucumbers, radishes, rhubarb, squash, zucchini and many others, as well as hemp, flax and other non-edible plants.

"What about potatoes?" he said. "You surely can't raise them in the air."

"Root crops like potatoes, yams and carrots take special consideration. We grow a smaller variety. Tomatoes – they're actually fruit, you know – are really popular. We can ripen them up to eight weeks faster than tomatoes grown in soil.

"We grow fruit and melons on the third floor – blueberries, strawberries, blackberries, dinner grapes, grapes for wine. Even dwarf fruit trees. I've heard that some other facilities grow lemons and bananas. Even pineapples." She looked toward the offices. "Maybe we ought to go see if Ms. Orlando and Doc have finished their meeting."

As they returned to the office Con thought about Lucille speaking as if NASA and their Mars mission could still happen. Had she made a mistake based on habit or did she know something Doc didn't about the revival of government?

Then he remembered to wonder where their electricity came from and asked her.

"Our generator. We're having some kind of trouble with it."

He wondered if Mrs. Orlando was asking Doc to fix the generator. He didn't think Doc's fitting a dune buggy with solar panels qualified him for repairing faulty generators. He thought of something else.

"Where do you get the fuel for the generator?" he asked.

"From the sun. I'm no engineer but I'll tell you how I understand it. Old-fashioned solar plants had rows of mirrors that concentrated sunlight onto water pipes that ran parallel with the mirrors' rows. That superheated the water to generate steam. The steam turned the turbine that produced the electricity.

"In our system, pipes carry water through a central tower behind the growhouse. Mirrors focus sunlight onto one place on the pipes. The water in that spot is a lot hotter than it was with the heat spread through all the pipes in the old system. So, more steam. That drives a larger turbine, which produces more electricity. It used to provide enough extra to store in batteries overnight. Now it doesn't. The batteries seem to be working okay but the generator isn't getting as much electricity to them as it used to.

"We also have solar panels on the growhouse roof; you can't see them from the ground. They power the lights, and some on the kitchen roof run appliances."

In the main office, Con and Lucille saw Doc and Mrs. Orlando talking quietly but earnestly in the doorway to her office. When Doc noticed them, he looked up, smiled and motioned them over.

"Here's the young man I told you about, Alejandra," he said to Mrs. Orlando. "Meet Con Colby. He's been a great help to me on the road."

Alejandra Orlando was a small woman with graying black hair drawn back in a loose bun. Con bet her dark snapping eyes missed little.

"I'm pleased to meet you, Con. You're a brave one to ride the roads with this maniac."

"Pleased to meet you too, ma'am. Maybe I'm a little crazy too."

She laughed. "That helps, I'm sure. Dinner will be ready in about an hour. Doc knows where the bunkhouse is if you'd like to rest till then. I'll send Dorothea for you when it's ready."

Con and Doc said their goodbyes and Con thanked Lucille for the tour. Outside, Doc led Con between the houses, frowning.

"Bad meeting?" said Con, and quickly added, "None of my business, of course."

"No reason to keep it secret. Among other things, we talked about the people outside. The natives are restless. And hungry. News travels fast. More show up all the time, too many for this place to feed properly with all its other obligations."

"Where the hell do they come from? The only places we saw where people used to live were that adobe house and the ghost town."

"They're probably living off stuff they get from stores and people's houses in places like that. After the food runs out, they wander around, hear about this place and show up. When the occasional truck brings goods here from the cities some of these folks go back with them. The last truck came over a month ago. On top of Orlando's worries about trying to feed these folks and places like Hardy Town, their main generator seems to be crapping out."

Con said, "Yeah, spraying water and stuff on all those plant racks takes lots of energy."

"Not only that. They run these big floodlights at night." He pointed to light fixtures mounted high on poles aimed outside the compound. "To intimidate the natives and to keep an eye on em." A red cross on the front of one building they passed identified it as an infirmary.

Con asked, "So Mrs. Orlando wants you to fix the generator?"

"No. She knows that's beyond my ability. Her maintenance guy thinks he can fix it with the right parts. She's hoping the next truck comes pretty soon so they can order the parts they need. She mainly wanted to talk to me about something concerning Hardy Town and places like that. They're gonna have to cut back on feeding them so she can help these folks out." He nodded toward the gate.

Con said, "Hardy Town's gardens don't produce enough yet. And they don't know much about hunting edible desert critters." Con grinned. "Have you told em about rattlesnakes?"

"Not yet."

"Why don't these lazy bastards" – gesturing toward the gate – "try getting their own food?"

"Alejandra and her bunch are working on that. Full-time creeks are rare out here, but they found one. They're helping the Outsiders build an irrigation system using it. And if the Outsiders bring in some critter they killed they'll trade them some vegetables for it. That fish you ate back at Hardy Town? One of them caught a string of them."

"That's a good lesson," said Con. "If you give a man a fish to eat he'll be hungry tomorrow. But if you give him fishing tackle he can fish and drink beer with his buddies all the next day."

That didn't get the laugh out of Doc he expected.

"Did I say something wrong, Doc?"

"Oh, no." They had reached the bunkhouse. Doc opened the door for Con. "I'm just thinking about Alejandra. She said she doesn't know how much longer the generator'll last. Oh, it won't crap out tomorrow but some day it will. Then they can't grow food for themselves or anybody else. Too bad we don't know how to eat cactus and stuff. The Indians used to live off this land. If I knew how to do that, I wouldn't have to run up and down this goddamn road."

Five – Beware: The Desert Gods Listen

After dinner that evening, Doc told Con he had some friends to visit in a manner that let Con know he couldn't come along. Con felt miffed at first, considering the adventures they had shared. Then, remembering the warm greeting between Doc and Lucille, he realized who the "friends" were. He wandered about the houses and other one-story buildings until he found the inevitable bar. He had suspected that Orlando's institutions operated like a commune – he had seen no evidence of money – and sure enough, they allowed him to drink without paying. The dozen or so other customers, most of them older than him, seemed a gloomy bunch. They questioned him about the world outside their walls, especially after they learned he had trekked several hundred miles from his home in Tres Robles and listened to his answers intently. But the journey to Orlando's had worn Con out, so after a couple of beers he apologized and went to the bunkhouse and to sleep.

The next morning, Con and Doc helped the Orlando workers fill their cart and the buggy's back seat with the supplies on Doc's list. The well-kept compound looked successful but Con sensed an air of tension among the workers, much like he had felt from last night's bar patrons. They understood their tenuous position.

After they finished loading and lunch, Doc left to visit his "friends" again. Con hadn't seen the poultry yards and rabbit hutches, so he rounded the far side of the growhouse to look them over. Though he knew nothing about raising animals, they looked extraordinarily well-kept. Hearing the happy squeal of children from the front of the growhouse he went back around its corner. Seven or eight children poured out of a side door of the church across the street into a fenced yard of brown grass. They ranged in age from about five years old to eleven or twelve. A thin priest in a black cassock stood watchfully over them. When two of the younger boys wrestled over a toy, he intervened. Con couldn't hear their conversation but when the priest stepped back, he saw him smile and the little boys laugh.

Relief welled in him to see that at least these children and those outside the walls had survived. And gladness to find this little moment of happiness amidst the gloom. He walked over to the priest and said, "I see you're good at settling disputes."

The priest smiled. He had a thin, ascetic face and a neatly trimmed beard. "I'm afraid my talent extends only to students, formerly at university and now at play." He had a slight accent Con couldn't place. He extended a hand. "Father Bartolomeo Carmioni, formerly of the University of Messina in Italy."

Con shook it. "Con Colby, barely a graduate of Tres Robles High. You're a long way from home."

"No. Home is wherever God needs me. I happened to be here on sabbatical when the sickness struck." And seeing Con examining the church, "I am a Jesuit, but many faiths gather together here so I have made the church an ecumenical refuge."

Con said, "We'll need you after we get civilized again. To settle disputes and gather people together."

Father Bartolomeo shrugged and smiled sadly. "I pray for that day. In the meantime, I use whatever I find at hand to help people. I care for the children so that their parents can work. We'll just have to accept what comes tomorrow."

"Sounds like you're making the most of all that comes –"

"— and the least of all that goes." Father Bartolomeo laughed gently. "So saith Doc Drennan."

* * *

Waiting for sleep that night, Con thought of the priest, stranded so far from friends and family. He must have been lonely, no matter what he said. As always, just before sleep, he spoke to Gloria. I miss you, Babe, but I'm glad you don't have to go through this shit.

* * *

Early the following morning, they took a last luxurious bath, shaved and started back to Hardy Town with Con driving.

As he had expected, the heavily loaded buggy and cart reduced their speed. He drove as fast as possible downhill to get a run for each upslope, but they slowed considerably before reaching the summit. Doc took over driving after their siesta, claiming they had reached the area too dangerous for Con to drive. Another of Doc's little secrets, thought Con irritably, but relinquished driving without comment.

As the morning passed, the ramifications of Orlando's eventual shut-down disturbed Con. It would mean disaster for the Hardy Towners and others like them who couldn't produce enough of their own food. The salvation of civilization depended on food banks like Orlando's. He didn't trust its revival in the hands of the few Hardy Towners he had seen or its ditch diggers. People had a better chance of raising their own food in the agricultural Midwest and the fertile parts of California than in the Nevada desert. That's where civilization would return first if it returned at all.

At the end of the day, Doc said they had made good time.

"If we do this well every day," asked Con, "will we make it back to Hardy Town in four days?"

With mock severity, Doc put a finger to his lips. "Ssh. Beware of hubris. The desert gods are listening."

Despite Con having risked the desert gods' displeasure, the next day started off much like the previous one. In late morning, as Doc drove, Con began to doze.

A brash noise behind them shook him awake, a familiar one he never expected to hear again: the sound of motorcycles with old-fashioned internal combustion engines. Looking behind and to his right he saw a cloud of sand in the desert coming straight toward them. One bike led. He saw another, no two, close behind it. He knew that the swirling storm of sand obscured more.

Doc saw them too. Since the buggy had started climbing a slight incline, he had already pressed the accelerator to the floor. He said, "Damn. Wonder where they got fuel for those old gasoline hogs? There aren't that many old cars to siphon it out of."

"Speculate later!" Con shouted. "Get us the hell outta here somehow!"

Even though patches of loose sand slowed the motorcycles down, they gradually drew nearer. They would move even faster once they reached the smooth paving. Con thought Doc should act a helluva lot more worried than he did. They approached the top of the incline. Con hoped they found the other side much steeper.

The bikes popped out of the sandy cloud and turned screeching onto the pavement, all too close to them. He counted five. If Doc had a plan, Con couldn't imagine what it was.

Con watched the bikes as the buggy started down a much too gentle slope. They wouldn't remain ahead of their pursuers for long. He wished they could jettison the cart. The food would surely satisfy the bikers.

"Now we got 'em," Doc cackled. "Roll your window up in case they got guns."

Con did, wondering if Doc had gone nuts.

Doc turned the buggy so that the right wheels ran on the shoulder.

The foremost biker did have a pistol. Con heard its bullet spang against the back window. Looking up front, he saw, oh, shit! they had nearly reached the bottom of the hill. And ahead of them rose a steep son-of-a-bitch.

He heard a loud crash behind them and turned. The leading motorcycle flipped rear over front. The driver flew forward, hit the road hard and slid face-down along the pavement. The bike crashed sideways into one coming up on its left. A third piled into them. A more distant bike turned into the median to avoid them.

Something bashed Con's door's window. He whipped around. A manic, bearded face grinned at him. A fist raised a tire iron to smack his window again. "Hey, Doc!"

They had reached the road's low point. Doc jerked the steering wheel to the right to strike bike and rider with the buggy, then straightened. Biker, motorcycle and tire iron shot airborne along different trajectories. The man, splayed legs kicking and arms windmilling frantically, followed the bike down into the dry creek bed under the freeway.

Doc glanced at the falling man and laughed. "Asshole over appetite. That'll teach im."

That crazy bastard's enjoying this, thought Con.

Con looked behind them. Just one of the men lying on the pavement stirred. The only one now standing, who had detoured into the median, had pushed his bike onto the roadway. He stood with hands on hips watching them go. He either didn't have the nerve to pursue them alone or care enough to fire at them if he even had a gun. Doc had the accelerator to the floor. Despite his levity, he apparently wanted away from them as badly as Con did.,

The highway had flattened. Con rolled the window down, leaned back and willed his nerves to settle down.

At last, he said, "Are you gonna tell me what happened to those guys or just let me wonder? And don't tell me the desert gods saved our ass."

"Oh, I'm gonna explain it." Doc sported a big grin. "It was too brilliant an idea not to brag a little. But I do wonder where they got the gasoline for those old engines."

"Probably siphoned it out of old internal combustion engine cars' and bikes' gas tanks but go back and ask em if you want to know. I'll go ahead in the buggy."

Doc laughed. "No, I'm sure you're right.

"But as to how those guys got their asses busted, you know those grates they put over the drainage inlets in these highways?"

"I guess so." Con had barely noticed them before.

"Well, I suspected somebody like these fuckers'd try to hijack those groceries someday. When I first drove along stretches of road with these grates in the paving, I pried them up and threw them in the weeds. If someone started chasing me, I figured I'd straddle the inlets with one wheel on the shoulder. Most people don't even notice them. They'd be more likely to watch the buggy than the road. It'd work just as well if they drove a car. Only one wheel needs to hit a hole like that to stop a car or even flip it if it's going fast enough.

"To be honest though, I wasn't sure it would even work. See, I told you we learn something new every day. But in case those guys and their bikes aren't as beat up as they looked, what say we forego our siesta and drive on through."

Con shuddered. "I second the motion. And I guess that's why you thought some reaches of road were too dangerous for me. You could've just warned me about the missing grates."

Doc grinned. "I don't want to let you in on all my little secrets till I have to."

They traveled through the afternoon heat and found a good hiding place for the night.

∗ ∗ ∗

The next morning, as they returned to the freeway, Doc said, "Two days behind us and we're halfway home."

"Let's not risk pissing the desert gods off," Con says. "I've seen what that leads to. Two more days to Hardy Town sounds good to me."

"I said two days behind us. I didn't speculate on how many days it'd take to get to Hardy Town. Hell, we might be ten days from there."

They drove on in silence, Doc looking all around as always. Con thought about the next leg of his journey beyond Hardy Town. He had dreamed of it every moment he dug the ill-fated ditch. Now, he could afford to leave. The time from Hardy Town to Orlando's and back would add at least ten days. Ten times the twelve chits per day Doc had promised him equaled one hundred twenty, less however much Doc deducted for meals. And he had saved twenty from the ditch work. That should buy him as much food as he could carry or more.

While they lay up hidden in a pile of rocks for their siesta, Doc said, "Y' know, Con, all my trips up and down the freeway aren't as harrowing as this one."

"Good. I'm glad for you."

"What I'm trying to say is, I could use somebody to help me with em."

"I don't see much future in what you're doing, Doc. Just running up and down the highway for lousy chits. They're not money. What'll they buy you?"

"I don't do it for the chits. I'm under contract with Hardy Town but they don't pay me much. I make the trips to add to my stash from what I find in deserted towns. Now I have camping supplies and water sterilizing equipment and arms and ammunition. All stashed in a safe place. Someday soon, I'll fill the buggy up with enough stuff and we'll take off. I got a few more items on my wish list to get first. But I'm getting too long in the tooth to carry this on alone. Until I'm ready to leave, I need some help."

"I wish you well, Doc. I think you're a great guy. But I gotta go on. I can't wait."

"To find a girl?" Doc had lost his usual aplomb. "That's why young men do stupid things. A girl who probably isn't even alive!?"

Con almost snarled. "Chloë was alive the last time I saw her. And she's a helluva lot tougher than you and I combined. She survived Chou's Disease just like you and I did and took off for Tin Cup. But I told you, it's not for love. I had my love, and Chou's took her away from me."

Doc looked away, through an opening in the boulders, out over the desert. "Sorry, Con. I was outta line." And a moment later, "I'm tired of this shit. I'm like Old Man River: Sick a livin but scared a dyin."

Con thought he looked older than ever. Doc had never disclosed that much of his inner self. But he had lost everyone important to him, just like Con had. "Shit, Doc –"

"Shut the fuck up and get some sleep."

As Con waited for sleep, it struck him that Doc had said he would pack the buggy with supplies for when we leave. That must mean Lucille. The second bathtub in the big house was for her. Maybe he invited Lucille to ride with him between the food bank and Hardy Town, but she refused because of the danger. No, he thought, she would have gone because she loved him. After setting up the bathing arrangements, he must have decided not to ask her for the same reasons: because of the danger and because he loved her.

Doc misunderstood his quest to find Chloë. He dreamed only of Gloria, never Chloë. He couldn't love Chloë with Gloria filling his heart. He had only spent a couple of weeks with Chloë, first as her patient while suffering from the infection, and after recovering, helping with the other patients. So why was he seeking her?

Because he had nowhere else to go. He would not give up his goal.

✳ ✳ ✳

On the fourth day, they took a long detour through the desert around the blockade of cars they had encountered on the first day. One of the motors stuttered, clogged with sand. As they exchanged it for one in the trunk, Doc said he had warned Alejandra Orlando about the blockade in case she knew of anyone heading in that direction. Con felt embarrassed that he hadn't thought to mention it.

Before the day's last light, they came to the rent in the right-of-way fence that gave access to the dirt road leading to Hardy Town. To Con's consternation, Doc drove past it.

"What the hell, Doc? Is this one of your little secrets? If you're doing it to piss me off, it's working."

With his eyes straight ahead and without humor, Doc said, "It's a secret known only to me that I'm about to share with you."

Con sat back with his arms crossed, irritated but resigned.

After about a quarter of an hour, they came to an exit ramp. Doc took it down to a paved two-lane road leading east across the flat land to one of the West's ubiquitous vast solar panel farms. They reached and passed an administration building on the road's south side and the beginning of the immense fenced field of solar panels on the north. Seemingly endless rows and columns of them extended to the east and north. Supporting structures set in concrete held them at a southerly angle to face toward the sun. Doc stopped at a gate hanging by one hinge that gave access to a footpath between the rows and Con got out when he did. Doc opened the trunk, took out a shovel and started down the path. Con followed, noticing him counting until he had passed over a hundred rows. Then Doc turned right and went down a row of posts supporting the racks holding the solar panels. Doc stopped behind one of the structures. The earth underneath it had been disturbed and roughly smoothed over.

Doc wiped the sweat from his face with his handkerchief. The heat remained even though the sun had begun its slide behind the low western mountains.

"You can see here," he said, "that I've been mucking around in the dirt. I can't compact it to match the surrounding ground, so I rely on the field's vastness to hide my handiwork. It's worked so far."

He took the shovel to the dirt, not to dig deeply, but to scrape away six inches or so of it. Soon, he had exposed a sheet of metal about four by six feet in size, green with a white border. Centered white letters proclaimed, "FREEWAY ENTRANCE."

"Your secret," said Con, "is a buried highway sign?"

Doc grinned. "A repurposed highway sign."

He lifted one edge and pulled it aside to reveal a hole slightly smaller than the sign. Rectangular translucent plastic containers, apparently empty, neatly filled the hole. Doc pulled one out and then another to expose another layer of the boxes. The vague shapes of objects of some kind lay within the second tier.

Doc said, "When all the empty ones are full, I'll be ready to leave. But tonight, I'll pay you for your trip to Orlando's before we get to Hardy Town."

"I don't understand, Doc. I thought you'd pay me in chits."

"Fuck the chits. You can't eat them. I'm gonna pay you in food out of the cart and stuff you need to survive out of these boxes. First, we'll replace that ratty knapsack, leaky canteen and holey blanket. And your baseball cap. It looks like it needs an oil change. You need a wide-brimmed hat like mine to protect you from the sun. I'll show you how to hide all this up under these racks for tonight." – he pointed to a space under the solar panels – "In the morning, turn in the Hardy Town chits for whatever food they'll allow you, come here to pick up this stash and be on your way."

Con, stunned, stood there for a moment. "Why, thanks, Doc. I don't know what to say."

"You earned it so there's nothing to say. Help me lift these empty boxes out of the way.

"And by God, that girl better be worth it."

* * *

A couple of hours later the buggy rested beside Wiley's bar, closed for the night, facing west, away from Hardy Town's somber stockade. They sat on its hood, leaning back against the windshield, drinking sour, bad-smelling beer Doc had drained from Wiley's near-empty keg. The desert's manifold species of plants and irregular landforms gave it an eerie, almost mystical, beauty at night under a waning moon surrounded by innumerable stars.

Doc asked, "Do you know how far this Tin Cup is?"

"I don't even know where it is."

Doc shook his head. "I don't know whether you're courageous or nuts. I'm beginning to believe it's probably a little of both."

Con took another drink of beer and felt his stomach lurch. Doc's scrunched-up face showed his beer had had a similar effect.

"But you're a tough kid, Con. You'll do okay. It's a scary world now, in case you hadn't noticed, and food will become ever harder to find. Every time you find an opportunity, like my buggy and I did hauling food from Orlando's to Hardy Town, take it. You don't have a set date to get to this Tin Cup."

"In other words," said Con, "make the most of all that comes."

"Exactly. You're learning. At the same time, if you miss out on an opportunity, don't mope about it. In other words…" Doc held a hand out, indicating that Con should finish the sentence.

"Make the least of all that goes."

"You got it." Doc held his fist up and Con struck it with his.

They suffered through another drink of beer, not because they liked it but because that's what friends did on their last night together.

God, I'm gonna miss this guy, thought Con. He couldn't tell Doc though, or he might talk Con into more trips to Orlando's.

"I'm gonna miss you too, Con."

Con looked down and blushed. He realized he had been looking at Doc in a way that betrayed his thoughts.

They talked far into the night. Not once did Doc again try to sway Con from his goal.

Six – A Fairy Rainbow

Con awoke in the night. He had slept deeply and free from his usual dreams as only the completely exhausted can. He sat up, stretched and looked about at the surrounding desert. Though eerily illuminated by a waning moon and starry ceiling, he couldn't see as far as the low, arid hills to the north that led to Las Vegas. He thought he had seen them the evening before but his profound weariness and need to reach it might have played tricks on his eyes. He got up and stumbled out of the shallow swale where he had spent the night.

We must be getting close, though, he told Gloria as he pissed on the fuzzy little cholla cactus at the edge of the swale. This will be our sixth day out of Hardy Town.

He didn't like traveling at night for fear of accidentally treading on a poisonous critter. A rattlesnake would prove deadly, and he had heard that the relatively mild neurotoxin in Gila monster venom, while not fatal, caused extreme pain. He didn't know if scorpions or other poisonous creatures lived in this part of the desert. His ignorance of astronomy kept him from telling the time from the stars, but he felt well-rested and needed to get to Vegas.

Doesn't it look light enough to go on, Babe? he asked Gloria. If I'm really careful, of course. My food's running low but I'll find more in Vegas. Water's a bigger concern. I got empty water bottles strapped to the backpack and a half-empty canteen. He chuckled. Yeah, Babe, you always bitched at me for being a glass half-empty sort of guy. Then choked back a sob. I could sure use your half-full optimism now.

When he, as a tyke, and his dad had camped out in the desert in the fall it had gotten chilly at night. Though it must now have been late October – Con had lost track – the nights after Hardy Town had been merely pleasantly devoid of the days' brutal heat, thanks to the warming climate. So, instead of unrolling his sleeping bag the night before, he had used it for a pillow. The backpack still lay beside where he had slept in the swale. He hadn't disturbed the wire food cart except to take out some hard cheese and bread for his dinner. He didn't like that kind of cheese very well, but Doc said it traveled better than the soft variety.

He sipped just enough water to wet his mouth and throat, then tied the sleeping bag over the top and sides of the backpack. He strapped on the belt holding his hunting knife and canteen and settled the backpack over his shoulders. After donning his wide-brimmed hat, he grabbed the two-wheeled cart's handle and set off, pulling it along behind, munching a shriveled apple for breakfast. He had left the solar panel farm with the cart full of food, with packets of more strapped on its wire sides. With much of that food now gone its much lighter load made pulling it easier.

The cart's still half-full, Gloria. See, I can be a half-full guy.

He trudged north with Interstate 15 a mile or so to his left and a few minor roads and barren hills a little closer on the right. As the sky grew brighter, he kept a wary eye on them. Traveling with Doc had taught him that almost deserted roads did not mean completely deserted or safe. At last, he saw the welter of hills into which I-15 disappeared to reach Las Vegas and the suburbs spilling south of them. He would reach them before his food ran out. Meanwhile, he would concentrate on finding water.

The temperature failed to rise past merely miserable, so Con continued without his usual midday shady hole-up. He only took a couple of rest stops, with some beef jerky for lunch, and drank sparingly of his water. Late in the afternoon, as he crossed a hillock, he saw a crevasse on its other side that widened and deepened into a miniature gully as it sloped gently to the north. Though dry now, flowing water had obviously shaped it during the infrequent but often fierce brief desert rains. It disappeared around a manzanita shrub some two hundred yards ahead. From his vantage point atop the little hill, it appeared to drop into a draw. Maybe it led to water and a sheltered place to spend the night.

Halfway to the manzanita bush, he saw that it fell into a draw broader than it had first appeared. Closer yet, he heard human voices, a man and a woman. He backtracked to a group of large yuccas and hid his food cart in their midst. He took the target pistol Doc had given him out of a side pocket of the backpack, shoved it through his belt at the small of his back and pulled his shirttail out to hide it. Then, backpack in hand, he crept toward the gully. After removing his hat to reduce his profile, he dropped to his hands and knees behind the manzanita bush. Careful not to disturb the bush, he looked through its lower branches into a gully twelve or so feet deep. A bearded, gray-haired, balding man dressed in faded dark clothes stood there with hands on hips. Facing away from Con, he seemed to be giving directions to a couple of women attacking weeds with hoes in a garden of droopy, dust-covered vegetables.

A dried-up channel ran down the center of the gorge. As Con began to wonder where these people got their water, two women carrying pails appeared from the upstream end of the gully. When the man turned to show the women where to pour the water, a large ornate medallion, perhaps a cross, glinted from a chain around his neck. The women poured the water into swales between the rows of vegetables. Con could get water from wherever they did, and they'd surely let him spend the night. Who would be safer to stay with than a preacher and four women? He crawled back from the draw far enough to stand up without them seeing him. He returned the pistol to its backpack pocket, put his hat on and walked to the edge of the drop with the backpack slung over one shoulder.

"Hello," he called down to them. "I'm unarmed." People had gotten shot for not announcing themselves.

The women started at the sound of his voice. Surprisingly, the man calmly looked up at Con as though he expected him.

"Hello, young fella. Come on down. There's a path over there." He pointed a short distance along the gully wall. "Take care. It's steep."

Con found the ladder-like path and carefully descended flat stones set into the gully wall.

The man met Con at the bottom of the path. He smiled and held out a hand for Con to shake.

"Welcome to Gaia's Garden, young fella. My name is Spero Peace, here to serve you."

"And I'm Conrad Colby. Just call me Con."

"Very well, Con. Come meet my charming posies." He led Con to where the women had stopped work and waited to be introduced. "Ladies, this is Conrad Colby – call him Con – and these are Verbena, Primrose, Daffodil and Iris, delicate flowers of Gaia that I care for."

Each lady put out a hand for Con to take as Spero introduced them. The hands of the three middle-aged "delicate flowers" felt rough from work, that of young Iris less so. He found her, hardly more than a teenager, petite, cute in a pixyish way and shy. She looked down demurely when introduced and murmured, "Pleased." The older women wore dark clothing, Iris, a blue skirt, a white blouse and a wide-brimmed straw hat.

Spero's terms, "Gaia's Garden" and "delicate flowers of Gaia," identified them as Gaians, the new pagan religion kind of like Wicca or Odinism. (His friend Henry had called the latter Onanism.) He noticed that Spero's chest bore not a cross but a figurine made of some hard, white material. It portrayed a very pregnant woman with huge breasts, thighs and hips. Small arms rested on her vast breasts. She tapered at top and bottom and had no hands or feet. Despite her featureless face, she wore an elaborate coiffure or headdress.

Spero said, "I see you're admiring my ivory Gaia."

"I, um, don't know much about Gaianism."

"We worship Gaia, who is Mother Earth herself. Paleontologists mistakenly called figurines like these 'Paleolithic Venuses' when they found them at Old Stone Age sites in Europe. They're actually symbols of Mother Gaia. We've worshipped Mother Earth ever since we became sentient. These figurines date back at least 35,000 years. Upstart religions elbowed ours out of the way."

"Upstart religions. Like…?"

"You know. Modern religions like Christianity, Islam, Buddhism."

"Oh."

"But come." Spero Peace took Con's arm and led him to a desiccated cottonwood log on the other side of the dry stream bed. Three crude pole structures covered with tattered plastic tarps sat against the gully wall opposite the one Con had descended. Gaps showed between the poles. The warmer climate no longer made solid walls for dwellings necessary, and apparently, Spero's group didn't care about privacy.

"Please sit." Spero Peace sat on the log. Con, laying aside his backpack, sat beside him. The women continued their tasks of weeding and watering the garden.

Con said, "How did you get such a… I mean, your name is…."

"Many of us Gaians who survived the Mother's pandemic took new names. Spero is Latin for 'I hope for.'"

"The Mother's pandemic…?"

"Why, yes. Mother Gaia sent the Disease to rid the Earth of all the false religions."

"I see." This guy's bonkers, Con told Gloria. And to Spero Peace, "I saw your women bringing water from somewhere. Could I go there to fill my water containers?" He started to get up.

Spero took his arm. "No, sit right there. Give said containers to me." Spero stood up.

At last, the lazy bastard's gonna do something, Gloria. Con unhooked the canteen from his belt, detached the water bottles from his backpack and handed them to Spero.

"Daffodil, dear," Spero called. "Could you please come here for a moment?"

One of the waterers set her bucket down and came over to them. She wiped sweat from her face with a rumpled cloth, leaving a dirty smudge. "Yes, Spero?"

"Con here needs some water." He handed her the canteen and water bottles. "If you would please…?"

"Certainly."

"Wait a minute," said Con. "I don't mind going…." He half rose.

Spero placed a hand firmly on his arm. "You don't know where the spring is."

Daffodil said, "I'll be right back, sir." She smiled tiredly at Con but didn't even look at Spero. Obviously, happiness in Gaia's Garden was not universal.

Spero expounded on the origins of Gaiaism and how the "false religions" had driven it underground until Daffodil returned with Con's canteen and water bottles. The shadows had grown long. The women abandoned their labors in the garden and took turns washing their hands in a wash basin set on a table between the lean-tos. Then they worked at preparing dinner at the table and the fire in the ring of stones near it.

Spero continued to talk as they worked. "You probably wonder how my desert flowers and I ended up here together. We all, except Iris, lived in a commune Gaia commanded us to create not far from here. Only we four survived. The community had too many memories for us and was too big to keep up, so we moved here. Poor, hapless Iris stumbled upon us a month ago, starving, half-naked. We took her in, fed and clothed her. As the Holy tells us, 'Whatever you do for the least of my creatures, you have done for me.' So of course –"

"Wait a minute," protested Con. "That saying's from –"

"As I was about to say," Spero said with a frown, "we provided her with food, raiment and love."

Clearly, Spero Peace did not like interruptions. Neither did Con. He had started to protest Gaia's theft and mangling of a verse from an "upstart religion's" Holy Book.

The women interrupted both by bringing a low table to place before Con and Spero and covering it with plates of food.

Dinner turned out better than Con had thought possible after seeing the pitiful garden: Spero bragged extravagantly on the dishes: a salad of desert dandelions and miner's lettuce with radishes from the garden, sprinkled with pinyon nuts; squash from the garden sweetened with honey; the pads of prickly pears called nopales, deprickled and cooked like a vegetable; and the little red fruit of the prickly pear cactus. Con had to agree that the meal was delicious and filling, though he didn't mention he would have liked some meat to go along with it.

After they finished eating, Spero continued talking while the women carried the utensil-laden table away and began washing the dishes. He described other foods provided by the desert: "The saguaro cactus provides food, drink and even building materials. The pulp, for example…" But the day's journey and a full stomach began to tell on Con. He gradually tuned Spero out as he watched a spectacular desert sunset paint the sky above the gully. Surely Spero would soon shut up and he could find a place to unroll his bedroll. Then Verbena and Primrose approached with another low and smaller table. Verbena placed it before Spero. Primrose placed two bundles and a clay jug on the table.

Now what? thought Con.

Spero said, "You're here on an auspicious night, young man, the night we hold this ceremony with my little sorcerer root plant."

Sorcerer root plant!? What the hell could that mean?

A cloth covered the top of the jug. Spero untied the thong holding the cloth in place and removed it. "We make this wine from the fruit of the saguaro. A short time into the ceremony, we mix a powdered bit of the plant's root into the wine –"

"The root of this sorcerer plant?"

"Why, uh, yes, of course." Spero's brows lowered.

He really hates interruptions, thought Con.

Spero cleared his throat. "When we consume the wine mixed with the powdered sorcerer root it connects me with Mother Gaia. But only me, not my Gaian flowers. I have been an adept for many years, but unfortunately, they are not. I perform this ceremony every week. Mother

Gaia gives me powers unknown to non-adepts. That's how I knew you watched us over the edge of the cliff."

Con remembered that Spero hadn't acted surprised to see him appear.

"Even though my lovely ladies are not adepts, the root enables them to see beauty denied those who do not partake. And by performing the ceremony with me they enhance my abilities. If you join us, you will see the world as my lovelies do and make me even stronger."

Con had never experimented with any drugs more potent than alcohol or pot. He wanted to know more about this one before partaking. "What is the plant?"

"Mondragora autumnalis. The mandrake." He unwrapped the largest bundle. A plant about nine inches long lay in it. Nearly its whole length consisted of a root covered by hairy growths. It had hardly any stem and a crown of leaves topped it. The root split into two long appendages at the end with two lesser ones sprouting from either side just below the stem. Con had heard that a mandrake plant looked like a little person. He supposed the bifurcated root at the bottom could pass for legs, the upper extensions for arms, the stem for a head and the leaves for a wild hairdo.

Con asked, "But isn't the mandrake plant supposed to be poison?"

"It has a reputation in connection with witchcraft and sorcery. But folk have used it in herbal medicine for centuries. In the Bible's Book of Genesis, it enabled Rachel to conceive Jacob. It's been used as an aphrodisiac, an anesthetic and medicines for various disorders. We brew it for all those purposes – it's been indispensable as an anesthetic – but drinking it in a naturally fermented liquid allows us to commune with Mother Gaia.

"But you have to be careful how much you ingest. It has deliriant hallucinogenic properties and –"

"Wait a minute. I know what hallucinogens are but what's that other word?"

"Deliriant? A deliriant hallucinogen can cause delirium. A subject might perform 'phantom' behaviors like plucking their hair out or disrobing. Or putting more clothes over ones they already wear. Or talk to imaginary people. While under the influence, my wife once didn't recognize herself in a mirror.

"A worse overdose can cause some kind of psychotic episode, make people lose control of their actions and do something horrible. They don't remember anything they do later. And of course, an overdose can kill.

"But oh, the proper dosage makes sex so wonderful!"

Con said, "And I guess you, uh, adepts learn all this stuff from other adepts."

Spero chuckled. "No, I was a pharmacologist before the pandemic, responsible for the preparation, uses and especially the effects of drugs. That's how I learned about my little magic friend."

While they talked, the women had knelt as closely as they could to the little table.

Spero said, "I perform the first part of the ceremony myself to commune with the Mother." He opened the other bundle, which held several objects and extracted a scalpel from a roll of cloth. "Verbena sterilized the scalpel and bathed and anointed the root. Now I exchange blood with my little sorcerer plant. During this part of the ceremony, no one is to speak."

Spero's next act convinced Con of the man's insanity. He poked the pad of his left forefinger to admit a bead of blood, then made a small slit in the plant to allow a bit of green fluid to seep out. Verbena bound the finger and root together with the wounds touching. Spero leaned back his head and closed his eyes in a trancelike state for a long moment. The ceremony felt surreal in the deepening evening gloom. Then he relaxed, smiled and looked at Con.

"My little sorcerer root friend has renewed me," he said. "After the ceremony, we'll replant him so he can grow ever stronger and more mature."

"Is this your only mandrake plant?" asked Con. "What if he gets some kind of blight or something and dies? Would you lose your adeptness or whatever you call it?"

Spero laughed as one would at a naïve child. "Oh my no, Con. We have a whole garden of the little creatures. I planted them near the spring right after we moved here from the commune so they'll stay well-watered. I'd never risk losing my power in such a foolish way."

He withdrew other items from the small bundle. He carved a thin slice off the root with the scalpel and grated powder into the bowl. Then he scooped up a bit of powder in a tiny measuring spoon and used a metal stick to level it off.

"This spoonful," said Spero, "will take us where we want to go tonight. We'll find our inner selves and see beautiful things. Twice as much acts as an anesthetic."

A scheme for using the mandrake plants began to form in Con's mind. He asked, "How do these plants reproduce? How do you plant them?"

"By seeds or offsets or by dividing the tubers. If you use seeds, collect them from the berries when they get overripe in the fall. Plant them in containers and leave them for a couple of years, then transplant them to your garden. But be careful that they're far enough away from food plants so nobody'll eat them."

"What are offsets?"

"See this short lateral shoot?" Spero pointed to a short spear on the side of the root. "That's an offset."

"Okay."

While Spero worked, Daffodil had brought up six mugs and a wooden stirrer. Daffodil filled the cups with wine. Spero ground more powder and stirred a carefully measured spoonful into each mug.

Con asked, "How much more of that would make a person do crazy shit?" The idea made him a little nervous.

"Two more spoonsful. Anything more than three would risk inducing a coma and death."

He picked up the mugs and passed them around. "Just a sip at first," he cautioned Con. "Let it slip up on you."

So Con took a tentative sip. The wine tasted weak, mildly sweet and rather woody, obviously of low alcoholic content. He felt nothing. He took a bolder sip. Maybe living on a vegetarian diet in this barren place had made the others more susceptible to alcohol.

Then he noticed a thin ribbon of colors roiling over the gully wall, the last of the dying sunset. Shades of pink changed smoothly from peach to coral to salmon to other shades for which he had no name, all resting on a bed of writhing purple that darkened through many shades from lavender to blue-black. He hadn't known so many shades of pinks and purples existed. The colors undulated, salmon and coral threading sensuously through deep purples. Seeing the band of colors approach, didn't surprise him, even when they drew closer than the gully wall. He took a deeper drink, hoping to see more colors before the vanishing sunset took them with it.

Someone urged him to look Up! Up! He did. The explosion of light took his breath away. The stars! He had never known they had so many colors. And the colors changed as the stars swirled around and around. No, not the stars. Someone holding his hand whirled them both about beneath those magic colors. Others danced around them, singing, shouting, laughing. Their voices turned to music. The scintillating colors from the stars filled the gully. He had finished the wine without realizing it. He flung the cup away.

Come, they whispered to him. Up! Up! To the stars.

And then, miracle of miracles! Gloria holds his hand. They dance among the swirling colors that become a bridge of light. A fairy rainbow! They danced along it, up out of the gully. He holds her body against his and strokes her angel's hair and kisses her and tells her how much he loves her and how much he missed her.

Swirling stars surround dancing Gloria. He sees their colors even through his closed eyelids. Though he holds her close something tells him not to open his eyes. If he does Gloria will be gone from him forever, like Orpheus' lost Euridice. He will not open them, in spite of hell and all its demons. He will allow nothing to take her away again.

They make love on the softest of clouds....

Seven – A Moveable Feast Heads to Las Vegas

He found himself awake, sitting up. As his stomach tried to leap into his throat, he clawed his way as far from Gloria as possible before he…

…heaved. And heaved. And finally rolled over onto his back, away from the mess. And looked up at the star-filled sky. It no longer spun. But instead of beaming with warm, bright colors, the stars looked down on him in cold, pitiless disdain.

He had to think despite the brain fuzz. And quickly. The drug must have tricked him into believing he had danced with someone. But not with Gloria, of course. He forced back a sob. And he had made love to someone. The drug couldn't make him imagine that. He looked back at where he had slept and the dark form lying there: a woman with her back to him, nude but curled on a pale garment that the moon- and starlight turned gray. He recognized the light blue skirt little Iris had worn as they danced. And her short, dark brown hair.

He wondered if Iris knew she had coupled with him. Or had she imagined a lost lover as he had Gloria? And what would Spero think about Con violating one of his "delicate flowers of Gaia?" He didn't know what rules, if any, he and Iris had broken. But he couldn't think about that then. He filed it for later.

The waning moon rode high, and no sign of dawn had appeared, but he knew he had to leave immediately. With the stolen mandrake plants. That would violate at least one universal rule, that of thievery.

He stood up tentatively. Despite his muzzy thoughts, he had to plan his next moves carefully: retrieve the food cart from the yucca patch and bring it down to the gully's floor, the latter a tricky move given his weakened state. Then get his backpack without disturbing Spero and the women. That might prove a more daunting task. He didn't know where they had fallen asleep in relation to the backpack.

He took a deep breath and went up the trail to the yuccas where the food cart was stored. He successfully made it back down the trail despite the encumbrance of the cart. Fortunately, Spero and his three middle-aged "flowers" slept soundly in one of the lean-tos, Spero nude and snoring loudly, the women in various stages of undress. Con thought, wryly, The guy must be a lusty bastard. Even though the backpack lay near them they didn't stir as he picked it up.

He found the spring from which Daffodil had fetched his water beyond the curve in the gully. It wasn't an actual spring, but a hole dug in a low point above an underground stream. A score or more of mandrake plants grew around it. Their wrinkled and crispy-looking leaves reminded him of pictures he had seen of tobacco leaves. Hoping the spring's moisture had kept the soil loose, he selected the four plants nearest it. The leaves lay only five or six inches above the ground, but they grew almost a foot and a half long.

He loosened the soil around the roots with his hunting knife. As he had hoped, water from the "spring" had soaked the soil. Otherwise, he felt so weak and giddy that he may not have been able to exhume all four. Their roots were longer than the one Spero had used for the ceremony. Those of one plant extended a good two feet. He returned to Spero's camp and commandeered two watering buckets. Placing two plants in each one, he packed the roots with damp soil. After putting some food from the Gaians' stores in the cart, he placed the buckets on top of it. The night before, he had attached the filled water bottles to his backpack. Somehow, he got the food cart and backpack to the top of the gully. Resting on top of his half-full food cart, the plants rose higher than his head.

He began his nightmarish flight in the dark. Along with weakness, he suffered bouts of nausea and occasional feelings of unreality. Wheeling the food cart, heavier because of the buckets of mandrake plants, was difficult. He used a long stick to pull himself along. Once he awoke lying in the sun, extremely dehydrated, without remembering passing out. He gulped down water and forced himself to continue well after sundown. He needed to put as much distance as possible between himself and Spero Peace.

He fared better the following day, no longer feeling the drug's effects but only weariness. And hunger. He realized he hadn't eaten the previous day. Some dried fruit assuaged his hunger somewhat. He would prepare a more substantial meal when he stopped for the night. As he emerged from a stand of course desert grass he saw a rattlesnake, about four feet long, on the other side of a barren patch of hard-packed sand. He and the snake regarded each other for a moment, and then both decided their business led them in opposite directions. Con stepped back into the desert grass.

Only to hear the unmistakable rattle of another snake.

It lay curled up about a yard away from him, ready to strike. Doc's killing and roasting of a rattler encouraged him to try supplementing his dwindling food supply. Doc had said the venomous creatures could jump about a third of their length. Lying there coiled made its length difficult to determine, but he estimated it at about three feet. He had to get it to strike while avoiding its fangs. His walking stick had a branch poking off one end, which formed a rough fork. Moving slowly and cautiously, he picked up a rock, aimed carefully and threw it. The instant it hit the snake's head, it struck. And nearly reached Con's foot; it was longer than he thought. The crutch worked perfectly. Once he had its neck pinned, he withdrew his hunting knife. Careful to avoid the deadly fangs, he severed the creature's head.

That night, he made a near-smokeless fire, another lesson he had learned from Doc, in a shallow ravine surrounded by juniper bushes. As he cooked rattlesnake fillets, he realized how much he missed his friend, even Doc's secrets.

The next morning, the third day of his flight, figuring Spero could follow his footprints across the desert, he broke a self-imposed rule and risked discovery by travelers by taking a paved road. Better to avoid the enemy he knew, Spero, than the ones he didn't. He found a paved two-lane road that roughly paralleled I-15 and made better time than he had through the desert. Having eaten and slept well the night before, he no longer feared an encounter with the nutty Gaian preacher or whatever he considered himself. Besides, he was armed, if only with a .22 caliber target pistol.

Later in the morning, from a hilltop, he saw the buildings of a small town in the distance, probably a southernmost suburb of Las Vegas. When he went down the hill, the buildings disappeared from sight. Clouds appeared over the mountains to the west in late afternoon, bringing only a light drizzle, and relieving the heat. It increased enough to soak him, though, which made him eager to reach the town.

Finally, through dusk and rain, an auto-con store appeared about a hundred yards away. It sat at the edge of the town he had seen earlier. Though eager to get out of the rain, which had become unusually heavy for this desert, and his wet clothes, he approached it circumspectly, from far enough away, he hoped, that no one inside could see him. He left the paving, crossed the shoulder and ditch and angled toward the corner of the automated convenience store. From there he surveyed the covered plaza of charging stations for electric automobiles. Abandoned cars sat there but nothing moved in the store.

He moved just far enough under the plaza roof to get out of the rain, swung his backpack off and took the target pistol out of its side pocket. Leaving backpack and food cart just under the plaza roof, he turned his attention to the store. He smiled to see that the elaborate chain-and-time-lock arrangement securing the front double doors remained while most windows on each side of the doors had been broken out. Post-pandemic looters hadn't worried about emergency units responding to security alarms.

His gaze swept the store's dark interior. Seeing nothing move and hearing only the susurrus of the gentle rain, he placed a foot over the two-foot-high sill of the nearest empty window frame, his feet crunching on glass shards.

With pistol raised, he examined the store's darkening depths for a long moment. Nothing moved and he didn't smell the noisome stench of death. Finally, he brought his other foot over the sill and lowered it gently, with hardly a sound, onto the glass. He lifted the backpack and food cart over the sill as quietly as possible. It felt stifling inside the building. The rain had at least given the illusion of relief from the heat.

The nearest row was blocked with empty food containers pulled from the shelving. Customers' phones had allowed access to the containers by scanning their doors. The looters hadn't bothered using their phones. They had removed the displayed item and those waiting to take their place.

With backpack slung over one shoulder and food cart in tow, he moved down the first clear aisle he found, and the next, looking for supplies and wary of other occupants. Under an overturned counter he found and put in his backpack some packages of snack food the looters had missed: potato and other vegetable chips, pistachios, beef jerky. He gradually covered the whole store but found only one other resident: a scrawny rat that scurried away from him. With so few people remaining, his kind would find life difficult. From a television special about rodent infestations, Con had learned that worldwide, the number of rats roughly equaled that of humans, on whom they depended for food, water and shelter.

One more task remained in the little daylight remaining, the most important. He never spent the night in a place without a second means of escape. Knowing most automated convenience stores shared the same floor plan, he went to the back wall. The doors were all where they should be, those to storerooms, restrooms and the one he sought: the office door.

He found it open – someone had broken its lock – and went inside. A little light shining through a small window from the alley showed sparse furnishings: an empty desk below a computer set into the wall, a score or so of blank screens flanking the computer that had once displayed security camera views of the store's interior, and a couple of chairs. A hook on the back of the door held a jacket some manager had left behind. He closed the door and stuffed the jacket in the crack between it and the floor to prevent light from escaping, then extracted the everlight Doc had given him from his backpack and turned it on.

He hung his hat on the door's hook, stripped and draped his wet clothes over the desk and chairs and dressed in dry ones. He wished he had an open fire to set his soaked boots before. In stocking feet, he crossed to the back door, his second escape access, and opened it just wide enough to look up and down an alley. The rain had stopped, and he found it clear of people, creatures and even rubbish.

He turned off the everlight and withdrew the jacket from under the door. In stocking feet, carefully avoiding broken glass or other sharp objects, he returned to the storefront with his pistol, some of the snack food and the manager's jacket. The rain had left behind relative coolth. After checking the auto plaza, he swept away glass shards with the jacket and stacked broken shelving to make a seat. He sat and ate zucchini chips and beef jerky. The clouds dissipated to display the last shreds of a sunset that only a desert could make so beautiful.

He thought of Spero's gully, called washes or arroyos by the locals. They said that, though they mostly remained dry, rainstorms like the one that had just passed could flood them, sometimes with deadly results. He hoped if that had happened to the Gaians' gully, they had gotten out in time, even nutcase Spero. After eating, he tossed the packages into the rest of the store's rubble and padded back to the office. He lodged a chair under the door's handle. It wouldn't keep a determined person out, but the noise would awaken him, and he slept with the pistol in his hand. And he didn't sleep that soundly anymore.

He hadn't allowed himself to think about Spero's ceremony-cum-orgy but concentrated only on getting away from "Gaia's Garden." He unrolled the bedroll on the office floor and lay down, intending to think about that drug-muddled night. But stretching out felt so relaxing, despite the concrete floor, and after the onerous last three days' travel....

* * *

The glow of early dawn illuminated the small window in the back wall. He got up and stretched, went out to relieve himself in the alley and completed his ablutions using as little water as possible. After breaking his fast on some dried fruit mixed with cereal, he opened the interior door just enough to admit a little more light.

Then, sitting cross-legged on his bedroll, he watered the mandrake plants. Though dust coated their leaves from the previous day's journey they looked healthy enough. Spero had inspired his theft when he showed him the small amount of powdered root needed to serve as an anesthetic. And his claim that people had used the root for other medicinal purposes. With the demise of pharmaceutical companies, the mandrake plant could save so many people so much horrible pain and illness. He wished he had more of the plants.

Spero had scooped the small amount needed to get them stoned in a little measuring spoon and told him to add another spoonful to use as an anesthetic. The spoon's size had been imprinted on its handle in numbers too small for Con to read from where he sat. He thought that if he could find a set of measuring spoons like his mother had had he would be able to recognize the right size.

He decided to spend the day looking for food and other supplies, including the tools he needed to powder the mandrake root. His fear of Spero receded. The drug from the mandrake root had probably contributed to his paranoia. Dozens of mandrake plants grew in Gaia's Garden. Spero would not likely pursue him for the theft of just four. And Spero probably didn't even know about his and Iris' liaison. They had been safely apart from Spero while he dallied with the other women. Though still worn from his flight, the night's sleep had refreshed him remarkably well. The last four months of travel and work had toughened him to a greater degree than he had believed possible. And taught him caution.

He had let his caution lapse in Spero's case. What could be safer than staying with a preacher and four women? he had thought. Meeting the Gaian priest had taught him a valuable lesson. Anyone could be a potential enemy, no matter how they appeared.

Though at the beginning of his journey, he had avoided towns, he now felt more comfortable in them. They provided more hiding places and escape routes than open deserts. But they also harbored more enemies. Survivors joined together for security and to glean and produce food and necessary supplies. Thieves preyed on them to steal or just for fun. The bikers who attacked Doc and him may have been among those who did it for both reasons. He avoided most survivors except when hunger forced him to stop at settlements to work for food. Even that was risky. He had heard of slavery and seen the brutal evidence of the passage of wandering bands. The great dying, which included Chou's Disease and the vicissitudes that followed it, had temporarily left plenty of food, clothing and other necessities behind. Despite the sophistication of modern food preservation, it wouldn't last forever.

He went out into suffocating heat, as bad as before the rain. Staying in the shade of buildings as much as possible, he went through the stores in a strip center. They smelled of rot and mold. He found their goods either missing or ruined by vandalism or weather. He turned down a residential street. The front of the first house had blown outward from the inside as though from an explosion. He skipped it and moved cautiously from house to house. A midblock home looked undisturbed. Windblown dust sealed the front door crevasses and coated the windows, indicating it had remained vacant for some time. Passing along its side, he looked cautiously through a broken window. Enough dirt had blown in to provide small plots of weeds. A bird nest perched on the corner of a china cabinet.

When he reached the back door, he went up its two steps and across the stoop. He broke the door's window to reach in and unlock it, entered and pulled his cart in after him. The dust-covered kitchen reassured him that no one else had been there. He went through the room quickly, found a grater that would produce fine powder from the mandrakes, a set of measuring spoons and a beaker to mix the powder with a liquid. Water would work as well as an alcoholic beverage. Hadn't he heard that injured people should avoid alcohol? He took canned food and a bag of flour from the pantry, even though the cans' contents may not have survived the heat. He had learned to fry a paste of flour and water to fill his stomach.

He went upstairs and, in the closets, found clothes that fit reasonably well. Shucked the clothes he had worn since leaving the Gaians and pulling fresh ones over his filthy, sweat-slick body made him long for a bath. He had hoped to find some sturdy boots to replace his worn ones but found no footwear that would fit.

He skipped the next two houses because of extensive fire damage. In the next one, he hit paydirt, an unlocked walkout basement door and signs of long vacancy. A pantry inside held more packets of pressure-sealed, self-heating meals than he could carry, so he tossed the canned food aside. And next to it a wet bar as well-furnished with utensils as a kitchen. It contained several bottles of wine, hard liquor and a twelve-pack of Pilsner Urquell beer. He dithered over how much alcohol to take. He had to leave most of it to make room for food. He decided on a bottle of wine for future use with the mandrake root powder and a couple bottles of Hennessey VSOP for trading purposes. And the pilsners for himself. He found two touristy canvas shopping bags to hold the booze: one advertising Virginia Beach, Virginia, and the other Alcatraz Island. These people, he thought, had gotten around, from sea to shining sea.

He explored the rest of the house. Leaving backpack, food cart and the bags of alcohol in the basement, he took his pistol and went up to the ground floor. The kitchen held little of interest; they had moved its most important utensils down to the wet bar. They must have known they would die, he thought, and wanted to go out partying. But where had they gone after equipping the bar so well? He went through the dining and family rooms and a library/office with a computer built into the wall and bookshelves. Then, up to the second floor. He looked briefly into a couple of guest bedrooms and, finally, the main bedroom.

And there they were.

They lay in the bed clasping hands. The folds of the clothing draped over their desiccated bodies lay deep in dust. The dried flesh clinging to their skulls resembled parchment. An empty bottle of Freemarket Abbey Cabernet Bosché sat on the little table by his side of the bed next to an overturned pill bottle. Dusty wine glasses sat on tables beside each of them. He wondered: Had one been sick and the other refused to go on alone? They wouldn't have feared starving with the well-stocked pantry below.

He opened the door to the adjoining bathroom and stepped inside. And stopped cold when he saw the bathtub filled with water.

The likelihood of bathing made him ecstatic. The couple knew the water supply would soon disappear. What better place to save a large amount than in the bathtub? They must have run the water before deciding to commit suicide, or growing ill from Chou's Disease made the decision for them.

The tub wasn't quite full; some had undoubtedly evaporated in this heat. And so what if a little dirt had sifted in? It would look positively muddy after he crawled out. He found soap, shampoo, razor, shaving cream, all the necessities of cleanliness he had once taken for granted. A quick look in the hall bathroom showed they had also filled its tub with water. He could have another bath before he left.

Then he forced his mania down. Security and survival came first. He returned to the basement, brought his belongings up to the bathroom, and then looked around the neighborhood from all the second-floor windows. From the master bedroom, he noticed he had come closer to Interstate 15 than he had intended, though he wouldn't change houses. He would be out of town before long. Back in the bathroom, he filled his water bottles and canteens from the bathtub. Then he prepared for his bath. He would get rid of the clothes he had so recently obtained, already fouled by his body's sweat and filth, and replace them with fresh ones after his bath.

First, he closed the door to the bedroom. He felt oddly guilty, as though he had somehow happened onto this couple's last, tragic, intimate moments together.

As he soaked and sipped a pilsner, he considered taking a couple of days to rest. He had eaten sparingly of his food supply since leaving the Gaians because he didn't know when he could replace it. That provided fewer calories than his faster pace required. A day of rest and filling up on food he couldn't take along would replenish his energy.

Once he finished bathing, shampooing and shaving, he passed into the bedroom and, without looking at its residents, entered the walk-in closet. The man's clothes fit him better than those he had found in the first house. He had lost an appalling amount of weight but added hard muscle. He dressed in fresh underwear, a cotton shirt and rugged canvas pants. He would take along another change of the man's clothes, a couple of changes of underwear and socks and toiletries from the bathroom: soap, shaving cream, a razor, etc. He hoped he had room for all that.

He spent the next day resting, eating and cleaning his backpack and its contents, food cart and pistol. He only knew how to dismantle the latter's cylinder to clean it but knew other parts, such as the trigger complex, had to be taken apart to do it properly. He wished he had asked Doc for more complete instructions. He grated a small amount of mandrake root and put it in a vial he found in the wet bar. He needed to experiment with it to determine the efficacy of various dosages but not in a town surrounded by potential enemies.

That evening, Con sat on the somewhat cooler second-floor deck, far enough from the edge to be hidden from below but with a great view of I-15 and the glorious sunset behind it. The freeway lay just a few blocks away at about the same elevation as the deck. He had just finished one of the self-heating meals featuring pad Thai and steamed vegetables with a glass of merlot. He planned to have another glass of wine and go to sleep early.

He saw a vehicle coming from the south along the freeway, a dune buggy that looked remarkably like Doc's, cart and all. As it drew nearer, he recognized it undeniably as the Moveable Feast. He couldn't see the driver on the far side, but the female passenger's dark hair peeking out over her forehead from her scarf reminded him of Lucille's. Doc! What were the odds of that? The old rascal had gotten his shit together and taken off with his true love. He watched them enviously as they passed out of sight.

The next morning after breakfast, Con went upstairs to shave and wash up. He would leave the next day, so would wait until morning to bathe in the other bathtub. The two days of rest had restored him and made him eager to resume his trip to Tin Cup. As he passed a guest room's open door, a distant motion from outside, a cause for alarm more often than not, caught his attention. Through the window, he saw a rather short man wearing a broad-brimmed hat walking just a block away. He walked with his head down and hunched forward, obviously exhausted, fighting for each step. He closely resembled Doc, but of course, he had seen Doc and Lucille driving up I-15 the evening before.

Suddenly, the man fell forward. During the few moments Con watched, he didn't move.

The survival lesson Con had learned on the road, to avoid strangers at all costs, warred with the compassion of helping those in trouble. His sympathetic side won but the cautious one made him keep his pistol at hand. Withdrawing it from his belt at his back, he went downstairs and out the back door. He crossed backyards, climbed over a few privacy fences and once crossed a street toward the one where he had seen the man.

He stopped at the last house on the street where the man had fallen and peered cautiously around its corner. He no longer lay there. He must have faked fatigue. His henchmen could have weapons aimed at Con at that very moment.

Con thumbed the pistol's safety off and backed farther around the side of the house. Then, remembering seeing a lilac bush on that side, a perfect place from which to ambush, he turned.

And faced a man wielding a baseball bat. The one who had fallen in the street.

"Doc! What the hell are you doing here?"

"I could ask you the same question," said Doc, dropping the bat.

They both looked at each other for a long moment.

Eight – "The desert gods have served us well."

oc sank down on his butt and leaned back against the house, breathing heavily. Con squatted before him. He wished he had some water for Doc.

"You need to be more careful, Con. I saw you leap some privacy fences on the way here. A baddie coulda spotted you a mile away."

"Yeah, I shoulda been more careful. But things've gotten weird. I'd've sworn I saw you and someone else, maybe Lucille, tooling toward Vegas in your buggy."

"Well, you're partially right. The buggy used to be mine."

"You sold it?"

Doc scoffed. "Not hardly. I did something stupid. Now it belongs to someone else." Doc looked at him sharply. "So, you figured Lucille and me out, huh?"

"It wasn't hard to do."

Doc looked down and shook his head. "Well, there isn't any Lucille anymore. And no Mrs. Orlando. And no food bank."

"My God, Doc! What happened?"

"The Outsiders and some allies got in, killed everyone, destroyed everything." He looked up and far away with a complex expression that mixed fury and abject sorrow.

"Did the generators go out? No, wait." Con looked around them. "We're sitting out here where your 'baddies' can see us and it's getting dark. I got a safe place for us to go. After you've had your bath you can tell me more."

"Bath? Bless you, Con." Doc's voice was just a whisper, as though their conversation had used up his reserves.

Con pulled Doc to his feet, looped Doc's arm over his shoulder and half dragged him back to the house. Once inside and after a quick meal, Doc sat soaking in the hall bathroom bathtub, sipping a Pilsner Urquell. Con said, "Now tell me. Doc. Orlando…."

"Some wandering gang, this one riding horses, joined the Outsiders and attacked the compound. Father Bart couldn't tell how many, but they were well-armed. They had at least one RPG. That's a rocket-propelled grenade launcher."

"So at least Father Bartholomeo survived?"

"Not for long. By the afternoon I arrived, the place was a smoking heap of ruins, every building burnt, some to the ground. Corpses everywhere. The stench… I tied my handkerchief around my nose and mouth. I chased off some vultures that were tearing at them. I thought everyone was dead until I heard Father Bart groan.

"He said the attack had come the night before. He heard a series of hellacious explosions from where he slept in the back of the church and ran outside. The gate and the tower were just a pile of smoking kindling. Men on foot and horsemen ran around everywhere. They pulled people out of their houses and killed them or burnt their houses down with them inside. Horsemen rode down the ones trying to flee, men, women and children. Father Bart ran among them, trying to stop the slaughter. He heard some talk about nailing him to the door of the church. Like a crucifixion." Doc shuddered. "But the one with the RPG knelt with the weapon on his shoulder and fired at the church. Obliterated the front half of it. Father Bart and some Orlando women saved some of the kids and carried them out of the stockade. Then he went back in. A horseman rode him down and he didn't come to until just before I got there.

"I wanted to move him out of the sun but he said he hurt too bad. He was soaked with blood. From the angle of one leg, I knew his pants hid a compound fracture. He waved away my offer of water. Said his guts were so torn up it'd cause too much pain. His breathing got shallower and his talk dwindled until he just quit speaking. I couldn't find any sign of a pulse. I got up and just walked around. Dazed at all the butchering. Most of the growhouse still stood but he had said the looters didn't get much food out of it. I went inside and saw why. A lot of fire damage. Most of the plants on the ground floor drooped dead over the edge of their troughs. The fire had damaged the stairs too severely to go upstairs.

"I found Lucille's body lying under some troughs. I won't tell you what they did to her. I sat holding her head in my lap for a time. And just wept. Then the horror of it all, the evil, got to me. The Outsiders had invaded for food, the horsemen just to kill. I flew into a rage, ran outside, hollering and cussing, wasted some bullets on the vultures and a couple of starving coyotes. Then I saw a body I could tell had been one of the riders from his boots with spurs. I grabbed a machete out of his dead hand and chopped him to pieces. I only saw one more horseman, rotting beside his dead horse. He had been a cop. I took his gun and all his other cop stuff. Then I hacked at him and anybody else not part of Orlando's. One starved-looking Outsider woman was still alive, just barely. She put up an arm but I chopped her too."

Doc quit talking. Tears ran down his cheeks.

"Then I stopped. Realized I was as bad as they were. Plopped down in the sun and cried the last of the venom out of me. No way I could bury all the Orlando people, so I got off my ass and started hauling them into the growhouse, Father Bart as well. But not the attackers. Left their corpses outside for the vultures and coyotes. A grisly job. There wasn't much left of some of them." He paused to wipe the tears and snot from his face.

"It took till way after sundown. I had to rest a few times. Put them all in a pile under the ground floor troughs. Collected all the flammable liquids I could find: turpentine and anything that smelled alcoholic in the growhouse tool room but in the infirmary, I bingoed: Hospital-strength Barbicide. It's used to kill viruses and bacteria. Mixing it with isopropyl alcohol makes it flammable. I saturated the walls, floor and – God help me – that pile of former friends and set it all afire. I don't know which of the stuff worked and which didn't but the growhouse sure lit up the night.

"I left as soon as the fire got going good. It was late, getting on toward morning. I drove back toward Hardy Town. Must've slept some along the way. Don't remember much that happened for a few days. When I got to Hardy Town, I just kept on going. What would I tell 'em? There ain't no more free lunch? Lots a luck? I dug up my stash at the solar panel farm and kept going."

Con remembered wondering, after Lucille's mention of NASA, if the governments were about to return after all and straighten things out. Now he knew that was fantasy.

Con asked, "So how'd you lose the Feast?"

"I did something stupid. The horror of what I'd seen turned into self-pity. I told myself I didn't give a shit what happened next, with Lucille and all those courageous people gone. So I just started camping alongside the freeway."

"That's not like you, Doc. You were always careful to hide your campsites."

"Yeah, like I said, stupid. A few nights after passing Hardy Town somebody kicked the bottom of my foot to wake me up. I looked up at someone standing there in the dark. The moon glinted off something in his hand. It turned out to be the pistol I'd taken off the cop. He had taken it out of its holster in the buggy. Another mistake, leaving my weapons in the vehicle. As you know, I always slept with at least a pistol. He made me get up, show him how to start and operate the dune buggy."

"What did he look like, this guy?"

"Hard to tell in the dark. Thin guy, gray beard. Fiftyish maybe."

"But he had a woman with him, right? I saw a woman in the dune buggy."

"Just a girl, really. Little slip of a thing. He had her frisk me for a weapon, all the while going on and on about some kinda god he had to spread the word about and the upstart religions he was getting rid of and —"

"And the name of his god?" Con had to know for sure.

"Goddess, actually. Gaia. We had Gaian cults in California."

"So you met Spero Peace."

"You know this guy?"

"I'm afraid so. Was the young girl kind of small with short dark hair?"

"Well, she was short, but hey, it was dark and I was looking down the muzzle of a gun, not in the mood to admire her hair. One good thing about her, though: The man was going to cuff me to a guardrail with the cop's handcuffs before they took off. She talked him out of it. Convinced him I couldn't catch them in the buggy. She also made him leave me some food and water. If not for her, I'd be dead now."

Con mulled that over. The woman had been Iris. He wondered again if the thunderstorm had flooded the Gaians' gully and if so, what had happened to the other three women?

Doc sputtered. "Are you gonna tell me how you know these nutcases? Have you met them since you and I split or are they old friends?"

"It's complicated, Doc. And you're too worn out to listen. Finish your bath and get a good night's sleep and tomorrow I'll explain all."

"There's no time, Con. I gotta get after them first thing in the morning."

"Sorry, Doc, but you're in no shape to do that. You need a rest day."

"No, I can't let them get any farther ahead of me."

"I can't believe you've become an atheist, Doc."

"What the hell are you talking –?"

"Have you lost faith in your desert gods? Do you honestly think this Gaia bitch is more powerful than them?"

Doc glowered. His lips formed a thin, hard line. "I assume you're going to enlighten me on the foolishness you're spouting."

"You certainly converted me. Remember, you told me not to commit hubris. The desert gods were listening."

Doc continued to glare at him.

"The desert gods will stop the buggy, Doc. And then we'll catch up to them. And the gods will show us how to get it back. Did you explain how to clear the wheels of sand to this Gaian Pope or whatever he styles himself?"

"He didn't know it could happen and I didn't feel the need to explain."

"There you have it. They sandblasted us on the way to Orlando's and back. Even while we were on the freeway. When the gods foul the dune buggy's wheels, the pope and his concubine's trip will come to a screeching halt."

As he talked, Doc's frown faded into a mischievous smile. The conflict with the bikers had shown Con how Doc loved dangerous confrontations.

"You're right, Con. How could I forget…. But wait. You said when we catch up to them. You're not coming with me. I fucked this up and I'll unfuck it."

"Of course I am. Two will have a better chance than one. And I have the only gun. I'm not gonna let you have all the fun."

"Absolutely not. I don't want to share the glory of taking the dune buggy back by myself."

"We'll talk about it tomorrow, Doc."

As Doc luxuriously soaped himself, humming quietly, Con went back to the main bedroom, gathered a set of the deceased man's clothes and laid them on the bed in the guest bedroom for Doc. Con listened as Doc rose from the tub, dried himself and dressed in the guest bedroom.

When he checked on the older man a few minutes later, he found him sprawled on the bed snoring soundly.

As he waited for sleep, Con thought of another way his journey had changed him. He had never been one to take charge. Unlike many people of his generation, he could afford to leave home, but it didn't seem worth the effort. Besides, his mom was a good cook and he hated to cook. She grew frustrated because he never gave her meal suggestions – why should he when she always fixed things he liked? – but he finally gave in to avoid her scowls and recommended dishes for her to repair.

Gloria got tired of choosing activities for them, like picking out which concert they'd attend, so he occasionally took the lead. Gloria and his mother bought clothes for him when his began looking too down-at-the-heels. He hated shopping. He always paid them back, his mother by adding to his rent payment. He always let the guys at work choose where to go for lunch. His drinking buddy Henry enjoyed bossing him around and Con didn't mind.

Con didn't consider himself very smart. It surprised him that he had, without deciding to, taken charge of Doc Drennan, a man who knew so much and had so many skills.

* * *

The next morning, Con told Doc how he had found Spero Peace's "Gaian Garden," gotten stoned with him and his "flowers" and the rest of it, except for making love to Iris. He showed him the vial of mandrake powder he had made and his plans for it.

Though Con hadn't seen signs of people living in the town, Doc had and suggested traveling at night, starting the next evening. Though Doc had spent most of the day sleeping, Con thought he still looked too worn out to travel. Con knew he couldn't talk him out of it, though, so he agreed to leave on the condition that Doc let Con do the most strenuous tasks. Accordingly, they set out that evening at dusk, Doc wearing the former occupant's too-large clothing. Con had covered the mandrake plants riding in his food cart with a tablecloth to protect them from the blowing sand. Using a grocery cart Doc had seen a few blocks away, they managed to take all the food from the house after all. Con went to the freeway and found the familiar dune buggy tire prints in the sand that had blown onto it, then rejoined Doc. They went north on streets within sight of the freeway. Another advantage of going at night was that, though it was still hot when they started out, it grew cooler as the night became darker. The night was clear, so their eyes quickly adapted to the light from the moon and stars.

Con again went up on I-15 at the next interchange to check the northbound lane. He found the Feast's tire prints; it hadn't yet left the freeway. That night, he thanked the desert gods for not sending the breeze he usually welcomed to ameliorate the heat. It could have blown away tracks or covered them with new sand. He wiped the sweat from the back of his neck with his handkerchief. From the interchange, high above the street passing beneath it, he saw lights in several buildings a mile or more to the west. As he watched, several winked out – people in a makeshift community going to sleep for the night.

When Con had started his odyssey, he went into towns only to find food. Otherwise, he avoided them because of the evidence of violence or damaged utilities, especially downed power lines, and not least because of the stench. The pandemic left myriads of corpses with too few people to bury them. In a few towns, enough survivors remained to perform mass burials or burnings. From the latter, the ghastly smell of roasted flesh stayed with Con for days. When he saw a huge column of smoke rising from a distant town, he detoured it as far as possible.

With the great dying almost five months past, the Las Vegas suburbs no longer smelled of death but lay silent by the absence of life. Which Con found almost as depressing, given its vast buildings where so many had once partied and played.

They took several breaks, more closely together as the night aged. Well before the first pre-dawn light glowed in the east, Doc's pace slowed and his breath became labored.

"Dawn's almost here," Con said. "We oughta call it a night." He knew if Doc kept this pace up without sufficient rest, he would literally walk himself to death.

"Nah, we gotta keep going. I think we're getting closer. We can't risk the wind blowing the tracks away."

"Well, I'm beat. If we ran onto them now, I couldn't even whip the young girl."

They took refuge in a minister's office in a church. As they ate, Con told Doc about his fear that the three women remaining in Spero's "Gaian Garden" had been drowned by flooding from the recent thunderstorm.

"You said they had lived in a nearby commune of some kind," said Doc. "That implies that they had lived in the desert for some time, long enough to learn about the dangers of flash floods."

"I don't know. They were naïve enough to fall for that dopey religion of Spero's. He did too."

"I'm no expert on why people fall for such stuff. But for Spero, Gaianism might've been a front. He could've just been looking for pussy, took the young one after the storm and left the rest."

It bothered Con to think that Iris had chosen to go off with Spero. He had hoped that, despite the effects of the drug, Con and she had chosen each other that night because of mutual attraction.

They slept soundly on the office's two large overstuffed sofas.

That evening, as sunset stained the western sky, they passed through Henderson, Las Vegas' closest suburb to the south, accompanied by a soft, soughing breeze. That early, the breeze hadn't cooled the evening yet and Con worried about what it would do to sandy tracks on the higher interstate. They felt exposed to the broad South Las Vegas airport but only it offered a good view of the freeway. Soon, up ahead, they spotted a complex freeway interchange.

Doc said, "That's where I-15 crosses I-215. There are several ways they could've gone from there. I'll go up there with you."

"You said you'd let me do the tough stuff, Doc. I can —"

"No. It'll save time for both of us to go check it. This is a more complex interchange."

They went up an exit ramp, wheeling the food and grocery carts. Buggy tire tracks approached from the from the south. But wind, brisker in the interchange's higher center, where I-15 crossed I-215, than the breeze had been on the street below, had swept away the old sand and brought in fresh, just as they had feared.

Con said, "Stay here, Doc, while I look north of here. I'll motion if I find tracks."

There were drifts of new sand but no tire tracks. He returned to Doc, sitting on a guardrail.

"Well, you were right, Doc. I guess your desert gods failed you. I didn't find diddly."

Doc stood up. "Oh, ye of little faith. No, the gods are just telling us that the miscreants have gotten off the freeway. C'mon. We'll find em."

They checked all the off-lanes to I-215 in both directions, to no avail.

"Doc, I hate to say I told you so but –"

"We're not through yet. Look down yonder." He pointed south. "See that off-ramp? 'Bout a quarter of a mile away? It looks like it goes down to South Las Vegas Boulevard, where we just came from."

Con sighed in resignation. "Lead the way, O mighty prophet of the dunes."

They went to the off-ramp and followed its curve northeasterly and then easterly without finding any sand that would have left a tire print.

Then Doc grabbed Con's sleeve.

"There. See that?" He pointed to the edge of the road.

Two wrappers stamped King Oscar Kipper Snacks and discarded tins lay there.

Doc said, "Those bastards ate my kippered herrings! I'd been looking forward to them."

"I'm sure you and Spero aren't the only ones who like stinky fish. Anyone could've –"

"But look here." Still holding his sleeve, Doc pulled him a little farther. There, the dune buggy's tires had imprinted the sand beyond the asphalt shoulder. "They stopped to eat. Young man, you restored my faith. Now I'm returning the favor."

"I'm a true believer now, O great prophet of sand. The desert gods have served us well."

They wheeled their food-filled carriers down the ramp to the boulevard but saw no further evidence of their prey. Con gave a now-what? shrug.

Doc said, "There's no reason to doubt they'll continue north."

They followed Las Vegas Boulevard to the north. Sand had accumulated in little deltas against the tires of cars parked along the street. The higher wind had not descended to this level, but only a gentle breeze. After two blocks, they saw the buggy's tire prints in several little piles of sand.

Con said, "Why would they leave the highway for the Vegas Strip? I'd think this would be a better place for them to get ambushed."

Doc shrugged. "Maybe Pope Spero wanted to try his luck at the casino's tables."

They watched McCarran International Airport on their right carefully as they passed it. Its terminal, on the other side of the broad runways, would have accommodated a lot of people, but they saw no lights in it.

Without life-giving irrigation water, the exotic plants in the street's median had given way to weeds and desert plants. Most of the royal palm trees lining the boulevard had died. Mark Twain had written that palm trees resembled feather dusters struck by lightning. Con thought these looked like lightning had struck months ago.

They took a break at the foot of the famous "Welcome to Fabulous Las Vegas" sign. It stood sadly alone, decrepit, bright paint scabrous, like an old prostitute who had been hooking too long. Beyond it lay the famous Strip.

Con wiped the sweat from his face and neck. "Walking down the Strip, even at night, probably isn't too good an idea, Doc."

"We don't have a choice. This is where his holiness is leading us. We'll just have to keep our eyes peeled and take our chances."

"The sky may steal what dim light we have pretty soon." Con pointed to the clouds gathering in the west as they got up and started off again. So far, they had been granted nights brightly lit by moon and stars.

Sweat had long ago pasted their T-shirts and jeans to their bodies. The thin, whispering breeze now plastered them with a light coat of dust.

After a time, without seeing any trace of the tire prints, Doc sighed. "I hate to admit this, Con, but I wouldn't mind making this a short night. I haven't been walking all over creation like you have since the pandemic. I've spent it herding a Moveable Feast."

"Okay. We won't be able to see much pretty soon anyway so let's watch for a place to stay."

The cloud cover reached them as they came to the line of casino-hotels. They passed Mandalay Bay's vast edifice rising up through the dark and then Luxor's faux pyramid, which looked mystical in the growing darkness. By the time they reached the center of the intersection of Las Vegas Boulevard and Tropicana Avenue, the dark had intensified. Excalibur's vast pseudo-medieval pile rose to the southwest, facing the Tropicana across the street to the east. MGM Grand vaguely loomed on the northeast corner and New York-New York on the northwestern one. The four edifices, each looking large enough to house the population of a small city, stood surrounded by acres of dying vegetation and parking lots filled with debris, tumbleweeds and a few defunct automobiles. Aerial walkways connected all four building complexes. Con remembered from previous trips that pedestrians weren't allowed to cross the intersection at street level.

"Okay, Doc, we're as good as blind now, so pick the place with the best suite and we'll pack it in for tonight."

"How about the Trop since it's the nearest. But no fancy suite. They're in the top floors and I hear the elevators aren't running tonight."

They entered the Tropicana. Con turned the everlight on as soon as they had gone far enough inside to hide the light from outside. They stopped in one of the bars where Doc mixed whiskey sours for them to sip while they ate pressure-sealed, self-heating meals in one of the restaurants. They took a room on the second level, undressed and shook the sand off their clothes while holding them over the railing of the deck overlooking the parking lot. After wiping sweat and grit from their bodies with hotel towels, they dragged bedding from the two queen-sized beds to the deck. Con fell asleep almost as soon as Doc.

They awakened at noon and breakfasted in a casino kitchen. Con thought Doc looked surprisingly fit and acted almost jovial.

Con hadn't dreamed of Gloria the night before. Indeed, he had missed her several nights lately. Upset by that and irritated by Doc's light mood, he said, "You seem unusually jovial this morning, for a man worn out by walking miles in sweltering heat, living from hand to mouth and missing his wheels."

Doc grinned. "That's because this is the day we find the Moveable Feast. Let's check out the lay of the land from one of those overhead walkways before we hit the streets, say the one from the Trop to MGM Grand. Then maybe we can hang out in there till dark."

After breakfast, from the high point of said walkway, the day felt uncomfortably hot after the previous night's relative comfort. They hadn't expected to see any evidence of the dune buggy from their vantage point, so Doc's earlier ebullience had not faded into disappointment.

The wind whistled a high-pitched threnody through cracks in the walkway's glass cover at different, dissonant pitches, which set Con's teeth on edge. Con couldn't see the front of the MGM casino from his angle. Tumbleweeds and other debris disappeared as it blew toward it. A lot of wind-born crap must be piling up there, he thought. He wondered why the wind didn't blow it around the building and down the street.

After looking in all directions, Doc continued north toward MGM Grand, pulling Con's food cart behind him. Con followed, pushing the grocery cart. Its right front wheel wobbled, reminding him they would have to stop in the MGM casino to try to fix it before moving on.

Inside the MGM, near the top of the escalator leading down to the main floor, the recalcitrant grocery cart wheel turned to one side and refused to roll any farther. Doc continued down the escalator while Con knelt to deal with the wheel. He found its axle clogged with sand. After he scraped most of it out with his pocket knife the wheel moved more freely.

Doc's face appeared at the top of the escalator, white as a sheet. He said, almost in a whisper, "You know how I said we'd find the Feast today?"

Con stood and nodded, wondering what the hell was going on.

Doc pointed downward while touching his lips with a hushing finger. Con crept to the edge of the stairs and looked where Doc pointed to the floor below.

There, in the middle of a large room, sat the dune buggy and cart, surrounded by wind-blown debris.

Doc whispered, "Now that we've found it, I'm not sure I like it."

Nine – "You defiled one of Gaia's delicate flowers…"

They stood at the top of the escalator looking down at the dune buggy and cart without speaking. Finally, Doc turned away and motioned for Con to come along. He led Con to the center of the walkway where they couldn't be seen from the lower level and watched the opening to the escalator.

"So," said Con, "it's like I said…." Doc made shushing motions. Con whispered, "The sand jammed the wheels and they couldn't fix em. The dune buggy just barely dragged itself and the cart in here. Then they went on their way. We go down, clean the wheels and we're on our way."

"Why would they go to the trouble of bringing it in here?"

"To hide it from someone, namely you, who might be looking for it, and for them."

Doc adamantly shook his head. "No. They drove it in here to fix it and couldn't figure out how. Now they're hidden someplace down there waiting for somebody who can. Like me. He probably thinks Gaia made him spare me so I can magically appear and make the buggy roadworthy."

"C'mon, Doc. Nobody's dumb enough to believe something like that."

"Sure they are. Religious people do it all the time. Say one of them drives to Walmart during a hellacious snowstorm, praying to find a great parking spot. Someone pulls out of a space right in front of the door. Voila! God answered his prayer. He has forgotten all the prayers the Maker ignored and made him trudge across a snowy parking lot."

"Well, this isn't a Walmart and –"

"It doesn't matter. The point's the same. They may not be lying in wait for us, but we have to treat this as if they are."

"Okay, okay. I'll go down and check it out."

"The hell you will. Give me the gun. You stay here. You couldn't hit the side of a barn with the thing unless you threw it anyway."

They both glared at each other for a moment. Then Con released an exasperated breath and, no longer bothering to whisper, said, "We'll both go down. Otherwise, we'll die of old age arguing up here."

Doc turned toward the escalator but Con pushed ahead of him and started down it, saying, "Remember, I got the gun."

Despite his earlier cocky words, he drew the revolver and scanned the immense opulent room decorated in shades of gold with dramatic black accents. Far to the left, sunlight streamed through a bank of double doors, which showed where the disappearing tumbleweeds and trash had gone. Spero and Iris had propped open one set of the doors and hadn't closed them after driving the buggy in. The wind had blown the debris inside, where it now lay around the vehicles. Check-in counters lined the walls to the right and left of the doorway. The area in front of the buggy opened into a long canyon of gaming rooms, the closest ones filled with ranks of slot machines. They grew increasingly dark the more distant they lay. Casinos used only artificial interior light. They didn't want outside light and activities showing through windows to distract gamblers.

Con reached the buggy and cart and began circling them, kicking away the trash and dead plants, looking for any apparent damage while still watching for Spero and Iris.

Doc stopped between the buggy and cart to examine one of the buggy's rear wheels.

Con raised the red handkerchief, which perspiration and dust had turned a kind of muddy pink, from around his neck and wiped his face,. He said, "I wish the wind that had blown those weeds in the door still blew."

A footstep crunched in the grit beside the escalator. Con looked up to see Spero Peace step from behind it. Con knew little about firearms, but he figured the one Spero pointed at him had once belonged to the dead cop at Orlando's.

Spero grinned. "I didn't expect you, lad, but I'm glad Mother Gaia sent you to me."

Spero couldn't see Doc, crouched on the far side of the buggy.

Terrified, Con blurted, "What? You're not gonna kill me over —"

"You defiled one of Gaia's delicate flowers, the gentle Iris."

"No, Spero!" came a young woman's voice. Con saw the girl running toward them from the room of slot machines. Iris! "Leave him alone."

Spero ignored her. "I expected the erstwhile owner of this jalopy but bless the Holy Mother for sending you." Spero stepped closer to Con, raised his pistol.

Iris reached Spero and gripped his gun arm in both hands. "He hasn't done anything to us. Let him be —"

Savagely, he pushed her away. She fell hard.

"Done nothing!?" the Gaian holy man cried. "He raped you, the fairest of the creatures in Gaia's Garden."

"He didn't rape me."

"Of course, he did! This latter-day demon warped your mind so you couldn't recognize seduction, then raped you physically and spiritually."

Con remembered that he held his own revolver. While Spero still faced Iris, he leveled it at him, holding it with both hands, and pulled the trigger.

Nothing.

Spero spun toward him at the click, sans smile, and aimed his pistol at Con's chest.

Hearing someone leap from behind the buggy, Con saw Doc from the corner of his eye. Surprised, Spero dithered, pointing the pistol first at Doc, then Con. Spero fired at Con as Doc stepped in front of him.

As Doc fell back against Con, knocking them both to the floor, he gasped, "Run, Con!"

Con didn't remember crawling out from under Doc but suddenly he was running. A glance over his shoulder showed Spero aiming slowly, confidently at him. Con turned away, winced, sure of his death. He stumbled over a vagrant tumbleweed just as Spero fired.

Spero missed because of that, though he wouldn't a second time. But Spero hadn't fired again by the time Con entered the forest of slot machines. And the darkness. He no longer had his pistol. It had flown from his hand when Doc fell against him. No matter; it hadn't worked anyway.

He heard Spero: "Get back here, boy! You can't get away!"

Though the darkness had increased, Con wondered that it hadn't become absolute until he noticed occasional luminescent strips along the bases of some slot machines. He could tell from Spero's footsteps that he ran roughly parallel with Con down another aisle between the machines to his left, though Con gradually pulled ahead of him. When Con came to a dining room, he had no choice but to enter it. At its rear he leaped over a counter into a kitchen.

The lack of lighted strips made its darkness almost complete. He ran into what might have been stoves or cutting blocks, knocking pans off tables and walls. Spero had, in effect, herded Con into the kitchen, perhaps hoping to trap him there. But Con felt he had left Spero behind by quite a margin. Just to be sure, when he burst from the kitchen into the relative light, he put on a burst of speed. Spero's steps on the carpeting sounded farther away than they had when he entered the kitchen. He put ranks and columns of slot machines between himself and Spero's estimated location, but the man needed not to be close to put a bullet through him. Finally, he no longer heard Spero's steps. That didn't mean he had given up the chase. The thick carpeting deadened the sound.

When Con stopped briefly to take some deep breaths, he thought of Doc stepping in front of him to take the bullet intended for him, of Doc buying Con's life with his own. Now his body lay by the dune buggy. Con tried not to think of how the heat would treat it if Con died, leaving Doc's body all alone. At least they had seen no sign of rats…

He couldn't let Spero get away with Doc's murder. He could surely find a way to ambush him in the gloom. He had never wanted to kill anyone before, not even the man he had run over with the gune buggy. But then, he had never seen a murder right before his eyes, not of just anyone but his best friend in this savage new world. He had only his hunting knife to use against the other man's pistol. But by God, he would do it. That meant he had to make sure Spero still followed him.

He shouted, "Come get me, you cowardly motherfucker!"

He resumed his run through the dark. In time, he again faintly heard Spero's footsteps. At a bell desk, an arrow on a free-standing sign with the legend "MONORAIL" pointed down an escalator. He might find an even darker, thus safer, place to ambush Spero down there. If that failed, access to the monorail should lead outside. He could probably lose Spero there and sneak back into the building to attack him when he returned. He took the steps two and three at a time, loudly enough for Spero to hear, into the darker underground. He followed the glowing arrows on the walls toward the monorail station through stifling heat and stale air. He wondered how the strips continued to give out light. The only other objects he knew of that glowed, like the everlights, had to be replenished by sunlight at times. Someday the strips' light and the technology that powered them would be lost forever.

He found nothing in the tunnel to hide behind to wait for his enemy. After what seemed like a long time, a glimmer of light appeared ahead. As he neared it, he saw that it came from another escalator. A sign beside it showed an arrow pointing upward and luminous letters proclaiming, "MONORAIL STATION." He reached and started up the escalator. The station above emitted a bright but ethereal glow like light refracted by water. Its bright colors were blinding after such a long time in the dark.

At the top of the escalator, a small landing separated him from double glass doors accessing the station. Beyond the doors, a half-cylinder of glass ran along the center of the ceiling and top half of the walls. Colors – red, yellow, blue and green – rippling in it caused the light show. Willing the doors not to be locked, he hit the horizontal bar of the right door running. And almost fell when it opened so smoothly.

He looked about anxiously, distressed to find no place from which to ambush Spero or even to hide. Large trash containers sat at regular intervals along the wall, big enough for him to hide in, but Spero would check them first. A low stainless-steel fence with stanchions holding ticket readers separated him from the rest of the station. Only a few messages and directions in dark blue stood out against the station's pristine, remarkably clean, white interior walls. To his left, the monorail track ran down the center of the station and into a brightly lit tunnel in the distance. Unlike the luminescent strips, he understood what powered these lights, which stayed on day and night for security purposes. They operated like the everlights. The sun charged their batteries all day, storing energy for nighttime and Las Vegas' few cloudy days.

He realized the sun had sunk a long way in its afternoon descent. The chase had taken longer than he thought, but the sun set sooner at that time of year. To the right, the track and station ended abruptly in a windowless, dark blue-painted and thus relatively dark round terminus.

He took a deep breath to calm himself, leaped the low stainless-steel fence and looked more closely at the dark end of the station. Where the wall curved up to meet the ceiling, a little higher than he could reach, he saw four horizontal slots covered in black glass, narrow but large enough for him to crawl through. He had missed them on his first look because of the station's brightness after being so long in the dark and the black glass against the dark wall. He pulled the nearest trash container under them and climbed up on it. With his hunting knife, he pried one slot open and looked out on an open space filled with once exotic but now dying ornamental vegetation. A hundred yards or so beyond the open space, another building rose, probably a wing of the massive MGM

Grand edifice. He could easily drop to the ground from the slot. But Spero could find him hiding in the open space too easily and if he crossed it, he didn't know if he could find access to the building. Spero might arrive before Con made it across the open space and shoot him from the slot. He didn't know how close Spero was.

Then a solution struck him. If he left the glass out of the opening and the trash can remained under it, Spero should assume Con made his escape through the opening. He jumped off the trash can and ran along the wall, past three trash containers to clamber into a fourth amongst desiccated refuse. If Spero followed Con's false spoor Con would have more time to find a better ambush site before he returned. Of course, as a middle-aged guy, Spero might find dropping out of the slot too strenuous. Or he might decide to check the trash cans first. Con readied his hunting knife.

A few minutes after Con hid, he heard his pursuer enter and stand for a moment, panting heavily, then crawl over the stainless-steel fence and walk toward the slots. The sunlight shining through the open one must have indeed attracted him. He grunted slightly when climbing on the trash can. Then Con heard nothing while Spero probably pondered whether to pursue him.

He evidently decided on pursuit because Con heard him, amidst groans and cursing, crawling through the slot. Con gave Spero time to drop to the ground, then crawled out of the container. He left the station and started back to the casino.

Though tired, and thirsty – he especially needed to find water – Con couldn't rest until he had found an adequate ambush site. He hurried back through the underground passage and came up by the bell desk. He started toward the dune buggy; Spero and Iris would surely have pitched their camp somewhere near there. He went more deliberately, looking for a place to jump the man. He didn't know Iris' status with him. If she believed she loved him, she could also pose a danger to Con. But maybe she had gone with him only for safety. He didn't want to think she loved the crackpot. She had seemed so sweet and innocent the night they had made love. Or had the drug made him believe that?

He came to the dark kitchen. Though he didn't like the idea of passing back through it, it was the only route he knew to the dune buggy. He entered it quietly, watching and listening in every direction.

Which made him aware of something among the shadows slamming down toward his head.

He jumped aside just as the object shifted to miss striking him. He drew his knife, then heard a sharp intake of breath and a feminine voice he recognized. "C-Con!"

"Con," Iris repeated, "I didn't know it was you. Honest to God. I thought it was him."

True, she had recognized him in time to turn the weapon aside. Still....

"Follow me out where I can see you," Con told her as he backed out of the kitchen, feeling his way without turning away from her, holding his knife defensively.

She did, after dropping the crowbar she held. She clasped her hands over her mouth and looked up at him fearfully. He stopped them between ranks of slot machines.

She said, "You do believe me. Don't you?"

He took her hands down from her face and saw a dark bruise that covered its left side from cheek to temple. The part of the eye that should have been white, the sclera, was blood-red.

"What caused that?" he asked.

"He hit me with his pistol."

"Why?"

"I spoiled his shot at you. When he was going to shoot you in the back."

So that's why Spero missed that sure shot at him. Pistol-whipping Iris took the time he needed for another shot before Con disappeared.

"Iris, I —"

"Don't call me that. Please. My name is Lois."

He sheathed his knife. "You saved my life, Lois. I don't know how to thank you."

"You can by helping me kill him."

Such determination coming from this waifish girl would have made him laugh under other circumstances. She had large, warm brown eyes; turned up nose; small, perfectly shaped lips; all framed in short, dark brown hair.

"If you hate him so much, why did you leave the arroyo with him?"

"I didn't have a choice. I'll explain later. Tell me what happened to him. Where is he now?"

The quaver in her voice betrayed her fear, despite her resolve to kill Spero. He told her about the chase to the monorail station and how Spero had fallen for his ruse and gone outside looking for him. "He won't be gone long. He'll probably figure I got away. He'll be easier to handle if he does."

"He hates you so much because we made love," she said quietly, looking down. "He thinks I'm his property." She looked away. "And I loathe him."

"Well, both of us can take care of him shortly. How well do you know this kitchen?"

"It's too risky to attack him there. He has a fire striker that'll let him find his way through the dark."

"You were taking quite a chance, then, attacking me in there, thinking it was him."

"I waited for him at the edge of the kitchen, hoping to hit him before he struck his fire striker. If he saw me before I attacked, I could say I was looking for a skillet or something. But if he saw you in there...."

"I get the picture. Then let's go look at where you sleep. I can take him after he's asleep." Though he felt a frisson of fear at that prospect, especially if Spero slept lightly with the pistol nearby. He picked up the crowbar Lois had dropped.

"Okay." She took his hand and led him through the kitchen by rasping her own fire striker on and off. She still held his hand through the relatively lighter gaming areas, and he didn't release it. They had set up camp farther from the buggy than he would have guessed. She said they did it to avoid anyone entering the casino's main entrance. Their camp consisted of mattresses they had brought from rooms upstairs, the camp cook stove and a low table from Doc's cart and odds and ends of cooking gear from the casino kitchen. She lit a candle with the fire striker, and they sat down on cushions by the table. *Like Doc and I did*, he thought.

Which reminded him of his duty to Doc, who had also saved his life that day.

At his frown, Lois asked, "What are you thinking of?"

"Doc."

"I've been thinking of him too. I know he's dead because I saw Spero's bullet strike his chest. I decided to check on him after I dealt with Spero in the kitchen. I didn't know when Spero would come back. I'll help you with Doc."

"I appreciate that, Lois."

"We only have each other now, Con. Until you came back, I felt so much alone."

Most answers to that could have inferred too much commitment, so he said, "Do you have some water? I worked up quite a thirst on that long run."

She dipped a cup of water out of the bucket on the table and handed it to him. "We found a big tank of water in one of the kitchens," she said. And then, nodding at a water bottle on the table, "He'll be thirsty too. He usually takes water with him, but he forgot this time."

"He was too intent on killing me…."

And then it struck him. He had put the vial of mandrake dust back in his pocket after showing it to Doc. He stood up, reached into his jeans pocket and pulled out the vial. He said, "He'll gulp down quite a bit of water, don't you think?"

"After a run like that…?" She nodded at the vial. "That's what I think it is, isn't it?" A malicious smile that seemed quite out of character spread across her pretty face.

"Yes. Powdered mandrake root."

"Enough to kill him." She poured water into Spero's bottle. "I'll fill it about halfway. It wouldn't do to fill it all the way and then he not finish it all."

"No, it wouldn't do at all."

A short while later, they heard Spero call from a distance. He must have just emerged from the kitchen. "Iris, darling, I'm back. The bastard got away, but I dare say he'll never come back."

Con grasped her hand and whispered, "I won't be far." And disappeared into the rows of slot machines. He hid in a dark corner some distance away but close enough to hear. When Spero arrived at the camp, Lois told Spero how thirsty he must be, and Spero blessed her for her thoughtfulness. After a pause, hopefully while he took a long, deep drink, Spero regaled her with a long imaginative description of the chase and how Spero had seen the terrified Con racing away from the casino.

"Let's eat," he said. "It's close enough to dinner time." He sounded strangely manic. Perhaps he believed Con, his only competitor for Lois' favor, had indeed fled.

"All right," she said. "How about a Vietnamese noodle bowl with lemongrass chicken?"

"Ah, one of my favorites."

Spero chattered on about his courageous pursuit of Con as Lois presumably prepared their meal from pressure-sealed, self-heating packets. In a few minutes she said, "Here you are."

Spero said, "Where's yours? Aren't you feeling well?"

"My stomach's a little fluttery."

"Eating something would settle it down."

"I'm sure it will feel better real soon."

Silence ensued while Spero ate. Occasionally, he made appreciative sounds. Then, silence again.

And finally, a loud cry from Spero. He shouted, "Melissa! These noodles are moving."

"I'm Lois, Spero. Melissa was your wife."

"Look at them wriggle. Just like little worms. They are worms. You're trying to get even with me, Melissa. You've always held it against me that you died of the Disease and I didn't, you bitch."

Lois said, "Why are you taking your clothes off, Spero?"

"They're crawling on me." In a panicky voice. "Mother, you and that bitch Lois did this to me. Where's my gun?"

"I hid it from you, Spero. You don't need it."

"Who are you to tell me what I need? Where are my pants, Mother? You've hidden them, you old harridan. How can I go to work without my pants?"

"Stay away from me, Spero."

Drawing his hunting knife, Con hurried toward them. He saw Spero, clad only in his shirt, stalking toward Lois with shaking legs. She looked prepared to make a stand, with feet planted solidly apart and a glare of pure hatred. She held the crowbar aloft.

Con said, "Step back, Spero."

Spero stopped and looked abruptly at Con with a quizzical frown.

"Ransom," he said. "Is that you, Ransom?"

"Sure is, Spero."

"Hey, wait. You're not Ransom. I was still George when the Chou's killed you." Spero laughed hysterically. "You wouldn't know my new name. I got you there, man." Then he turned serious and shook his finger at him. "I know something else about you, Phil Ransom. You always wanted to screw Melissa."

"Oh I did, Spero," said Con. "I fucked her any time I wanted to, and everybody knew it. She said you weren't any good in bed."

Spero moved away from Lois and toward Con. "I always wanted to kill you, Ransom. Now I'm going to. Just as soon as I find my gun…" Spero stumbled about, making the motions one would in opening and closing drawers in mid-air. He turned and wrenched the crowbar from Lois' hands.

Con leaped toward Spero with his knife.

"Aha!" said Spero gleefully. "Now I've got my unfaithful wife and her lover here together. I can finish both of you." He swung the crowbar wildly and clumsily at Con's knife hand. Con dodged him without difficulty.

A roar reverberated behind Con. Spero's head exploded in a mass of blood and brains and shards of bone. He collapsed prone to the floor.

Behind him stood someone who looked like Doc, holding a smoking shotgun.

"I kept trying to get a bead on him." His voice even sounded like Doc's. "But you kept getting too close to him, little girl."

Ten – "All Ye Who Enter Here..."

Con starevd in disbelief, but his senses could not lie. Doc stood before them. After a stunned moment, careful to avoid the mess around Spero's head, he stumbled over to Doc, grabbed his shoulders and looked him up and down. Pain twisted Doc's face and he held the hand free of the shotgun over his chest.

"Come lie down, Doc," was all Con could say. Doc could not have survived a direct shot to the chest. No blood appeared on the strange, thick, gray-green vest Doc wore.

Doc chuckled. "Hell, I've made it through worse than this." His laugh ended in a cough.

Lois had reached them. She helped Con lie Doc down on the closest mattress.

"Hello, dear," Doc said to her. "I'm so glad to see you again. This is the young lady who saved my life, Con. Kept this asshole," with a head-wag toward Spero's corpse, "from attaching me to that guardrail."

Lois blushed prettily. "You're not as glad as we are to see you, Doc."

"And your shotgun," said Con. "By the way, Doc. This is Lois, not Iris. She saved my life too. I owe both of you for that."

While she took Doc's shoes off, Doc unfastened one of the vest's shoulder buckles and said, "Help me get this damn thing off."

Con unbuckled the other shoulder one. "A bulletproof vest, huh?"

"Yeah. Without it, the bullet would've probably passed through me and you both. The proper nomenclature, by the way, is a 'ballistic vest.'"

"Where'd you get it?"

"Remember that dead cop at the food bank I told you about? I took it off him."

"But it didn't save him."

"No, somebody whacked him in the back with a machete or a big knife or something and, as you can see, it doesn't cover the back. It's a new generation of gear, sheets of laminated woven polymers, superior to old-fashioned Kevlar."

They finished unfastening the buckles and Velcro closures from the tough elastic straps holding the vest in place. Doc fell back with a groan and said, "Unfortunately, even though it stops the bullet from penetrating it doesn't absorb the whole force of the impact. It hit me right in the center of my chest, knocked me out. When I woke up I thought it had broken some ribs or maybe even my sternum. But I'm walking around too easy for that to be the case."

"You don't look so hot to me," said Con. "How did you find the vest?"

"I was squatting behind the dune buggy when Spero showed up, remember? While he was blathering, I slipped around to the back of the cart. I didn't have time to get the shotgun or one of the rifles hidden in the buggy. They were too valuable to leave in the cart. But I had stashed the vest in the cart where I could lay hands on it in case of emergency.

I pulled it on as quick as I could – that's why not all the buckles were fastened – and got in front of you just in time."

"So you had time to get the shotgun after you came to."

"Right. When I woke up, I saw the sunset fading outside MGM's entrance, and no one was around. I had an extra buggy key in my shoe so I unlocked it and got the shotgun from the compartment behind the back seat. After making sure it was loaded! Then wandered around looking for you. Finally, heard you and Lois talking. Then Spero. I stumbled toward the voices, keeping behind the one-arm bandits. When I got here I saw Spero acting weird, talking about eating worms. I got him in my sights but either one or both of you got in the way. At last, I had him."

Lois timidly unbuttoned his shirt over his chest to expose a large dark-purple bruise.

She said, "Oh, Doc, that looks so terrible. All we have is some aspirin from the buggy's first aid kit. I've got it right here."

Pointing to the bruise on her face he said, "You don't look so hot either, little girl."

She blushed and grinned, then got up and went to the table, carefully not looking at Spero's corpse and the pile of gore that had been his head.

Con said, "So what'll we do, Doc? We can't stay here." He glanced at Spero. Already a few flies had found him. "Lois couldn't stand it and he'll start smelling soon. We can move deeper into the casino."

"I'm for getting on the road."

"You're not fit to travel."

"Sure I am if you do all the work. Y' know, clean the wheels, drive. We can shift stuff around in the back seat so I can stretch out there."

Lois had returned with aspirin, a cup of water and a soaked towel. After Doc took the aspirin she spread the towel over his chest. "I'm sorry, Doc. This is all I could think of."

"It feels wonderful, sweetheart. Just what I needed."

She continued, "And I'm with Doc on leaving, Con. I can fix Doc a comfy bed in the back seat. And I'll pack the dune buggy and cart while you deal with the wheels."

She looked so distraught and haggard, Con quickly said, "What are we waiting for?"

✳ ✳ ✳

Con drove them up the Strip under a cloudless sky blazing with stars, while Doc lay on hotel cushions in the back seat with the shotgun across his lap. Con and Lois had repacked the buggy to accommodate their food, belongings and kitchen equipment from the casino. Con had placed the mandrake plants in their buckets in a corner of the compartment behind the back seat, wedged in securely so they would remain upright. He watered them before they left the casino. Lois had filled a five-gallon lidded container from the water tank in the kitchen.

Moldering vegetation cluttered the median to their left. Dirty cars lined the curb to their right. The casino-hotels looked so different without their lights and surrounded by tangled, dying vegetation that Con could recognize most of them only by their signs. They passed the Mandarin Oriental on their left and Planet Hollywood on the right, facing each other across the street, as did the Cosmopolitan and the Paris. Evaporation had left the Bellagio's lake with only a sludgy film and the overhead walkway that connected it to Bally's across the street had collapsed. Con threaded their way through its remains with difficulty. A vast shopping ziggurat rose across the street from the Cromwell, the Flamingo and the LINQ Hotel. Lights gleamed in its depths.

"Smart survivors," said Con. "Moved right in amongst the supplies."

"But the food'll begin to spoil some day," said Doc. "I don't see a good place to grow any around here."

Lois had been gaping at all the buildings they passed with awe.

"I bet you've never been here, little girl," said Doc.

"No. I've never seen anything so ritzy but, well, overdone. Corny, you might say. And huge. Even the little bit of the MGM Grand I saw was monstrous."

Doc said, "The MGM Grand is the largest hotel in America. It's got almost 7,000 rooms."

The water features in front of the Mirage and Treasure Island had suffered the same fate as Bellagio's. Lights also flickered deeply in the Venetian. They figured more survivors lived in the fancy ruins than they had seen evidence of. In a couple of places fallen palm trees forced them to make detours. They saw a fox peering cautiously at them from a tangle of foliage in front of the Palazzo.

At Con's request Lois told them about herself as they drove. Lois, nineteen years old, was a sophomore at the University in Los Angeles. When her mother succumbed to Chou's Disease she returned home to San Bernardino, an hour and a half east of the university.

"They all died, Con," she said, "one after the other, my mother, my father, my little sister still in high school. All my aunts and uncles except one uncle. All my cousins. And I didn't even get sick!" She burst into tears.

Con squirmed uncomfortably. Everything he thought of to say sounded trite and dumb.

Doc leaned forward, placed a hand on her shoulder and said gently, "There's nothing I can say to lessen your grief, little girl, but you must not give in to the guilt. I went through the same things you are, the loss of everyone and the grief and yes, the guilt for being the only survivor. Then I realized I couldn't have done anything to change things. We don't know why some died of the disease, others like Con recovered and a few like you and I never got it."

She put a hand over his and wiped her eyes with the other. She forced a smile. "It was just a crap shoot, Doc. Right?"

"Right. And I still have the grief, always will, but I put the guilt behind me."

"You're right, Doc. That's what I'll do. In time." She straightened and faced the front. Doc took his hand back and lay down.

Con wished he could think of something consoling to say to Lois.

After a while Lois said, "My little sister Margery had the worst of it. By the time she went to the hospital the rooms were full and gurneys holding patients lined both sides of the hallways, most of them dying. There were too few doctors and nurses. I suppose a lot of them had died too and others stayed away to keep from catching the disease. There weren't even enough people to give the patients water to drink or take them bed pans, no one to take out the dead ones. I wasn't strong enough to take Margie out so I had to leave her there. I gave the patients water but I couldn't stay after poor little Margie passed. The smell…."

She looked out the side window for a long while.

About midnight Con suggested they stop for a picnic lunch in front of the Wynn casino.

"We don't know if anyone's lurking in that building," said Doc. "There's a golf course behind it. I suggest pulling deep into it where we can see anyone coming and eat there."

They found that the relentless Nevada desert had taken back much of the golf course. Only a few patches of sere brown grass remained among invasive desert plants. Lois spread a blanket on one of the anemic grass plots while Con brought food from the buggy. Doc hobbled from the buggy, using the shotgun as a cane.

He handed Con the pistol he had dropped during Spero's attack. "It'll work now."

"How do you know? It didn't work for me, and I had cleaned it."

"I cleaned it properly. I'll show you how after we eat."

Lois asked Con, "I see you liberated some of Spero's mandrakes. Powder from those can keep you high for a long time."

Con frowned. "And it'll spare people a lot of pain and suffering. That's why I brought it."

Lois blushed. "I'm so sorry, Con. I shouldn't have jumped to such a conclusion. I –"

"No. You couldn't know. My only problem is I don't know the proper dosage. I couldn't read the little numbers on Spero's measuring spoon, so I didn't trust myself to give Doc any for pain."

She smiled and reached into the pouch on her belt. She extracted a little spoon identical to Spero's and held it up. "Sometimes we 'flowers,'" she spat the word, "measured out the dosages. I'll mix one for Doc now. I was too freaked out to think of it at MGM. Sorry, Doc."

Wonderful, thought Con, with a grin. He said, "Mix one for yourself for that bruise Spero gave you too."

"All right. Am I forgiven for my faux pas about you taking the mandrakes to get stoned ?" she asked.

"You bet," said Con, wondering what a faux pas was.

She said, "I've been so busy feeling sorry for myself," as she mixed mandrake powder in a glass of water for Doc, "I haven't asked you guys where you're from and where you're headed."

Doc said, "My story's a lot like yours, little girl. I'm from San Diego. I watched my family die there, then fired up the buggy and headed east without any particular goal. Just needed to start over somehow." He related how he had stopped at the food bank, met Alejandra Orlando and began delivering food from her food bank to Hardy Town for her. He told her about the sacking of Orlando's and the murder of its people and how he came to be where Spero had found him.

Con told how he had left his little town of Tres Robles because he had too many memories there. "Everyone I had known were gone. If not for Chou's Disease my girlfriend Gloria and I would've been married by now."

"And you have a place to go now?"

"Yes. I'm on the way to Tin Cup, Colorado."

"Tin Cup?" said Lois. "Is that a town?"

"Yeah," said Con. "The nurse who helped me through my second bout of Chou's, Chloë, was headed there. She was the only person left that I knew and respected, so I decided to follow her."

"Where is this Tin Cup?"

Con shrugged again. "Some place in Colorado."

"You don't know where?"

He shrugged. "Somebody in Colorado'll know."

After they finished eating, Doc showed Con how to completely disassemble and clean the revolver.

Back on the road, Doc said, "Let's make a rule that we always keep a firearm handy. And no one goes anywhere apart from the others without one. Do you know how to fire a gun, little girl?"

"Yes. My Uncle Eddie was a gun nut. Kind of a survivalist. Before the pandemic, he thought there would be a revolution to take back jobs that the computers and robots had stolen. Against my mom's wishes, he taught Margie and me how to fire his pistol and rifles."

"Well then," said Doc, "you'll be a better shot than Con. But once you pull a gun on somebody, be prepared to use it. That's the hardest lesson of all. Otherwise, they'll just walk up, take it away and use it on you.

"And as far as jobs go, computers gave some people like me jobs. Though I admit quite a few people were on the dole because technology stole their livelihoods."

"And some of us got jobs without college degrees or relying on computers," said Con.

Lois asked, "Have either of you thought of us joining one of these settlements of survivors?"

"I joined a few of them temporarily," said Con. "To work for food until I moved on. But I only went up to the ones who seemed to welcome folks."

Doc said, "The ones without a way of producing food are dead ends. When the existing food gets scarce they'll kill each other for what remains. Then whoever's left'll starve after the last of it's gone."

Con asked Lois how she had come to be so far from Los Angeles.

"My Uncle Eddie, my mother's younger brother, was the only one of our family to survive the Disease. When he found out I was still alive, he invited me to leave with him. Said he was going to join some friends in the mountains in Utah. They were some kind of survivalists but I didn't care. I'd be with Eddie. I'd always liked him. He was a lot of fun. And survivalists had to be able to, well, survive, hadn't they?

"So we packed up and took off in his car. We found plenty of charging stations that still worked. But Uncle Eddie got sick again. I don't think it was Chou's. It was more his stomach, vomiting and diarrhea. I took over driving, but he started running a high fever and had to stop a lot. I was really worried about him. When I saw this big solar farm, I decided to stop there where he could lay in the shade of the solar panels."

Con wondered if it had been the same solar farm Doc had used to stockpile his goods. Of course, a lot of solar farms existed in that sunny area.

"I woke up early in the morning to this terrible smell. He had died in the night and…and…"

"Voided himself," said Doc. "Sounds like a water-borne disease. And you didn't have any symptoms?"

"No, but I had filled jars with water from our house. I don't know where he got the water he brought. Not at his house. He said it didn't have any because a water line burst nearby. At any rate, when I went back to his car, I found it gone. Electric cars make so little noise I didn't hear anyone take it."

Con asked, "How could they have started it?"

Doc said, "It's not hard for a mechanic who knows what he's doing."

Lois had nothing to dig a grave with so she covered Eddie with all the loose dirt, gravel and rocks she could find. Then she started walking up the highway without food or water in the sun. That's how Spero found her, dehydrated and sunburned. He added her to his "Gaian flowers" to work in the garden, carry water, cook and help with the rest of the work, except for tending the mandrakes. Only he could care for them. In a few days, after she had recovered from her debilitating trek, he took her to his bed like he did the other women.

"I was a virgin," she said. "It was horrible. I can't talk about it." She gasped and looked away for a moment. Then, "He came to choose me over the others. From then on the women ostracized me from their group. I felt so alone. Then one day, while he was with his mandrakes Verbena sent me to fetch him. I was used to her bossing me around, but nobody gave Spero orders. I delivered the message and he stomped back to confront her.

"Only to find Verbena standing between the other two women, holding his rifle on us. She had obviously found it in his personal lean-to. She told him, 'We've packed some food and water for you. Now take it and your little whore and get out. This is our place now.' I was stunned. I couldn't think of anything more horrible than being alone with Spero day and night. At least in the gorge I had work to do during the day. Being with the three women who hated me all day was far better than being with Spero all the time. He thundered and cursed them, then begged and pleaded until Verbena pointed the rifle right at his balls. She said, 'You got to the count of three to start moving.' So we got. Two days later we found Doc. And you know all about that."

Lois resumed looking up at the giant buildings. They passed Circus Circus and others.

Con could think of nothing to say to her. To distract her, he said, "Impressive, the first time you see these buildings, huh? But just think of this. All the money they cost is now gone forever."

"And," she said, "all the money that passed through them while they were open. Now they're just useless ruins."

Doc said in a voice one used to quote the work of another, "'Look on my works, ye Mighty and despair! / Nothing beside remains. Round the decay / Of that colossal wreck, boundless and bare / The lone and level sands stretch far away.'"

"'Ozymandias,'" said Lois. "Percy Bysshe Shelley."

"I'm impressed, Lois," said Doc.

"You shouldn't be. I was a literature major." She sighed. "A degree now as worthless as Ozymandias' great works and the wealth of Las Vegas."

"Never think that," said Doc. "We have to preserve Shelley and all other great poets and literature. And whatever technological information that's necessary to fight our way back."

How different, thought Con, from the Doc who had preached the futility of trying to save civilization. Perhaps he meant it to raise Lois' spirits. And Lois had passed from shy, helpless stray to mature cynic. Con had passed high school without distinction with no desire to continue his education. Doc's knowledge, which seemed to come from a mix of college and experience, seemed boundless. Lois' education put her on a level nearer to Doc than Con. He felt left out.

Suddenly, Lois grasped his arm. "Con, what's that!" She pointed out the windshield to the left side of the street.

"What is what?" He stomped the brake and looked where she pointed.

"Hey, watch it!" hollered Doc as the buggy skidded to a stop.

"Sorry, Doc." He would try to be more careful because of his injury.

"That white tower."

Con leaned back in the seat and chuckled. "That's the Stratosphere tower. The building behind it is the hotel and casino and parking garage."

"Oh, my. It looks like some kind of weird spaceship. The wide part on top could be the quarters for the crew and passengers with the spar pointed toward their destination."

Con smiled, relieved that he could explain something she didn't know about. "No, it's just an observation tower. You can see all over Vegas from there. There was a good restaurant there and cocktail lounges. There used to be rides, a sky jump, a rollercoaster and other fun stuff. All scary."

He put the buggy in gear and drove past it, but slowly so Lois could keep watching it.

Beyond the tower, Con stopped, thinking of Doc. "I'm sorry this ride's so rough on you, Doc. Shall we stop for a while?"

"No, let's go downtown and take a look at Fremont Street. Maybe from a distance. If we decide to explore it, daytime's better."

So Con drove down Las Vegas Boulevard's northernmost, less glamorous, reach. They passed pawn shops, tattoo parlors, wedding chapels, bars, restaurants and shops. A few clouds drifting over the moon and stars made their light come and go so Con drove more carefully to avoid trash that might flatten a tire.

When Lois gasped, "Con, look!" he stepped on the brake, but gently for Doc's sake. He looked up. With his attention riveted on the street, Lois had seen brightly lit sky seconds before him.

"Doc," he said, "you need to see this."

Doc, lying behind the front seats so he couldn't see ahead, said. "Yeah?" And when he sat up, "Wow, those lights are bright. And they're coming from downtown."

Con said, "We can't see their source but they gotta be electric. That can't be."

"Remember your Sherlock Holmes," said Doc. "'Once you eliminate the impossible, whatever remains, no matter how improbable, must be the truth.' The light looks like it's coming from the covered pedestrian mall portion of Fremont."

"So, what do we do about this 'improbable truth.' Just go up and say hi?"

Doc said, "Let's be more circumspect. Take a right at this next street and let's sneak over to the part of Fremont Street south of downtown where we can look the lights over from cover."

Con drove down a series of side streets leading to Fremont Street five or six blocks southeast of downtown. He parked behind a liquor store that hid the buggy and cart. They got out, crept to the edge of the store and looked around the corner. Floodlights illuminated the intersection of Fremont and a broad cross street.

A high wall crossing the street from building to building blocked it. A vast banner spread across the entire mall entrance. It stated in huge red letters, "WELCOME TO DANTE'S MARKET." Smaller letters in the second line, barely legible at that distance, said, "All ye who enter here embrace hope." The third and fourth lines said, "We keep any weapons we find on you / and you will be banned forever."

"I suggest we wait until morning to approach them," said Doc. "Nighttime visitors may not be welcome."

Con and Lois nodded without question. Con noted how curiosity had driven them to tacitly agree to check out the market. A grassy area beside the liquor store made an appealing-looking campsite.

Eleven – A Return to the Fairy Rainbow

They awakened a little after dawn. After morning ablutions, they ate a cold breakfast sitting on the curb in front of the liquor store. The entrance to Dante's Market looked rather down-at-the-heels by daylight. The cover over the pedestrian mall behind it looked intact. The stained banner slouched listlessly over a wall of bricks, concrete blocks and stones, crudely mortared together. It did look quite solid, though, with a stout wooden double gate, wide and tall enough to admit a truck, in its center. A small brick kiosk with no door stood beside the gate. It had horizontal slots at eye level on the two sides they could see.

Con asked Doc, "So how do we approach them?"

Doc shrugged. "We don't until I check it out."

"Until you check it out?"

"We can't all just drive over there in a dune buggy bristling with weapons. Read the banner. And we can't all go and leave the buggy here unattended, loaded with all our stuff."

"Yeah, I know. But why don't I go? You're more important to our little group than me. You and Lois are better with guns." He didn't add, *and you're smarter than me.*

Doc said, "That's true. That's why I'm leaving Lois here to protect you." He grinned at Con and smacked his shoulder. "And if there's any negotiating to do, I'm more experienced at it."

Con sighed. "I can't argue with that. If you don't come back I have dibs on your bulletproof vest."

"That's okay," said Lois. "It's too big for me. But I get his shotgun."

"Thanks for your support," said Doc. He turned toward Dante's Market, walking slowly. Con could tell his injury still caused him pain.

Con felt Lois' hand slip into his. She said quietly, "You're as important as any of us, Con Colby, and maybe braver. You faced Spero with just a knife."

He couldn't think of a suitable response, so he squeezed her hand and held it, looked down at her and smiled. He wanted to kiss her, but she had turned to watch Doc and the Market. So he did too.

Lois asked, "What's beyond the wall?"

"That part of Fremont used to be a pedestrian mall. They projected light shows on the underside of the canopy that showed birds, rockets and weird critters flying down the mall."

When Doc got within a half block of the wall, one of the gates opened. A large black man came out. He stood with arms akimbo until Doc reached him. Though Con and Lois couldn't hear what they said, they saw the two greet each other, shake hands and stand talking. Doc looked shorter than usual standing beside the big man. After a few minutes, the black man called to someone through the open gate. A blond man came out and said something to Doc, who raised his arms straight out to the side. The man frisked him. After a few more words with the black man,

Doc shook hands with him again, turned and started back toward Con and Lois.

Con and Lois' curiosity made Doc's return seem interminable.

When he finally reached them, Lois asked, "Was the big guy Dante?"

"Yes. Dante LaFarge himself. He tries to meet everyone personally who comes to his compound, as he calls it. He welcomes us and says we can stay as long as we like if we're willing to work."

Con said, "Work at what?"

"They got lots of jobs. It's not just a market. It's a community. They make things to sell to other people."

Lois said, "What other people?"

"I don't know. Let's go find out. We'll have to give them our guns. They'll give them back when we leave. You'll have to turn that over too." Doc pointed at Con's hunting knife.

"Wait a minute," said Con. "We don't know anything about this guy. Maybe he just wants to collect guns so he can start a war."

Lois asked, "Did he pull a gun on you, Doc? From here it didn't look like he even had one."

"He didn't. Neither did the guy he called to come out, Joe Emerson."

Con said, "Of course, the guy in that little kiosk with the slots could've had a gun."

"True. Still, Dante didn't try to talk me into anything; just said we could either come in to shop and leave or take his offer to join them or go on our way."

"Well," said Lois, "why don't we all go talk to him and then decide."

They piled into the buggy, Doc in the front this time, drove to the gate and got out of the vehicle. A third man had joined Dante. A buzz of voices and the sounds of activity came from beyond the wall. Doc introduced Con and Lois.

Dante took Lois' hand gently and said in a deep, resonant but gentle voice, "I'm glad to meet you, Lois. Doc told me what a fine young woman you are. I see he was right. I'm Dante LaFarge and these are my right-hand men. This is Joe Emerson. The little fellow that just came out is Manuel Cuzco."

"Most people call me Manny," said the newcomer.

The blond man, Joe Emerson, had looked small from a distance because of his proximity to Dante LaFarge, but he stood about six feet tall and his polo shirt revealed a muscular frame. Manny Cuzco only looked small standing beside Dante and Emerson.

After introductions all around, Dante smiled and shrugged. "So, what do you think? Want to give us a look? You can leave anytime you want."

The three looked at each other. Doc said, "Let's check the place out."

Con felt nervous about giving up their weapons but finally gave a "what the hell" shrug, loosened his belt to slide off his sheath and knife and handed it to Dante. As he submitted to a search by Emerson, he saw Lois fidget.

Before he could protest her search, Dante said, "Don't worry, Miss. You'll see Martha once we get inside. She's as gentle and sweet as a spring flower."

Con and Doc took their weapons and ammunition from the buggy, including even Doc's bulletproof vest, and handed them to Emerson, who unrolled a plastic sheet he had brought from inside and wrapped the weapons in it.

"While I show you around the compound," said Dante, "I'm sure you won't mind if Joe and Manny search your vehicle and cart. It's a routine procedure that we ask of every visitor." His voice, deep and gentle, nevertheless evoked a sense of quiet power. Dante motioned them into the open gate and followed them in. The voices and noise of activity sounded more distinct inside. Dante stopped them and took Lois inside an enclosure against the outer wall he called the "front office" to see Martha.

Once he emerged, Dante said, "We're chronically short-handed in case you'd like to consider staying."

Con looked around. A score or more of stalls, tents and lean-tos of various sizes stood haphazardly over the mall for two blocks. Some were mere frameworks draped with sheets of plastic or canvas. Their lack of order surprised him.

Martha's examination of Lois didn't take long. After Lois appeared, Dante led the three down the unoccupied center of the mall on a surface of colorful mosaic tile laid in abstract or geometrical designs. Dante called it their "promenade." Moribund hotels and casinos formed the mall's boundaries along each side, their doors and windows bricked over. The sounds of wood- or metalworking came from a few sheds and smoke rose from some of their chimneys. People worked inside the structures or walked among them. Everybody looked busy but many found time to talk or laugh with each other. Bright spots of sunlight, varying from a few inches to several yards across, shone through holes in the canopy. Avoidance of those must have largely explained the slapdash locations of the little businesses.

Dante explained as they walked, "Like I told Doc, we make things for people who don't know how or don't have time or don't want to be bothered to make. They pay us mostly in food or things they've pilfered from the hotels and casinos." He stopped at one of the larger tents and pulled aside the blanket over the doorway. "Hello, Claire," he said to a short, squat middle-aged woman arranging candles on a table just inside.

"Hi, Dante." She looked the three newcomers over. "What kind of candles you folks lookin for?"

"They're not customers, Claire. At least not yet." And to the three, "Claire and her daughters are our chandlers."

"What do you make them of?" asked Lois. "Bees' wax and tallow must be scarce around here."

Claire laughed. "Soy wax. Our biggest customer raises soybeans hydroponically."

Dante said, "Claire's business is growing more important as the hotel candles get used up. Thanks for letting us disturb you, Claire."

Con made a mental note to acquire more candles before they left.

Dante dropped the doorway flap and they moved on. They passed what had once been an intersection of a cross street with the pedestrian mall. Similar walls to that at the entrance blocked the streets. Each had a solid-looking door in it, not a double gate like that in the entrance wall but a person-sized door, expensive looking, that must have come from inside a casino. Con bet guard kiosks like the one at the main entrance set outside the doors.

Dante pointed out a couple of pottery shops, another whose owner wove baskets from the sturdy fibers of desert plants and others that produced soap, clothing, dyes and other items. Partway along their walk, One door in a casino had not been sealed off. A small balcony with tables and chairs protruded from the second floor above it. It had obviously been used recently. Con resolved to ask Dante about the door and balcony during a break in his monologue.

They reached the end of the compound, blocked by a wall similar to that at the entrance. Dante turned to face them, hands on hips. "Well, what do you think of our little empire?"

"An interesting setup," said Doc, "but I have a couple of questions."

"Fire away."

"First, how many solar panels does it take to illuminate the nighttime light show at the entrance? And second, how do your shoppers find enough food to feed themselves and pay you?"

As Doc spoke, Dante's smile broadened. "Those are related questions, my friend. We use rooftop solar panels for day-to-day needs in the kitchen and some of the light in our rooms, but they wouldn't provide enough electricity for all our needs. By the way the 'light show' on our outside walls isn't to show off. It's for security. Our compound is not without enemies. But we can generate all the electricity we need and enough to sell to the food producers. They use it to grow enough food for themselves and for us. A sound economic system, right?"

"And I suppose how you produce this power is secret."

"Not at all. We use pedal-driven generators."

Doc shook his head. "That can't be, Dante. Bicycle-driven generators are too inefficient. Even with a hundred people pedaling day and night, you couldn't keep your entrance lit all night, let alone enough to produce enough watts to export."

"You're right, but I didn't say bicycle-driven. I said pedal-driven. Bicycles weren't invented to power generators. Energy is lost from pedal to chain and chain to sprocket. Our workers pedal the wheel directly. It operates generators that produce 110 volts of alternating current."

Doc asked, "How do you sell electric power to your customers?"

"We recharge their vehicle batteries. If you look under the hood of the cars, trucks or heavy equipment anywhere in town, you'll be lucky to find a battery."

"But how long will car batteries last? Despite the advances made in electric car batteries."

"Right, again. Their days are numbered. We don't use them for the compound. We use compressed air energy storage. That's been around for small-scale use for a long time. I found plans for a system that powered nine locomotives. We store energy in these compressed air units, release it to power our generators and charge our clients' batteries."

Doc grinned. "Sounds like you got the power problem covered. And I thought I was handy making mechanized things. What's your background?"

"I'm a mechanical engineer. Had my own company. But come with me. I have to get back to work soon."

Dante turned to retrace his steps with the others following.

Doc asked, "What brought you to Vegas? It's not exactly a hotbed of cutting-edge technology."

Dante looked down. "An email from my son. He got Chou's Disease. My wife had died of it, but I survived. Had to be here with him in his last days. He was a magician on tour and –"

"Dante's Inferno!" said Lois. "That was his show?"

"Musta been!" said Con. "His banner said, 'All ye who enter here, enjoy.' I thought something about your sign had a familiar ring."

"So that was your son," said Doc. "He never used his last name, so I thought 'Dante' was a show name."

Dante looked up and smiled sadly. "Yes, Dante Junior. He put on a good show, didn't he?"

Con said, "Yeah. Black curtains opened to a dark stage. Then bright red lights and explosions. Hot female assistants with skimpy devil outfits."

"So anyway, I was numb from my son's death and the pandemic. By the time I forced myself to get off my ass to leave, all the airports had shut down. I didn't have any place I wanted to go anyway. But I always gotta tinker and I met some people as lost as I was. We got hit by some bad ones, too, so we built this fortified compound and started our market."

Doc said, "So how do your customers use charged car batteries to produce enough food for themselves, let alone for you? In case you hadn't noticed, Las Vegas lays smack dab in the middle of a desert. Where do they get their water? For that matter, where does your community get its water?"

"Las Vegas got almost ninety percent of its public water supply from Lake Mead, which is only a big pond now. But did you ever notice the astronomical amount of water the hotels used back in the day? Everywhere you looked you saw water features, fountains, waterfalls, even canals. The fountains in the lake out front of the Bellagio blasted towers of water into the air every hour. Most hotels solved the problem by tapping their own aquifers for water. So when we set up our pedal-driven electrical system, one of the first things we did was activate a hotel pump.

"A guy name of Chris Abend from a big mall out along the strip asked how we got our water. He wanted to set up some kind of a hydroponic system in the mall, but it would take a huge amount of water. I'd been worried about what we'd do after the food from the hotels ran out. This was the answer to our prayers. So we sell them water for produce from their gardens."

Doc grinned. "Shows what I know. I told these kids that the people in that mall would starve after the hotel food spoiled or ran out."

They had reached the hotel with the unbricked door and the small balcony above.

Dante said, "I'll show you one more thing before I go to the office."

He led them inside and down a dark corridor, obviously made since the compound's construction. A few closed doors appeared in its walls. Muted sounds issued from behind one.

Con asked Dante, "What's going on in there? Or maybe it's none of my business."

"It's no secret. That's our pedalers. Except for work, we pretty much live inside this casino. This next door leads to the refectory. Head in there when you hear the dinner bell. Couples and families eat in their own apartments but our single residents, about a third of our people, eat in there." At the next door, he said, "This goes to the school and nursery. That's why you won't see any little ones running around outside until evening."

They climbed a motionless escalator to the second floor. At the top, light entered from two windows and a glass door leading out to the balcony. They walked between ranks and columns of the ubiquitous slot machines. Dante opened the door to the balcony and gestured for them to go out. It only took a few tables and chairs to fill. An ornate wrought iron railing surrounded three sides. They sat around one of the tables.

He gestured to the mall's ceiling. "When they ran the light shows, the view from here was exhilarating. Tourists used to look longingly up from the mall, saw us with drinks in our hands and wished they were important enough to join us. Not knowing the balcony was public, open to everybody. Only natives knew that." Dante's laugh was deep and resonant.

"And you didn't tell them," said Doc.

"Indeed not. My wife and I wouldn't have known about it if my son hadn't told us and then swore us to secrecy.

"But let me change the subject and tell you our deal. Everybody can stay here a night or two if they're just passing through. Or they can stay as long as they're willing to pitch in and work. Which we encourage you to do. Our population of a hundred and thirty-three can't handle all the jobs."

The door opened and the blond man, Joe Emerson, appeared. He looked distraught.

He nodded greetings to them all and said to Dante, "That new guy, Rick Skinner, he didn't make it back again last night. He's been gone two days now."

Dante shrugged. "Well, not everybody fits into our little community. As I recall, he wasn't our hardest worker."

"No, I had to stay on his ass to get him to do anything. If he comes back, I recommend we send him packing."

"Maybe just a stern talk. Let's give him one more chance. Keep in mind what the world's like now."

Emerson shrugged resignedly. "You're the boss, but I don't trust him. He hasn't straightened out in the month he's been here despite my riding him." And to the others, "Dante's too mild a guy. He'd support every lazy bum in the world who wants to stay here if he had his way."

Dante said, "One more chance, Joe. Then you can do as you like."

Emerson smiled briefly at the three, said goodbye and left.

Dante stood. "Now I have some work to catch up on, work schedules, checking the battery inventory, exciting stuff like that. First though, if you like, I can introduce you to Beulah who can show you where to take a shower."

"A real shower?" said Con. "The last one I had in Hardy Town wasn't even a real one."

"Well, you might not think this one's 'real' either, but it's the best we have."

They followed Dante down the escalator and through gaming rooms that looked like those in MGM Grand, right down to the luminescent strips on the slot machines. Dante ushered them into a large room at the rear of the casino with people washing clothes in big tubs and hanging them on lines strung from wall to wall. Near the far wall stood a dozen or so plastic-sided stalls. A smiling, attractive woman stood near them folding towels and placing them on a metal table. Though she appeared to be about Doc's age her café au lait skin remained smooth. Silver threaded her great bush of reddish-black hair. She smelled of lavender, undoubtedly some expensive scent obtained in a hotel boutique. Dante introduced her to them as Beulah.

She said, "I bet you-all are the proud owners of that 'Moveable Feast' beast settin out yonder in the garage." She turned and opened a door, which revealed a large garage. About twenty vehicles sat with their noses facing the washroom wall: cars, trucks, dune buggies and motorbikes, all electric. The Moveable Feast sat near the door.

"That we are, ma'am," said Doc.

"My Virgil an me had one kinda like her." She looked away to hide her trembling chin. "He'd a sure nough liked to a seen yours." She looked up at Doc and smiled. "I'd be much obliged to have a ride in her someday. I had Manny move it close to the door so you-all could get whatever you needed for your shower."

"You're a saint among women, Beulah," said Doc as he appraised her lithe figure. "We'll take a ride in her as soon as possible."

She smiled. "I'll hold you to it. Might give us a chance to get to know each other better too."

He pointed to a large double door and a smaller, person-sized one in the garage's far wall. "Do those doors lead outside?"

"Yes, sir, out to what used to be a public street. Now, how bout them showers?

Beulah indicated three stalls that were ready for use. She explained how they worked. Half a metal drum rested on a rack above each. They had sat, filled with water, in the sun all day. The drums' bottoms had been perforated with small holes with a moveable cover that kept them from leaking. The bathers stood beneath the drums and levered the cover aside for an initial soaking, then closed the cover, soaped themselves and opened it again to rinse clean.

Soon after they finished showering, a bell summoned them to dinner, which consisted of a salad of greens and tomatoes, roasted potatoes and roasted chicken, so delicious after weeks of pressure-wrapped, self-heating meals.

Con, seeing Doc frown, said, "You don't like it, Doc? These roasted potatoes are to die for."

"No, the food's wonderful. I'm just thinking about the double door in the garage."

"It had a steel bar across it and looked pretty solid."

"But I saw sunlight through cracks around the edges of the door."

Con said, "Yeah, but Dante seems to have everything under control." Besides, he thought, I'll soon be on my way to Tin Cup whether Doc and Lois go with me or not. Though he sure hoped they would.

Doc shrugged. "Even if the bar held, a heavy enough blow could snap the hinges off."

After dinner, they found the bar, conveniently located behind the refectory, or mess hall as Doc called it, but they were too tired for more than two beers each, one for Lois. They decided to put off talking about staying until the next day. Beer was free to anyone merely passing through on their first day.

"Something worries me about this place," said Con.

"What's that?" said Doc.

"It seems too perfect."

"You sound more like me all the time."

Con grinned. "That concerns me too."

Barracks for visitors had been prepared on the third floor, one room for men and the other for women. Con and Doc bade Lois good night at the door to her barracks. She looked wistfully after Con as the two men walked away. He smiled back at her, thinking of how her hand had felt in his that morning, a hand slightly roughened by work in Spero's garden but not as much as his from jobs on the road. And the thrill of her hair brushing his face, greasy from traveling so long without a chance to wash it. Like his. The vagaries of travel, both alone and together, had drawn them close. He remembered how badly he had longed to kiss her.

Doc said, "You're a fool."

"What?"

Doc looked back at Lois and then at Con but only shook his head and kept walking.

Con and Doc found their room nearly filled with beds, though they were the only occupants. Con let Doc have the bed nearest the door and the bathroom. The hallway had received a little light from widely spaced candles, but their room was utterly dark except for a thin, dim line under the door. They had candles and fire strikers in their bags but felt too tired to dig them out.

Doc fell asleep immediately but Con lay awake, thinking of Lois. Doc had been right. He should have gone back to Lois to hold her and kiss her good night. With a twinge of guilt, he realized he hadn't thought of Gloria since they had begun the ride with Lois.

Light lanced across the room from the opening doorway. He recognized the small form silhouetted against it that entered and quietly closed the door behind her. He sensed her approach in the dark. Her weight on the bed excited him. He felt her slipping under the sheet. Yet she didn't touch him.

He could barely hear her shy whisper. "I'll leave, Con, if you think I'm being too presumptuous. I just wanted to be near you." She indeed sounded like Spero's gentle flower. "I've thought of you ever since the night in the gulch."

He slipped an arm around her, remembering the fairy rainbow.

Twelve – Christmas Shopping in Las Vegas

The distant breakfast bell woke Con and Doc. Lois had slipped away sometime before. On the way down to the refectory, Doc asked with a conspiratorial grin, "Did you sleep well last night?"

Con shrugged nonchalantly. "Better than usual. And you?"

"Not as well as you. But I got more sleep."

They joined Lois, already there; Con sat beside her. She placed her hand on his thigh under the table. He put a hand over hers. She smiled demurely. He returned it with a lascivious one.

Doc said, "We need to decide what to do. I, for one, could use a rest for a while. This looks like a good, safe place. Of course, none of us are bound by the others' decisions." He looked at each of them in turn.

Con said, "I agree. For a little while since they said we can leave any time." He looked questioningly at Lois, though they knew she could hardly leave alone.

"I'm for that," she said, then smiled at them. "In fact, this would be a good time for it. December must be half over by now. Christmas is coming up."

Doc smirked. "Hey, you're right, and I haven't ordered your gifts yet."

After breakfast, they found Dante in his so-called "front office" just inside the front gate. With him were Martha and an old man named Earl Hudson with skin the color and wrinkled texture of an ancient walnut. Dante introduced him as his "runner." Con thought that ironic since he barely looked able to walk. Martha, a businesslike, gray-haired, middle-aged lady, had searched Lois the day before.

"We've decided to take you up on your offer to stay," Doc told Dante. "Put us to work."

Dante had been adding a column of numbers. He leaned back in his chair and studied them for a moment. "Good. Doc, the questions you asked yesterday show your technological bent. Joe and Manny are good supervisors, and they have competent foremen under them, but they need help to keep equipment running. And I could use a hand with the compressed air storage energy batteries. Let's try you out on stuff like that."

Doc nodded. "Sounds good."

"And Con, we need a strong young man like you. We can switch you from one job to another so you won't get bored. You can start off pedaling. Okay?"

Con shrugged. "Fine." But thought, *He needs a strong back/weak mind type of guy. Like me.*

"Lois, you probably don't know much about making candles, but you seem like a quick learner. Our candle business is growing. Claire and her daughters could use some help. How's that sound?"

"Interesting."

"Good. Settle in today and report here in the morning for your assignments. You'll get a day off every week. Consider yourselves citizens of Dante's Market from now on if you want to be. Any questions?"

"Yes," said Doc. "Can we three have the same day off?"

Dante said, "I don't see why not."

Lois asked, "What is today's date?"

Martha indicated a calendar above her desk. "It's December twelfth, 2072."

Lois thanked her.

"Okay," said Dante. "And I suppose you'll keep the same dorm rooms…?"

Con cleared his throat. "Lois and I would like a room together if possible."

Con heard an intake of breath from Lois and from the corner of his eye, saw Doc grin.

After the briefest pause, Dante said, "Why, of course. Martha will see to it."

* * *

Con soon came to hate pedaling. His shift lasted six hours, from 8:00 a.m. until 2:00 p.m. He pedaled for an hour at a time with fifteen-minute breaks in between. Manny made rounds occasionally to make sure everyone pedaled over the minimum rpms. He frowned as he checked speedometer dials and chastened the laggards but said little to the others. The strength of Con's legs, thanks to his long trek, surprised him. The exercise would have exhausted the sedentary pre-pandemic Con. He easily maintained the required speed but found the monotony, the exercise and the unrelenting heat excruciating.

Men manned most of the machines, but a few stout women also pedaled. Manny harassed a dozen or so workers more than others. He threatened to throw those who couldn't maintain the minimum speed out of the compound. He especially hassled an undernourished-looking kid named Artie. Once, he hollered at him, "How long do you think your skinny ass'll last out on the streets? Unless you find some sugar-daddy who thinks yours is cute."

On the first afternoon, a big guy several stations behind Artie stopped pedaling and approached the two. He hovered over Manny. Though Con couldn't understand them over the hum of the wheels, he saw them argue for a time. When Manny pointed to the big man's station, the man returned to it and went back to work. Though Manny hadn't backed down in the argument, he didn't harass the kid for the rest of the shift.

Despite his stamina, Con's legs began to ache toward the end of the shift. And they cramped when he got to their room that evening.

The next day Manny put Con to work at the loading dock, where customers waited with their carts and other contrivances. He and the other dock workers helped them unload goods they had scrounged from hotels and deserted homes that they wished to trade, especially vehicle batteries that needed recharging. After the customers finished shopping, Con and the others helped reload their vehicles with the Market's products and charged batteries.

Back to pedaling the next day. To keep the singing of the wheels and the enervating heat from driving him crazy, Con allowed his mind to wander, thinking of the resurrected technology he had seen in his travels. He changed his mind again about the revival of civilization. Doc must be wrong after all. Soon all would return to normal. Dante's Market seemed the most sustainable attempt he had witnessed. On the other hand, concerning Tin Cup, what if found it abandoned with winter snows covering its ruins?

That evening, after their third day of work, the three talked about their jobs over dinner.

Lois asked Con, "Did you have to ride the bike today again?"

"Yeah. They tell me it's nothing like a bicycle, but it sure feels like riding one. A bicycle to nowhere. And I think I'm stuck on it."

"What do you mean?"

"Manny told me I'd only have to pedal every other day this first week to keep my legs from cramping, to give them a chance to 'muscle up.' That sounds like it'll be my permanent job after this week."

"If that's the case you'll have to take it up with Dante."

"I will if Manny means to keep me pedaling. But how's candle making?"

"It's interesting for now but I can see it becoming boring pretty soon. We do the same stuff over and over." She explained how they dipped the tapers into melted wax again and again until they reached the desired diameter.

Con said, "I'm sure your job's a lot more interesting than ours, Doc."

He shrugged. "I'm learning a lot about compressed air storage energy batteries and how your pedaling generates electricity."

Con grumbled, "I've learned all I want to know about 'pedal power.'"

Later, in their room on the third floor, Lois said, "You're not yourself, Con. You're so gloomy. I know it's because of the pedaling. You need to speak to Dante."

"I want to talk to Manny first. I've learned never to go over my boss's head."

"That sounds wise." And after a time, "What do you think of Dante's Market? I mean, if you get your job situation straightened out. It seems like a safe, comfortable place. At least, given the rest of the world."

He brooded for a moment without answering. He was anxious to resume his trip to Tin Cup. And to convince Lois to join him.

She nudged him playfully. "Thinking about Tin Cup aren'tcha? And that nurse you know up there. I'll bet she has big tits. Not fried eggs like mine."

He laughed and lunged for her. "Let me show you how much I like fried eggs."

* * *

In truth, Con enjoyed only the part of his new life he spent with Lois. He didn't know how to ask her to go to Tin Cup with him. For safety's sake, she might decide to stay at Dante's Market. A student of English literature, she had read books he had never heard of. He read little, only the occasional thriller. And she was smart like Doc. They often talked and laughed about subjects he knew nothing about. Awkward silences occurred when they tried to draw him into those conversations.

If the pandemic had not depopulated the world, she wouldn't have had anything to do with him. Hell, they never would have met, her destined to be a college grad and him a small engine tinkerer.

He hoped Doc would go to Tin Cup with him for a lot of reasons, mainly because he liked, admired and respected the man. he liked, admired and respected the man. Then, too, the Moveable Feast would get them there much quicker, and traveling with Doc would be safer. He had to think of a way to broach their leaving to Doc.

One night, for the first time in a long while, he dreamed of Gloria. She stood a long way from him across a stretch of desert. He walked toward her. Though she didn't move, she stayed the same distance from him. He tried to call out to her but could make no sound. At last, she smiled sadly, blew him a kiss and disappeared.

He awoke sweating in the heat, disturbed by the dream. It took him a long time to get back to sleep.

✳ ✳ ✳

On Con's fifth day of work and third of pedaling, his break coincided with that of the burly guy who had defended Artie. Wiping sweat from his face with his handkerchief, he walked over to where the man drank water from a community pitcher.

Con said, "Hi. I've heard you called Kane. I'm Con."

"Glad to meetcha, Con. But wish it was in a different place." They shook hands.

"Me too." Con also took a drink from the pitcher. They sat on a nearby bench. "I've got a question for you, Kane. But you don't have to answer if you don't want to."

"Go ahead, shoot."

"I've noticed you and Artie are friends and I'm wondering why Manny bullies him so much and why Artie takes it. He could complain to Dante and get an easier job."

Kane scoffed. "Artie's my sister's kid. Manny bullies him because he can. Dante turned this operation over to him and lets him run it however he wants. He don't fuck with me though. He knows I'd kick his ass. If you've noticed, there's about twenty here that Manny bullies the worst, though not as bad as Artie. Y' see, them and me and Artie ain't citizens here."

"What? Dante told us anybody who worked could be a citizen."

"Well, it ain't quite like that. See, we belong to Chris Abend's horticulture mall? And it needs lotsa water. Artie and me are mongst the twelve Abend sends over to help pay for the water."

"But Dante said the horticulture outfit pays for the water in food."

"Dante's Market don't have enough workers, so they charge warm bodies along with the food. They's eleven of us Abend guys pedalin and five from Bennet's folk. And a few more from other groups."

"Wait a minute. You said Abend sent over twelve of you. Now you say eleven. And who is Bennet's folk?"

Kane scoffed again. "No, I said Abend sent twelve and eleven are pedalin. Manny took a fancy to the twelfth one, Lola, and keeps her for himself. And Bennet? He's a pretend merchant who's really a crook. His gang captures people passin through town and locals dumb enough to roam the ruins alone, and sends em here to pedal. Bandits gotta have water too."

"How does this Abend decide who works for Dante's Market?"

"Mainly, he chooses us that fucks up. Me and Barker, that big guy settin over there? Got drunk and had a fight in a bar, wrecked some furniture."

"You two seem to get along now."

"Oh, yeah. We're buddies. We just get fucked up sometimes. Anyhow, he sent us here to pedal these damned wheels for six months. Three to go and then Abend'll send somebody to replace us. It ain't so bad for Barker and me, except for the boredom – we're big guys – but poor Artie…" He shook his head. "He mouthed off to one of the Abend's sub bosses. Thank God he's only got a month left."

Con asked, "Manny couldn't just kick Artie out on the street, could he? Wouldn't Abend take him back?"

Kane shrugged. "I don't know. Some that Abend sends here don't come back home."

"At least the shift is only six hours. That gives Artie time to rest up."

"That's for you residents. We have eight-hour shifts."

Con wondered if those who didn't go back to Abend's mall made a run for it across the desert or joined criminals like Bennet. He wondered how many survived.

He longed to leave on the next stage of his journey to Tin Cup.

* * *

Dante had reserved a hotel bar for his managers, "soldiers" and their spouses or lovers, a couple dozen or so. A conference room between the refectory and the hotel bar served as a bar for regular workers. Wine, beer, spirits and mixes for both came from the hotels, casinos and liquor stores, some brought for trade by the Market's customers. Managers' drinks came gratis, without any limit. Workers earned three beers or glasses of wine or two mixed drinks for each shift, recorded by their names on a slate behind the bar; no sense risking the hoi polloi getting so loaded they missed work the next day.

After his shift on the fifth day and a couple of beers in the workers' bar, Con waited for Manny outside the managers' lounge. When he emerged, a little wobbly, Con confronted him.

"Could I have a moment, Manny?"

Manny stopped, surprised. "Who the hell –? Ah, yeah, you're the new guy, Conner or something."

"Conrad. I'm wondering about next week. For my every-other-day job,, can I have some shifts in one of those guardhouse things?" He had noticed six of them. They had no outside access, only entrances from inside the compound.

Manny chuckled and shook his head. "Ah, no, no. Only long-time residents stand guard. They have to be armed. They're the only ones we trust with guns."

"I guess loading customers' carts is okay. Or carpenter work. I heard a couple guys talking about moving a wall to make a bigger apartment. Or maintenance, or –"

"No, no, no." Manny held up his hand, his grin wavering. "I only gave you a break in the first week to get your legs strong. You're too good on the pedals. That's your job."

"But Dante told me –"

Manny's grin changed to an angry grimace. "I don't give a fuck what Dante said. I run the laboring jobs, and I say you pedal."

Though no fighter, Con barely resisted hitting Manny. He turned and stormed away. He would confront Dante soon.

* * *

Finally, their day off arrived. At breakfast, Lois seemed unusually excited.

"I know this sounds silly and old-fashioned to you men of the road," she said, "but it's just a few days till Christmas and I'd like to get you guys a gift."

"Great," said Doc. "Just google me a new computer."

Con said, "How about a drone to check out the hottest new casino."

"No, I mean it," she said. "These abandoned hotel shops are full of treasure and it doesn't belong to anybody. Plus, I think exploring them would be a lot of fun. C'mon."

Con said, "You mean right now? Today?"

She said, "We won't have another day off for a week."

Doc shook his head. "We don't know what kind of people roam these ruins. They could be full of Speros."

"And even more dangerous birds," said Con.

Doc scowled. "Calling them birds seems a bit old-fashioned."

Con shook his head. "Not sparrows, those little birds that peck the ground around your feet. I'm talking about vicious birds like harpy eagles, peregrine falcons, vultures."

"Oh, I gotcha. We don't know how many harpy eagles are there, Lois."

She laughed. "You cowards. We'll only go into the casinos along the mall just outside the compound."

Doc grimaced. "I've gotten too used to feeling safe without looking over my shoulder every minute. That's what we'd be doing outside the compound. Remember, when you fall into a good thing, make the most of it. There's too few of them."

"Besides," said Con, "Dante's people will have already looted them. Haven't you seen the jewelry and clothes these people wear?"

Lois countered, "There's only a hundred and thirty-some people here. They couldn't've taken everything. They stocked these boutiques to accommodate millions of customers a year."

Doc sighed. "I know you won't give us any peace until we agree, so we'll do it. Right, Con?"

"Sure." Lois seemed determined to keep them there until at least after Christmas. That gave him a reprieve from asking her and Doc to leave with him.

"But," said Doc, "Con and I got something to do first." He stood. "Meet us by the back gate. Won't take us but a few minutes. C'mon, Con."

"What's up?" asked Con as he followed Doc to the washroom.

"We're going to see Beulah."

"Is she going shopping with us?"

"My God, I hope not. Shopping with one woman's bad enough."

Con sensed another of Doc's annoying little secrets.

In the washroom, Beulah greeted them with a big smile, directed especially at Doc.

Doc said, "I don't suppose the powers that be would object to me looking at the Feast."

"They might if they knew," she said, "But I ain't gonna tell em." She encircled Doc's arm with both of hers and pressed it between her breasts. "You ready to take me on that ride, sugar?"

"Sorry, love, not today, but soon." He grinned wolfishly and took his time freeing his arm. "Then we'll get to know each other a lot better."

Still vexed by Doc's latest secret, their flirtation irritated Con further. He went out into the garage and the buggy alone. A large, ungainly shape with a tarpaulin thrown over it sat about halfway down the cart, yet another of Doc's mysteries, he had no doubt.

Doc appeared and made an exasperated sound at having his coquetry interrupted. "Wait a minute, Con. You don't know what you're looking for."

"Well, you won't find it either until you get your ass out here." It pleased him to irritate Doc for a change.

Doc shut the door, which usually remained open, behind him, hurried over to the dune buggy and opened its back door. "I'm sure you remember the strongbox behind the battery." As he talked, he unfastened the brackets holding the battery in place.

"Sure. That's where you keep the drop cloth we spread parts out on to clean."

"Right. We'll see if Manny found it when he searched the buggy." He unbolted the frame securing the battery, pushed it aside and opened the strongbox. "Good. He didn't. The drop cloth's still there."

"I'm sure glad to know that. Can we go now?"

Doc removed the cloth, now wrapped around a small bundle. "I put these in there after the night I showed you my stash in the solar panel farm. Thought they'd come in handy."

After glancing over his shoulder to ensure the washroom door remained closed, he placed the bundle in a pocket and replaced the battery pack in front of the strongbox. Then he said, "Now, c'mere," went behind the buggy and sat on its bumper. No one opening the washroom door could see them there. Con sat beside him.

Doc extracted the bundle from his pocket, laid it on his lap and opened it. It contained two objects wrapped separately. He opened one to reveal a small revolver and a box of shells and put the other in his pocket.

He said, "I was lucky enough to find these two relics in an antique firearms store. Smith and Wesson 32-caliber pocket pistols, something your great-grandmother would have hidden in her bosom. It'll stop an adversary better than the 22 I gave you but is lighter to carry than a 45 and has less of a kick. And it's small enough to hide in your pocket." He handed the gun and a box of shells to Con.

"And you think we'll need these out there?"

"I doubt it, but I don't want to find out that we needed them too late."

They met Lois at the back gate. The heat had risen despite the early hour. Doc went up to the guard in the kiosk to tell him why they wanted to go out. As they exited, the guard said, "Be careful out there, Mr. Drennan."

"I certainly will, Charley."

Once out of Charley's hearing, Lois said, "Wow. "Mister Drennan. I'm impressed."

Doc shrugged. "People who see me with Dante all the time think I'm part of management."

They decided to go to the end of the mall to casinos less picked over by compound residents. To Con, walking the vacant, trash-strewn mall, bounded by giant, silent buildings seemed strangely eerie after the noisy, hectic compound.

Doc said, "There's something I wanted to tell you two that I'm probably not supposed to know. That's why I waited till we got beyond earshot of the Market."

"Because," Lois said, "even the walls have ears."

"Right," said Doc. "Yesterday, after I finished working on one of those compressed air storage energy batteries, I went up to Dante's hotel office to ask him a question. He has several offices, you know. I heard someone arguing so I stopped outside. I couldn't hear them very well but recognized Dante's voice. He called the other guy Chris. I wondered if it was Chris Abend. The guy raised his voice a few times, so I got the gist of the argument and found out he was indeed Abend. He called Dante's charges for water outrageous. Finally, he hollered, 'We're not gonna stand for this much longer,' and stomped toward the door. I split before they saw me."

"So, there's trouble in paradise," said Lois.

"There's even more trouble," said Con. "A lot of the pedaling is done by slave labor." He told them about his conversation with Kane and his confrontation with Manny after work.

Doc said, "From now on, let's keep our eyes and ears open and each other informed."

Suddenly, Lois laughed, pointed and exclaimed, "Look at that sign. That's the ugliest cowboy I've ever seen."

They looked up to see a large sign resembling a grinning cowboy with a cigarette dangling from one side of his mouth and a hand raised in greeting.

"Careful," said Doc. "You don't want to insult Vegas Vic."

"Oh, he has a name. I'm sorry, Vegas Vic."

"He used to be a friendly cuss, waved that hand and greeted everybody."

But now, Con thought, faded and without his neon lights, Vegas Vic looked pretty seedy.

The Fremont Street Mall ended in a T at a north-south arterial street named Main Street. On its other side a large building faced the mall. A sign identified it as the Plaza Hotel & Casino.

"Okay," said Doc. "Let's pick a casino to do our shopping in."

Lois said, "But we have to split up."

Doc said, "No way. Just leaving the compound was risky enough."

She insisted, "But I don't want you guys to know what I get you."

Con said, "It'll be okay if we go into the same casino and stay within earshot of each other."

Doc scowled thoughtfully for a moment. "I don't like it, but I'll agree if we stay close together. Let's go in here, the Golden Gate."

They entered the last casino on their left, bordering Main Street. It felt marginally cooler inside. Behind the gaming rooms and a snack bar, they found a labyrinth of hallways lined with boutique-style shops with glass walls and doors. Luminescent strips near the floor provided the only light. They agreed to meet at the snack bar after they finished "shopping." They took different hallways that seemed to run roughly parallel with each other so that, hopefully, they could stay in contact in case of trouble. Doc made Lois take the center one. Con had never considered even entering such exclusive shops in his past life. Now he only needed to break through a door or window to get in.

As it turned out, he didn't even have to do that. Without electricity, the electronic locks no longer functioned. When he pulled on the door of a jewelry shop it opened so freely, he almost fell. Pillagers had ransacked the store, leaving the remaining contents heaped in broken display cases or scattered on the floor. They had left plenty of loot behind, so it didn't take him long, even in the dim light, to find a gold and bejeweled set that included a matching necklace, bracelet and earrings for Lois and a diamond-encrusted gold watch for Doc. The watch still ran but Con had no way to tell if it kept the correct time. He placed his finds in the bag he had brought and returned to the snack bar. He sat at one of the tables. Doc soon joined him.

"No Lois yet, huh?" said Doc worriedly.

"You know how women like to shop. And today the price is right."

But after roughly a quarter of an hour Con said, "Shopping fun shouldn't last this long."

"Yeah, we shoulda heard something if she ran into trouble. Maybe she wandered off too far. Let's check on her."

They went down the hallway she had taken. Near its end, they found her full bag lying in the middle of the hallway. A faint but brighter light came from around a corner. Recognizing it as daylight, Con ran toward it. Doc followed. They found a door to the outside, a minor door like one for employees. Wedged open with one of Lois' blue canvas shoes.

Con said, "She left us a sign. She's in some kind of trouble."

Con started to open the door further. Doc grabbed his shoulder. "Remember Main Street out there? And the Plaza Hotel across it? If she was abducted her kidnappers could be watching for us to show ourselves, aiming guns at this door. We gotta be smart about this."

"How in the hell do we do that? They could be raping her right now. Or worse." His voice broke.

As he talked, Doc dropped to the floor and edged the door slowly open just a bit farther.

"What do you see, Doc?" Impatiently. "Anything?"

"Yes. I see a door set deep in the Plaza Hotel's wall almost directly across the street. And there's a blue shoe laying on the sidewalk outside it. Just like this one."

Thirteen – Even More Trouble in Paradise

oc scooted away from the opening and stood up.

Con asked in a tremulous voice, "What the hell we gonna do, Doc?"

Doc jerked his head to one side. "Follow me." And led Con back through the shopping hallways, past the snack bar and through gaming rooms toward the rear of the casino. They entered a lobby lit by daylight shining through a glass wall.

"This opens on the Golden Gate's parking lot," said Doc. "If we cross Main Street here, they can't see us from that Plaza Hotel door. It's too deeply recessed. Then we'll slip up on them."

They went out, half blinded by the raw sunlight, crossed the broad street and flattened themselves against the Plaza Hotel's wall. The morning sun had heated it so fiercely it burned Con's back through his shirt. They edged along it to the recessed door.

Doc pulled out his pistol and whispered over his shoulder, "Take this side of the door and be prepared for anything." He ducked under the door's peephole – it had no window of course – crossed to the its other side and waited for Con to draw his pistol.

The bastards are bound to be armed, thought Con. I hope they have their weapons drawn so I'll have an excuse to shoot them.

"Wait till after you hear me firing," Doc hissed, then whipped open the door and went in.

After hearing three shots, Con raced in. Two men and Lois lay on the floor, the men lying in pools of their own blood. Lois, very much alive, looked up at him with large eyes, her arms behind her back and a handkerchief covering the lower part of her face.

"Doc, you coulda hit Lois!" Con joined Doc at her side.

"Nope. She lay on the floor. They stood over her. I shot them before they could raise their weapons. Missed one that got away."

Con unknotted the handkerchief and Lois spat out the gag. Handcuffs confined her wrists behind her back. She began to silently weep.

Con held her, rather awkwardly. "Did they…?"

"No, no."

Doc appeared with both dead men's sets of keys. He found one for the handcuffs and unshackled Lois' wrists. She sat up, rubbed her wrists, then folded her arms around her knees. Con held her closely and gently.

Pistols lay on the floor near the dead men's hands. He had intended to wait to fire until he saw them draw their weapons, but they already held them when Doc burst in. He would be dead now if he had waited. Belatedly, he remembered Doc's instructions to be ready to fire as soon as he drew his weapon.

"Were there only three of them?" Doc asked Lois.

Con wanted to tell him to leave her alone for now, but they had to know.

Lois said, "No, four, but their boss left these three to decide what to do with me."

"What to do with –" blurted Con. "Why those bastards!"

"One wanted to kill me, one to rape me first. They said they couldn't afford to let me live and rat them out. But the little one who originally caught me – the others called him Rick – wanted to spare me, keep me for himself. He's the one who got away. Except for the boss, he seemed the most important, so I imagine he would've had his way." She shuddered.

"What did the boss look like?" asked Con.

"I was too terrified to notice much. A big guy. With a red, pocked face."

"What the hell were they doing here?" demanded Doc.

She said, "They were spying on Dante's Market. They split up to watch from different angles high up in the hotels. Looking for ways to break in. This little guy Rick was going through the Golden Gate from his spy post to join the others when I accidentally blocked his escape route. He backed up as I got near him, hid behind some crates by an outside door. When I looked behind them, he grabbed me. I was so scared I peed in my pants." She put her face in her hands and wept.

Doc had watched the entrances to the room as she spoke. Now he encircled Lois and Con with his arms and asked her gently, "Can you stand now, little girl?"

"Oh God, yes. I want out of here so bad."

They helped her up and went outside, where she grabbed her canvas shoe. Then they edged their way along the side of the Plaza Hotel until they could safely cross Main Street to the Golden Gate's parking lot. Both men held their pistols ready. Then back through the casino's gaming rooms.

At the snack bar, Lois exclaimed, "Oh, wait. I have to retrieve my bag."

"Your what?" asked Con.

"My shopping bag. I dropped it at the end of the hallway when that Rick guy grabbed me and put his gun to my head. But you two have to come with me. I can't be alone right now."

Doc sighed resignedly. "This is my last shopping trip with a woman." But he put his arm around the trembling Lois.

They went down the hallway and picked up Lois' bag. Con went around the corner to close the outside door and retrieved her other shoe. On the way to the main entrance, Con said, "Doc, they probably heard the shots from the compound. They're sure to check. If they see us here, they'll know we were involved."

"Good thought," said Doc. "They'll know we did the shooting if they find our guns and smell the burnt gunpowder." He held a hand out to Con. "Give me your gun and box of shells."

Con handed them to him. Doc led them deep into the forest of the Golden Gate's slot machines. He stopped at a row of potted faux pygmy palm trees and asked Con to hold one of the pots steady. He heaved on the tree until he freed it and lifted it up, exposing the fake root ball. He put the revolvers and ammunition in the bottom of the pot, replaced the tree and tamped the top of its root ball down with his foot until it looked like the others.

Con asked, "Why didn't you just hide them on top of a one-armed bandit?"

"Because one of them might have a sharp enough nose to smell the burnt powder."

Lois wrinkled her nose. "They won't need a sharp nose to smell my pants."

Doc continued, "If they find the guns, but not on us, they can't prove they're ours but they'd confiscate them so we couldn't get them back." He sat down on a slot machine stool, swiveled away from the machine, and frowned thoughtfully.

Con and Lois sat on stools near him. Con said, "Should we head back to the compound, say we heard the shots but didn't know anything about them? Came back because they scared us?"

Lois cleared her throat. "Guys, I hate to tell you this, but I lost a hair ribbon somewhere. Somebody from the compound might recognize it as mine. If I lost it out on the street, we could get it back but…."

Doc said, "We have to tell them about your kidnapping in any case. Dante needs to know somebody is spying on his compound. Besides, it's also important for our security as long as we're there. And even if you hadn't lost the ribbon, one of the other of us could've accidentally dropped something. When we report this to Dante, let me do all the talking. Now, let's get our story straight."

Doc, of course, came up with their story.

They met the investigating party just outside the casino, over a dozen armed men led by Dante himself, approaching under the colonnade-supported portico. They all huddled together nervously except for the always unflappable Dante. He stopped and halted the others with an upraised hand. His other hand went casually to the handle of his pistol in its holster.

Doc raised his hands, palms out. "Let us explain what happened. Among other things it'll keep you from walking into an ambush."

"We'd appreciate that," said Dante. His deep, resonant voice sounded ominous to Con. His hand remained on the pistol butt. His mouth's faint smile didn't extend to his narrowed eyes.

Doc nodded toward the Golden Gate's doorway. "Let's go inside. We'll tell you what happened."

As Doc led them toward the retail section, Dante said, "What're you carrying in those bags? I think we oughta have a look in them."

To the surprise of all who knew shy little Lois, she stopped and exclaimed, "No! These are surprises. We three got Christmas gifts for each other and have to keep them secret." She clasped her bag to her breast.

Dante said, "Well...." Unsure of what to do.

"Damn, Dante," said Emerson. "You let that asshole Rick Skinner get away with all kinds of shit, but you can't let a sweet little girl keep her Christmas gifts secret?"

"Yeah," said another. "Where's your Christmas spirit?"

The others laughed, partially in relief at being in the relative safety of the casino's interior.

"Okay, okay. Keep the damn bags."

Doc led them past the snack bar and through the boutique section to the door that opened onto Main Street. He explained how Lois had inadvertently trapped Rick at the end of the hallway and how he had put a gun to her head to force her to accompany him across the street.

"Describe this Rick for us," Emerson said to Lois.

"Kind of a small guy, wiry, with thinning black hair."

Emerson said, "That's our Rick, Dante. Rick Skinner."

Dante waved dismissively. "We don't know that. There's lots of little Rick-looking guys in the world. Even in Las Vegas' small population."

Doc said, "He took her out this door. She left one of her shoes here to wedge it open." He opened the door just far enough to show the Plaza Hotel across Main Street. "She kicked the other one off just outside that door over there. Now, follow me and I'll show you how to cross the street and get into the hotel without getting your asses blown off, in case the baddies have come back."

Lois grabbed Doc's sleeve. "Doc, I'm sorry. Let me wait here. I can't go back over there."

Doc took her hand and looked at the Market's leader. "She's been through too much, Dante. Let Con take her back to the compound. I'll guide you across the street."

Dante hesitated, then looked at Lois and Con. "Okay, go straight to the compound."

So they went.

On the way, Lois said, "Thank God. I really couldn't have gone back over there and I desperately need to change these pants."

Doc had told Con and Lois that their concocted story must stay as close to the truth as possible. He would tell Dante that he and Con had heard shots coming from inside the Plaza Hotel. When they reached it, they found two men lying dead on the floor and Lois handcuffed but unharmed. Lois had told them that four guys had had a shootout amongst themselves, and the victors had left, reason unknown, leaving her behind.

"What if they don't buy the story," Con had said.

"How can they refute it?"

Doc's story sounded thin at best. Why would the winners of a firefight abandon their captive and flee? And Dante's Market having unknown enemies made Con nervous.

* * *

Con and Lois waited nervously for Doc in their room. Just before the dinner hour, he finally came.

"It's about time," she said. "Are you trying to give us heart attacks?"

Con told her, "You shouldn't have worried. He's gotten him and me out of worse scrapes. Of course, he's the one who usually got us into them."

"Con was worried about you whether he admits it or not," said Lois, "What took you so long?"

Doc took the nearest chair. "Dante had us search for traces of these guys throughout the Plaza Hotel. Found nothing. Then we looked outside. Nothing there either. But I retrieved these." He grinned, reached into his bag of Christmas gifts and pulled out the two pocket pistols and the boxes of bullets.

"Wow," said Con. "How'd you manage that?"

"After I left the Plaza Hotel, I checked the Golden Gate. Found these under a certain potted plant. Since Lois had shamed them into not checking our bags, I felt safe putting them in mine. But I accomplished something even more important. I convinced Dante to return our weapons."

Con said, "How in the hell did you do that?"

"I said we no longer felt safe in the compound unarmed. He probably caved for fear of losing us. You know how short-handed he claims the compound is."

"Especially of people with your expertise," said Con.

Doc shrugged self-deprecatingly. "And I got a respite for you, Con. With Manny standing right there, I told Dante that since you now would have your rifle, you should be posted in the kiosks on half your workdays. Dante turned to Manny and said that that seemed reasonable, didn't it.

The young man had shown a lot of courage. You could tell Manny didn't like it, but Dante is the boss. So tomorrow, right after breakfast you'll report for duty at the rear kiosk." He stood up. "Let's see if we have time to get our weapons back before dinner."

* * *

Immediately after breakfast the next morning, Dante called a meeting of the whole community to tell them about the attempted kidnapping. He even relieved the citizen pedalers, though not non-residents like Kane and Artie, from duty for the half hour or so of the gathering. The guards couldn't leave their posts, but Con could hear the announcement from his. Dante made it from the second-floor balcony through a loudspeaker. He finished by telling the assemblage that they must remain on high alert until the miscreants could be identified and put out of action.

"And I assure you," he said, "that we will find and prosecute them." Then he answered peoples' questions.

Though Con couldn't hear the questions clearly, he did Dante's answers. Someone must have asked if he had any suspects because Dante answered, "We don't have enough information to name a guilty party for sure, but I can tell you that Chris Abend of the horticultural mall has threatened me. At one point he said he wouldn't stand for our water policy anymore. He wants more of our water. He doesn't understand that we must provide water for ourselves as well as others, like the merchant Herschel Bennet's people and for smaller groups."

After Dante dismissed the assemblage, they returned to work and the kids to school, under a pall of gloom.

Dante's speech brought up several questions. Abend's argument that Dante unfairly withheld water from the horticulturists made Dante the culprit. But Dante claimed he furnished them all the water he could spare. Con wondered why, if all these hotels had pumps to the aquifers below, Abend couldn't activate the one in his domain like Dante had? And why couldn't they get one of these compressed air battery things? Also, was Bennet a bandit like Kane said or a legitimate merchant as Dante implied. In addition, Dante treated the pedalers from other communities like slaves. Maybe the time to leave had come before they got caught in some struggle between Dante and Abend. Or with Bennet. He would discuss that with Doc and Lois.

Christmas would arrive in a few days. Everyone said Dante made a big deal out of Christmas Eve. All work except manning the kiosks would cease on that evening. Dante's people and even the indentured pedalers would party late into the night.

The attempted kidnapping had dampened even Lois' enthusiasm for Christmas.

As they finished dinner the following evening she said to Con, "I wonder what Dante's doing about what happened. Apart from affecting me, it's a threat to the community."

"I saw Doc this morning. He says Dante's spent the last two days in locked-door meetings with Emerson and Cuzco and a few others. And he's sent teams of guys out to reconnoiter. Including Manny, thank God. He hasn't been around to hassle us much."

"Where is Doc anyhow? He usually joins us before now."

Con smirked. "As you know, I went to the bar for one more beer last night. He came in a little tipsy and smelling of lavender."

"Beulah's scent! The sly old fox."

"And she's the vixen to his fox."

They both laughed.

Then she said, "This place is creeping me out, Con. I don't know how safe we are."

"Me too. We need to talk about it but with Doc too. Tomorrow when he's sober." Good! Con thought. Time to leave Dante's Market had come.

✳ ✳ ✳

They found Doc waiting for them at breakfast the next morning. As they ate, Con recognized the tension underlying his wise-cracking. After they finished, while depositing their plates and utensils at the dishwashers' window, Con said, "Okay, Doc, let's have it."

"What?" said Lois, looking at Con, puzzled.

"When he acts like this," said Con, "something is stuck in his craw. I also have something to discuss with you two. Let's find a private place to talk."

"We can go to our room," said Lois.

Doc shook his head. "No. I don't know the limits of Dante's ingenuity. For all I know, he has some way to bug our rooms. Let's go to one of those picnic tables along the promenade."

They occupied a plastic table toward the rear of the promenade beyond hearing of any of the businesses.

Doc said, "Let's hear what you have to say first, Con."

"I don't understand the fuss between Dante and this Chris Abend. For example, why can't the horticulturists use the pumps that reach down to their own aquifers like Dante does? And why can't they come up with one of these air storage battery things?"

"You got to know a lot about pumps to get them started again, to draw water up from 800 to a thousand feet below ground. As a mechanical engineer, Dante has that expertise. He may be the only one left in Vegas' small population. As to the compressed air energy batteries, Dante downloaded plans for building them before the computers died. He's not inclined to share them."

"Well," said Con, "the fight between those two makes me nervous. And I don't know how this Bennet fits in."

"Their conflict bothers me too," said Lois. "It may be time to think of moving on."

Doc said, "My news might confirm that."

"So there's even more trouble in paradise?" said Lois.

"Yes. A certain lovely little lady has listened in on some of Dante's secrets."

"Beulah," said Lois.

"Correct. She was Dante's main squeeze until about a month ago. Then he traded her in on a young frump – Beulah's word, not mine – from the kitchen. Beulah didn't mind after his payoff. He put her in charge of the washroom, which requires little work, and gave her spacious rooms adjoining it, furnished with a king-size bed from upstairs, a kitchen, the works. Easy duty and comfy digs.

"She tends to be a nosy little thing. While she shared Dante's quarters, she eavesdropped on meetings between him and others held in his second-floor office, top secret ones. He held day-to-day meetings in his other offices. The main voices she recognized were Joe Emerson's and Manny Cuzco's, but sometimes others. And get this, Lois: One of those 'others' was none other than your buddy, Rick Skinner."

"No!"

"What did they talk about?" asked Con. "And how did she eavesdrop?"

"She only heard parts of the conversations because she didn't know when they would occur, so she missed a lot of details. But sometimes she heard mention of Clarence Abend and his mall. As to how she listened in, workmen are joining some rooms together to make an apartment on the third floor, right above Dante's office. She went up there at night after they finished work. They had taken up some flooring when they removed a wall. But not Dante's ceiling. Beulah could hear them through it."

"So," said Con, "even the floors have ears."

"What about this Rick guy?" asked Lois. "What did he and Dante talk about?"

"Beulah heard them discuss 'secret missions' Dante had sent him on and plans for another one. That's probably why he left right before we got here. Dante and Rick seemed to have kept these missions secret from everybody else, even Joe and Manny. By the way, she heard them say Rick had belonged to Hershel Bennet's group before he came to Dante's Market. In spite of all that, she didn't remember Rick as a bad guy."

"I don't agree with her on that," said Lois.

"To be fair though, little girl," said Doc, "Rick protected you from his cronies."

She crossed her arms over her breasts, looked down and grudgingly said, "True."

"Dante has always defended Skinner," said Con. "Even on the first night we got here to Joe Emerson. He can't any more, though."

Doc said, "Dante and Skinner are plotting something now, and it's gonna hit the fan pretty soon. We've made the most of our break from traveling. Now it's time to make the least of it and go."

Lois said, "Maybe we should leave right after Christmas."

"I second that," said Con. "But how about these Bennet guys? They'll be waiting to ambush us along the freeway if Kane's right."

Doc grinned. "Not if they're honest businessmen like Dante says. But in case Kane's right I'll have a little surprise for them. Have you ever heard of the Kreuzer impact rifle?"

Lois shook her head but Con said, "Yeah. It's some kind of military weapon, isn't it?"

Doc nodded. "Yeah. They're deadly. They use some kind of electromagnetic force to propel their bullets at tremendous speeds. They can pierce armor. The recoil of these things is brutal."

Con smirked. "So, I sense another of your little secrets. You have one of these suckers tucked away somewhere. Like you did the bulletproof vest and the pocket pistols."

"No, but Dante has one in his armory. I saw it when we went to get our guns out of hock. Didn't you see it?"

"I wouldn't know a Kreutzer from a calabash. But I suppose he either leaves this armory unlocked or you miraculously have a key to it."

"I'll have a key when the time comes. After Dante threw Beulah over for the kitchen frump, she had a few intimate liaisons with a certain Manuel Cuzco. During one of them she relieved him of his armory key. Like us, she figured things were going south and wanted to be prepared. When Manny realized it was missing a few days later he confronted her. She said she didn't know anything about it, of course. In the process of ransacking her room and the washroom looking for it he roughed her up a bit. He finally admitted he must've lost it, wanted them to get back together. But she warned him to stay away from her if he valued his life. She claims she's handy with a knife and he believes her."

"Sounds like your girlfriend gets around," said Lois.

"What'll happen when Dante finds out Manny lost it?" asked Con.

"Manny's still in good with Dante, which means Dante doesn't know he lost it. I'm sure he prays Dante never asks him to unlock the armory."

"And," said Con, "when you ask Beulah nicely she's just going to hand this key over to you."

"Yes, as long as we take her with us."

Fourteen – Christmas Eve at Dante's Market

The following Thursday, Con pedaled the afternoon shift which lasted from 2:00 p.m. unvvvtil 8:00. After the shift, he grabbed the clean clothes and towel he had brought along that afternoon, left the pedal-room and stopped at the workers' tavern for a beer. Since his position was the farthest from the pedal-room's exit, if he had gone directly to the washroom, he would've had to wait behind a long line of pedalers for one of the eight showers.

In the washroom the single candle burning there and a second in the garage barely pricked the darkness with their light. By reaching the room late he had it all to himself, except for Earl Hudson, Dante's ancient errand boy, asleep in the high guard's chair just inside the garage. Con hung his clean clothes and towel on a bar for that purpose outside the shower's waterproof curtain, then stripped and dropped his sweat-soaked clothes on the floor outside the curtain. After showering and drying off, he dressed in the shower out of habit despite the unlikely chance of anyone appearing that late.

As he finished buttoning his shirt, he heard a knock on the garage's pedestrian door. When Hudson didn't answer the newcomer pounded louder and called, "Hudson, you old fart, wake up and let me in."

Con heard the oldster groan and mumble, "Awright, awright, don git your shorts in a wad."

Something told Con to remain hidden. He grabbed his dirty clothes and towel and brought them into the shower. He heard Hudson hobble to the door and unlock it and its creaking open.

The newcomer said, "You worry me when you don't answer, old man." He spoke in a loud voice because of Hudson's poor hearing. "If you die on me there won't be anybody to let me in. That is if only you and the boss still know about my visits."

"I ain't plannin to die on you, Rick Skinner." Hudson chuckled. "In fact, I'll dance on your grave. And yessir, just me and Dante knows bout your visits."

"I'm just shitting you, Earl. I know you got a lot of years left. Dante's lucky to have somebody he can trust as much as you."

"Well sir, I'd be dead now if Dante hadn't taken me in so you bet I'll keep his secrets. He knows I can't work much because of my arthritis. I'll be here every Thursday night in case you come."

"I'll come if I got something to report. Like I do this week."

Earl said, "I don't spose you'll let me know what it is."

They had crossed the garage and washroom as they spoke, and now paused by the casino door.

Rick said, "Nope. Dante made me promise to only tell him. It'll all be over in a week or two, so everybody'll know." The door whished as he went through it.

And, thanks to Beulah, Con knew how to listen in on him and Dante. He first had to tell Lois where he was going so she wouldn't worry.

Con heard Hudson shuffle back to his chair. He didn't wait for the oldster to doze off again; the chair faced away from him and toward the garage doors. And his deafness would keep him from hearing Con leave, especially since Con wore his pedaling slippers instead of his boots.

Once in their rooms, Con told Lois about the conversation and his intent to eavesdrop.

He said, "Doc told us he thinks whatever they're plotting will happen soon and Skinner verified that. This meeting might tell us what it is and when."

As he started for the door, she grabbed his sleeve. "You don't think you're going without me, do you? Especially since you're going off half-cocked." She opened the bag she had been filling as they talked. It held candles and a fire striker. "How do you expect to see in an apartment with no light?"

"Good point. But it's too dangerous a job for you, sweetheart. I'll –" He reached for the bag.

She pulled it out of his reach. "You can't leave me out of this. This Rick creature kidnapped me, not you, so I've got an interest in whatever this is."

"Listen. I could get killed up there."

She pushed past him and went out the door. "Then I'd never know what they're planning."

The third-floor room from which Beulah had eavesdropped lay just down the hall from Con and Lois' apartment. No candles lit the hallway but the lights over the banner in front of the Market showed through the window at the end of the hall. By its dim light they quickly found the room's door. It must have been unlocked when Beulah entered it and still was. Once inside, they lit one of the candles. Three rooms were being joined to form the apartment. Con found Beulah's listening post between the rear two where workmen had removed the flooring along with the wall that had stood on it. They knelt silently over it.

They recognized Rick Skinner's voice below. "Where's your new girlfriend?"

Dante said impatiently, "You know we can't let anyone see you. I told her to spend the night with friends."

"And she didn't ask why?"

"She'd better not ever."

"Is she younger than Beulah? Prettier?"

"I'd rather have kept Beulah – she had more spunk, more fire – but I couldn't quite trust her. She seemed to have a secret agenda I couldn't figure out. I didn't want to make a mistake, like what happened with a certain kidnapping."

"Look, Dante. We've been over that. I fucked up, okay? I panicked, didn't know what to do with her. It won't happen again."

"As you say, we've been over that. What do you have for me tonight?"

"Herschel wanted me to tell you that we're ready. All we need to know is when. We've drilled the men on how you want them to attack. They'll drive up to the front gate and fire a few rounds at the wall. But stay a good distance away from the wall and the guardhouse so they won't get shot. In the end they'll throw a few smoke bombs over the wall and retreat. Act like you guys drove em off. The women made green shirts like Abend's people wear. They've even got the logos on the left side. See mine?"

"You shouldn't've worn that in here."

"Nobody saw me cept Hudson and he won't tell anybody. He's absolutely loyal to you."

"Remember, Rick. Nobody gets hurt. Nobody in here sees Bennet's men's faces. Our people need to believe, beyond any doubt, that Abend's men are attacking us. I want them so mad they'll want to get even with Abend."

"Yeah, yeah." Rick sounded impatient. "Bennet's men won't shoot directly at any of your folks. And to protect themselves they'll wear body armor and helmets that they appropriated from the National Guard armory. And masks."

Dante said, "The ultimate goal is to annex Abend's hydroponic mall, then the small groups of people scattered here and there. I want control of Vegas from here south to the airport. Bennet runs everything from here north for me. If you manage Bennet and this attack right, I'll let you run the town south of the mall. You'll answer only to me. In fact, right now I'm having an apartment built for you, right above this office. You'll stay there when you come to report to me."

"I really appreciate this, Dante. I'll do you a good job. So when? Herschel's chomping at the bit. He wanted to do it on a holiday because nobody'd expect it then but knew you didn't want to do it over Christmas."

"That's right. My people work so hard, and they enjoy Christmas so much I won't spoil it for them."

"So when?" insisted Rick. "Herschel'd like it as soon as possible, especially on a night where everybody's partying and drinking."

"Okay, how about New Year's Eve? Everybody will be so drunk and happy then, including the guards that…."

The door began to slowly open in the room they had entered. Lois grabbed Con's arm and blew out the candle. They crawled quickly around the corner into the farthest room.

Christ, thought Con. We've been caught. The ominously gradual opening of the door meant someone had seen them come in and was about to apprehend them, probably a watchman. He listened, heart pounding. At least two people walked stealthily. How had he and Lois betrayed their presence?

Then he heard a young girl's voice. "Oh, Reggie, it's a king-sized bed." Followed by a giggle.

"Nothing but the best for my angel." A teenage boy.

There followed giggles and the rustling of bedding and passionate disrobing.

Con whispered ever so quietly in Lois' ear, "We're stuck until they get through fucking. Teenagers can do that all night."

Lois shook her head. "We're not stuck."

As they squatted there listening to giggles, impassioned whispers and rutting sounds, Lois stood and said, "Now!" aloud as she rasped the candle's wick alight with the fire striker. She stalked into the lovers' room. Nonplussed and anxious, Con followed.

"What have we here?" Lois demanded peremptorily. The stunned, wide-eyed kids blinked at the sudden bright light. They hunkered down under the covers. "This is Mr. LaFarge's room," she said to Con. I wonder what he'll do with them?" And to the kids, "Well, why haven't you gotten up yet?"

"But…but…but…," blubbered the boy. He glanced at his clothes lying on the floor. The girl broke down into sobs.

Getting into the act, Con said, "I think we should take them down to Mr. LaFarge's right now." Standing at the foot of the bed, he grasped a handful of bedspread and sheet as though he intended to yank it off the bed. "Dressed just as they are."

Lois rubbed her chin, pretending to deliberate, "On the other hand, you know how long the boss takes to punish trespassers. And we'd have to wait until he finished to drag them off to their cells."

"Yeah, and it's so late," said Con. And to the kids, "Tell you what. We'll let this pass this time. After we leave, you have five minutes to disappear. If we see you any place on this floor again, we'll take you directly to Mr. LaFarge. He'll have you pedaling for the rest of your lives."

Lois said, "We're probably being too easy on them…." as she and Con left.

They waited in their apartment, barely able to suppress their laughter, until they heard the teenagers race down the hall. They returned to their listening post but heard nothing further. The meeting had ended.

* * *

When they met Doc the next morning for breakfast, Con told him, "Last night we found out what's gonna hit the fan and when. We need another private talk."

"Okay," said Doc. "This is our day off and it's only a few days until Christmas Eve.

Why don't we go on a shopping spree today? We can talk then."

"Are you nuts?" said Con. "Go where? Back to the casinos?"

"Well, of course, to the casinos."

Lois said, "We could hardly get you to go shopping for Christmas gifts. Now you want to go again?"

Doc grinned. "We need to go shopping for trade goods. And clothes. I don't know about you two but the only things holding some of my duds together are patches."

"Yes," said Lois. "I wondered which set of rags I'd wear to the Christmas Eve wingding."

"And by trade goods, I don't mean jewelry," said Doc. "People with extra food will be more likely to trade it for sets of dinnerware or pots and pans. Tools, clothes, blankets. We skip the hotel shops and hit the kitchens and rooms."

"You're always a step ahead of us, Doc," said Lois.

Outside the compound, as they walked along the mall and into the first hotel, Con and Lois described the conversation between Dante and Rick Skinner.

Doc said, "These meetings explain why Dante defended Skinner to Joe Emerson on our first day here."

"And that day in the Golden Gate to his men," said Lois.

Con told him about their interruption by the lovers and how Lois had terrorized them, which got a hearty laugh from Doc.

"So," summarized Con, rather smugly, "we learned not only how the attack is supposed to happen but the very night of its occurrence. But now that we know Dante's intent, I don't know what to do about it."

"I do," said Doc. "We get the hell out of here before New Year's Eve. We're not revolutionaries and we can't stop something like this. This won't be so bad for Las Vegas. Most people will continue to live like they always had, only more securely. Dante is a complex character, an empire builder, but one with compassion for his subjects. An enlightened twenty-first-century despot."

Lois said, "So we've gotta leave before New Year's Eve. Say, right after Christmas?"

"Right," said Doc.

Yes! thought Con.

They spent the rest of the day raiding hotel kitchens, guest rooms, lounges, bars, lobbies and reception areas. They gathered cooking and dining utensils, bedding, throw rugs, soap, wax candles and other goods. They chose sturdy clothing from the shops for themselves. About mid-afternoon, Doc declared that they had gathered enough.

"Are you sure this'll all fit?" said Con, thinking of all the room the tarpaulin-wrapped object took up.

"We can load any excess on top of the buggy," said Doc. He pointed to a sturdy-looking metal frame he had laid against one side of the pile. "I found that rack on a Jeep in a parking garage. "It'll fit on the Beast with a little modification. Let's wait till dark to lug this stuff over there. No need to clue Dante that we're leaving."

Lois said, "But he said we could leave anytime we wanted."

"It'd be just like Dante to search the Feast before we leave like he did when we first got here. And there's – ahem – a few things in the cart I don't want him to see."

Con frowned. "And, of course, you won't tell us what they are."

Doc shook his head, suddenly serious. "Yes, one of my little secrets. But an important one this time. If he finds what I'm taking, it's better you don't know what it is. I doubt if you can fake ignorance well enough and I don't want you blamed for taking it." Doc stood up. "Let's get this stuff organized."

They boxed and bagged the goods and stacked them in a hotel lobby facing away from the compound, then started back.

Doc said, "We can't put all this stuff in the cart and the Feast until we're ready to leave. Someone would be sure to notice. I just happen to have a friend with an apartment adjoining the washroom who'll be glad to let us store it there."

Lois said, "You made a judicious choice for a girlfriend, Doc."

"She chose me. But I didn't object."

"But what about the night watchman in the garage?" pressed Lois. "We have to pass through it to the washroom and then Beulah's."

"Dante increasingly trusts me to do more nuisance work for him, like scheduling the garage guard postings, except for when he wants a specific person there for some reason. I've arranged to have you stand watch from eight till midnight tonight. If there are still people doing their washing that late, we'll wait till they're finished."

"So I won't have to help carry all that stuff from the hotel."

Doc patted her arm fondly. "Right. I take care of my little girl."

Once in the compound, they went to Beulah's rooms.

"Wow," she said, "I didn't expect so much company." Doc had never brought Con and Lois with him before. "But you all look so serious."

"'Deed we are, Love," said Doc. "We've decided it's about time to hit the road. We've been getting ready today." He told Beulah about their plans and how they had spent the day gathering goods. "Since your rooms are next to the washroom and garage, we hoped you'd let us store them here. The night we leave, we'll pack the buggy and cart and take off."

Beulah said, "So when you plannin this getaway?"

"Soon after Christmas. Before New Year's. I'll tell you why later."

Beulah shook her head. "You're missin the best night for leavin."

"Which is…?" said Doc.

"Christmas Eve night. Everybody'll be partyin, Dante's soldiers'll be drunk. By midnight nobody'll know or even give a shit if we're gone."

"Perfect," said Doc. "We should've thought of that ourselves."

Beulah slipped her arm around Doc's waist. "Had to show you how much you need me. Come get me after dark tonight and we'll go get your loot."

"Our loot," corrected Con.

✳ ✳ ✳

Christmas Eve arrived. Work ended at five o'clock and everyone went home to dress in their Christmas finery. Con, Lois and Doc changed into their travel clothes and packed their personal belongings. Then they met, as previously agreed, in Beulah's rooms to exchange gifts. Goods from their "shopping" day filled her small living room. Beulah had left only four chairs and a table clear. She also wore sturdy clothes, though Con thought she looked striking in a pale yellow shirt with a fitted bodice, snug canvas trousers and hiking boots.

"Let me give you my homemade gifts first," said Beulah, "to get your disappointment outta the way."

She handed them each a flat package. Like the others, Con's contained a tan canvas garment. He shook it out to reveal a vest equipped with multiple pockets.

Beulah said, "I used to work for a company that made costumes for video actors. I designed vests like these for 'The Moon is a Harsh Mistress.' It was based on an old-timey science fiction story, but they updated it to match modern moon colonies."

"I saw it," said Con. "Great characters, lots of action." He realized that, after the pandemic began, no supplies would reach the colonies or scientific research stations in outer space. He hoped authorities had sent space shuttles to fetch their occupants home.

She continued, "Each pocket has a use, some to hold ammunition, others for first aid kits, emergency food rations, stuff like that. I just guessed at your sizes. I hope they fit."

Con tried his on. It fit perfectly, as did Doc's. Lois' was a little large.

"I can take it in a little, honey," said Beulah.

Lois smiled. "No, I like it the way it is. In fact, I can use it starting right now." She took a small packet out of a trouser pocket and put it in one in the vest. "Fits just right. A sewing kit. I found it when we 'shopped.' Wondered how I could carry it."

They exchanged the other gifts. Con gave Lois the jewelry and Doc the watch from the Golden Gate. On their latest shopping foray, he had found Beulah

a broad-brimmed Stetson with a decorative silver chain around the base of the crown and a matching silver necklace. Lois and Doc both knew Con badly needed new boots. Each, without knowledge of the other, had found him a pair.

He felt abashed, having given them expensive gifts that would, on the road, draw thieves like garbage drew flies while they gave him rugged gifts for traveling. But once on the mall, it pleased Con to see his friends wearing the gifts he had given them. Lois' and Beulah's jewelry and Doc's watch made their rugged garments look less plain. Beulah wore her Stetson over her reddish-black bush of hair, cocked jauntily over one eye.

Tables sat end to end down the promenade. Every other one held dinnerware with chairs along their sides, while others remained bare except for islands of soft drinks for the kids and booze for the adults. People wandered around to show off their finery, visit with friends and drink.

Dante and his soldiers wandered among the people, shaking hands and joking with children. After a time, Dante disappeared, but soon they heard the loudspeaker's squawk and Dante clearing his throat from the balcony. Everyone looked up. He called out, "Merry Christmas, everyone!" To which the crowd responded, "Merry Christmas, Dante!" It had the feel of a long-cherished ritual. Then Dante gave a short speech, complimenting the citizens of Dante's Market for their hard work and integrity. After the crowd's applause, he said, "And now for the ceremony we've all been waiting for. Parents, make way for your children just below me here. Kids, move in close to the building. That's it."

The kids pressed forward eagerly. Dante's men moved among them, passing out gifts wrapped in brightly colored, patterned paper. Con wondered what they would do after they ran out of gift wrap. For that matter, how would Dante keep his records and tout up numbers after the hotel stationary ran out.

And what a fight would ensue over the last bottle of booze. Of course, Dante would hide a cache of it for himself way before that happened.

Soon kitchen workers began filling the drinks tables with food, most of it from Abend's mall: steaming plates of chicken and fish, roasted potatoes and steamed vegetables, salads and desserts. People, including the kitchen help, took places at the tables, as did Con, Doc, Lois and Beulah. Doc recommended a wine he favored but the four drank sparingly. After they finished eating they hung around the drink tables and talked with acquaintances.

Doc poured two fingers of a 12-year-old single malt scotch. He looked a little guilty because the four had promised to drink lightly that night. He sniffed the glass's contents and then held it up to admire the liquid's color. "Don't worry," he said to the others. "I'll drink just this one. It's been years since the last taste and it'll be years more, if ever, before I get to have another."

As Doc sipped his drink, Con looked up at the huge atomic clock above Dante's balcony. Its hands gave the time as five minutes to eight. He said, "It's time." and went down to the garage. Doc had scheduled him to replace Earl Hudson at the guard station at eight o'clock, after which Doc would replace him at midnight. Doc, along with the women, would actually appear at eleven-thirty. That would give Doc plenty of time to get the Kreutzer. Then they would help Con finish loading the vehicle and cart. They hoped to leave at midnight but with Doc responsible for guard duty they could leave later if something went awry. Doc didn't feel guilty about abandoning the guard post for a few hours. During that time of night, he felt it hardly mattered.

Con had asked Doc why he scheduled Hudson for the guard post the shift before his.

"I didn't," Doc had answered. "Dante did. Maybe the old man doesn't care much for Christmas anymore. A lot of people miss their families too much to celebrate it. But Earl spends a lot of time on guard duty. He can't do much else and it frees up a healthy worker."

Con awakened Hudson who sat dozing in the guard's chair. He said, "Hurry on over and join in all the food and festivities, Earl."

As the old man climbed painfully down from his seat he grumped, "I don't eat much anymore and I'm too old for festivities." and shuffled off.

Con had promised to load the cart while he kept watch so they could leave sooner. Accordingly, he went to Beulah's apartment, unlocked the door with the key she had given him and strapped on his holstered pistol as required for guard duty. Then he began carrying boxes, bundles and bags to the cart. While adding to the cart's cargo, Con couldn't help but look under Doc's mysterious tarp. It concealed a number of packages, containing objects Doc's importance to Dante kept others from investigating. He stashed the weapons they wouldn't be carrying, Doc's shotgun, two rifles and the pistol he had taken from the dead cop in the compartment behind the back seat under bundles of clothing. Doc had left two pistols in Beulah's apartment, one that he carried as they traveled and another he had given Lois. They would pick those up when they arrived at her apartment. He couldn't figure out how to attach the rack Doc had found to the top of the Feast by himself so he left that aside. He left the few boxes he couldn't find room for inside Beulah's rooms.

After he finished, he climbed onto the guard's seat. It rose high enough to allow him to see the garage doors over the vehicles. Time passed interminably. He couldn't help but think about all the things that could go wrong, somebody catching Lois and Beulah looting the pantry or finding him and Doc loading the rest of their goods. Con had no way of telling time. It moved so slowly he began to think something had gone terribly wrong, that their plot had been discovered and the others already apprehended. At last he leaned back on the guard's chair and forced himself to stop fidgeting.

Finally, he heard the casino door open. He looked around to see Lois and Beulah appear.

Lois laughed at his startled expression. "Do I look so scary?"

"N – no. I was just, just expecting Doc, coming to relieve me. Where is he? What time is it?"

"It was eleven-twenty when we left the mall. As for Doc, Dante and Joe Emerson got him into a friendly conversation. He didn't think it'd seem natural to blow them off for a while. He sent us to tell you he'd be late before we head to the pantry."

"He started yawnin a lot," said Beulah, "pretendin to be tired. He'll leave 'em pretty soon."

"I got most of the stuff packed in the cart and buggy," he said.

"Good," said Lois. "We'll go to the pantry now. We decided to take a little food along. We'll be able to leave when Doc gets here."

After they left, Con leaned back, relaxed and turned toward the garage doors. His fears had been foolish. Everything had gone smoother than he had expected. They'd be on the road in less than a half hour. The casino door opened and steps approached. Doc had appeared sooner than he expected. He turned when the steps drew near.

To see a small, dark man with thinning black hair training an automatic pistol on him. Rick Skinner.

Fifteen - "You're gonna get us killed, Doc!"

"Okay, kid," said Rick Skinner, "step down fromv that seat. Keep your hands where I can see them."

Con did, his heart in his throat, eyes darting from Skinner's face to his weapon, then to Earl Hudson, shuffling up to his side.

"Now look, Rick," said Hudson reasonably. "You ain't plannin to shoot this nice young fella. Dante said no killin."

"Depends on how he acts, old man."

So, thought Con, Dante had posted Hudson here to admit Skinner. Apparently, they met on nights other than Thursdays. But what did Skinner have to report on Christmas Eve?

Skinner said to Con, "I don't want to shoot you, friend, so here's what you're gonna do. About midnight we'll hear someone knocking on the small door. You and old Earl here will slide that steel bolt outta its keepers on the double doors and open them. Then move aside and let a bunch of men in, Herschel Bennet's men. He don't wanna kill nobody either. He just wants to be your new boss. If you cooperate with him, you'll be fine. If you don't, you'll be dead."

Hudson said, clearly shocked, "Whadda you mean, Rick. Dante ain't gonna stand for that."

"I'm afraid the regime's a-changing, Earl."

"But Rick —"

Hudson grabbed for Skinner's gun arm. Still watching Con, Skinner smacked him with the pistol. Con started toward Skinner but halted when Skinner swung the pistol back to cover him.

"Stay where you are," said Skinner, "or Earl will be opening those doors by himself."

Hudson crouched on one knee and one hand. The other hand held one side of his forehead. Blood ran down his wrist.

Through clenched teeth Con said, "That wasn't necessary. Earl trusted you."

Skinner took two steps toward Con. "I decide what's 'necessary' — Ah!"

With both hands, Con had grabbed and twisted Skinner's wrist and pistol upward before Skinner could fire. Con had height, strength and youth over him. He took a hand off Skinner's wrist, clenched a fist and hit him in the face with all his strength, simultaneously wrenching the pistol out of his hand. Hands covering his bloodied nose, Skinner fell on his butt, eyes on the pistol now aimed at his chest.

Doc said from behind the erstwhile gunman, "Never get too close to the man you got the drop on, Skinner."

Doc stood behind Skinner in the doorway to the casino, leaning against the jamb, grinning, and holding a scabbard that Con assumed concealed the legendary weapon called the Kreutzer.

Con said to Skinner, "Don't you move a muscle." and to Doc, "I coulda used some help here."

"Didn't look like it to me," Doc said as he approached them. "But honestly, I got here too late to help. You had ahold of his wrist by the time I showed up. And I wasn't about to get closer with that gun whipping around like that. Earl or I could've gotten shot." And as he helped Earl stand, "Let me look at that head, old friend." And to Con, "Let's get these two into Beulah's apartment and find out what's going on. You go first with your prisoner. You've got her key. I'll lock the Kreutzer in the buggy."

Covering Skinner with his own gun, Con gestured for him to get up and pushed him toward Beulah's apartment. Con made him stand with his hands against the wall while he unlocked the door, motioned him in with the gun, pointed toward a chair and said, "Sit!"

He kept the gun pointed at Skinner while Doc gently washed Hudson's wound and wrapped his handkerchief around his forehead.

"This wasn't part of the plan," said the old man. "I don't know what happened…."

"Just what was the plan?" said Doc.

"Dante said Rick might have some news for him tonight," said Earl, "so he wanted me down here from four to eight to let him in. I figured Rick went up to see Dante. But he didn't. He hid out some place, prob'ly here in the garage. For me, the promenade was too 'festive,' as Con called it, so I came back to visit with Con for a while when I saw Rick holdin a gun on the boy."

Con said, "But it wasn't news he had for Dante. It was a bunch of Bennet's armed men."

"What?" said Doc.

Con told him Skinner's orders to Earl and him to open the double doors when Bennet's men arrived.

Doc picked up a piece of twine left over from tying the boxes and bound Skinner's wrists tightly to the chair's armrests.

"What're you gonna do to me?" Skinner's voice shook, his tough-guy façade gone.

A knock came at the door, followed by a strident voice. "Hey! Are you guys in there? What the hell's going on? We got a load of groceries out here." Beulah.

Con unlocked and opened the door.

Beulah and Lois entered, looking about in surprise.

Lois glared at Skinner and said, "You!"

Skinner repeated, "What're you gonna –" and Doc said, "Shut up." Just as Lois asked Con, "Are you all right? Where'd Skinner come from?" and Beulah repeated, "What the hell's going on?"

Doc shouted above the others, "Everybody shut up so we can find out what's going on." He turned to Hudson. "What do you know about Dante and Skinner's meetings, Earl?"

"I know that Dante thinks Abend's people are gonna attack us. I don't know what him and Rick met about, but I think he had Rick spyin on the hydroponics mall or something. Dante said they were plannin something that'd be good for all of us. That's all I know, Doc."

Doc turned to glare at Skinner. "Now it's your turn." He pulled up a chair facing Skinner, sat down and grasped the little finger of his right hand. "Here's what happens. You're gonna tell us what's going on. In detail. Every time I think you're lying or hiding something…" He lifted the finger far enough to make Skinner squeak. "I'm gonna break a finger. Begin at the beginning. I've got a feeling we don't have much time."

"Sure, sure. I won't lie. I promise I'll –"

"Stop blubbering. Everything'll be cool as long as you don't try to bullshit me."

Con had seen many sides of Doc, but never the hard-nosed interrogator.

Skinner told them about Dante's plan to have Bennet's men, pretending to be Abend's people, attack the Market on New Year's Eve, and then withdraw. "He only wanted to piss his people off at Abend so they'd attack his hydroponic mall and take it over. His ultimate goal was to conquer all of Las Vegas. He'd let Bennet and me help him run it."

Doc said, "But Bennet had other ideas, didn't he?"

"Yes, he wanted to make the attack earlier to help Dante convince his people – ow! Please."

Con winced at how far Doc had bent the finger.

"Okay, okay," said Skinner. "I'll tell you. Just let my finger go."

"As soon as I think you're telling the truth. You used to work for Bennet. Why did he send you to Dante?"

Skinner spoke in a rush. "Bennet sent me because I knew Dante when he first came to town, and he trusted me. One night when we were drinking, Dante told me he wanted to take over all of Las Vegas. I gave him the idea for the fake attack. We set the attack for New Year's Eve." He explained the details of the attack. Doc looked at Con and Lois. "Is he correct?"

They both said yes.

Skinner looked surprised at their knowledge of the plan but said, "Please let go of my finger." Doc lay his finger flat on the armrest but, ominously to Skinner, kept hold of it.

Doc said, "But Bennet came up with a new plan, didn't he? Decided he'd run the Vegas empire instead of Dante and moved the attack up to tonight. Clever for him to make it on Christmas Eve when nobody would expect it. And through the garage, the least likely place."

Hudson shook his head. "I shoulda seen through that."

"No way you could've, Earl." Doc released Skinner's finger and leaned back, frowning thoughtfully.

Lois and Beulah acted edgy. "Midnight's coming up, Doc," said Beulah.

But Con knew Doc had something to work out.

Presently, Doc let a breath out and stood up. "We're in a complicated situation. For our own safety, we need to leave as soon as possible. Yet, despite his despotism, Dante treats his people fairly, like he has us, so we owe him a warning. But we don't want him to catch me with his Kreutzer. So he needs to be warned, but after we're gone. He shouldn't have any trouble defending the Market. Emerson says he has more men than Bennet." He turned to Lois and Beulah. "Ladies, why don't you load those groceries while Con and I affix the rack to the top of our chariot and load the last few boxes of supplies."

Doc checked Hudson's wound. He had washed the blood from it but a sizeable swollen bruise remained. Then Hudson stood up. "Whadda you want me to do?"

"Your job comes later. You'll go warn Dante after we're safely on the road."

"What about me?" asked Skinner plaintively.

"You'll be lucky if Dante doesn't skin you with a dull knife," said Doc.

They left Skinner helpless in the chair and went out to the garage. They all worked quickly, but Doc with a sense of urgency.

While Doc and Con attached the rack to the buggy's top, Doc said, "I like the way you handled Skinner, boy. I don't think the Con I first met could've done that as well."

"Thanks, Doc." Con didn't think he could've either, such a short time ago.

According to Doc's new watch, they finished with time to spare until midnight.

Doc said, "Okay, Earl. We're taking off. Time for your job."

"Yeah, I'll go find Dante. So you're gone for good?"

"I'm afraid so. Sorry, but we don't have time for long, tearful farewells."

"I ain't cryin," said Hudson as they shook hands all around, "but good luck." Then he turned and shuffled his way back to the casino.

Con asked, "Where you gonna put the croaker, Doc?"

"Croaker?"

"Yeah, you know, that big fuckin gun."

"The Kreuzer. In my lap and ready till we get up the road apiece."

Standing on the passenger side of the buggy, Lois said, "I suppose we women get stuck in the back seat."

"You guessed it," said Doc.

Beulah said, "Hey —"

"Neither of you has driven the Feast or fired a Kreutzer and you're smaller than us so…."

"Okay, okay," she said grumpily and got in. Lois followed her.

"And Con, since you've never fired the Kreutzer either, you'll drive."

The cart's rear pointed toward the garage doors. He would have to turn the buggy and cart around somehow. Con said, "But I've never —" Backed a vehicle pulling a cart, he had started to say.

A knock on the small garage door to the outside interrupted him. He got in the driver's side and Doc the passengers'. They sat quietly, listening.

"That can't be Bennet's men this early," whispered Con.

"You expecting someone else?" Doc whispered back.

Another knock.

A few moments later, somebody outside asked, in almost a whisper, "Rick, you there?" and knocked again. Another pause, then louder, "Hey, Rick." Followed by the muted murmur of several people consulting. And finally, "Okay, Rick. We're coming in. They musta got you."

They heard nothing for a time. Then came the sound of a vehicle, not of its silent electric motor, but the singing of tires on pavement, moving rapidly. It crashed against the door. Which shuddered. Con thought that if Earl hadn't had time to announce Bennet's arrival to Dante, his bashing against the door would.

Doc said, "Those doors won't hold for long, Con. You need to back around to your left and point us toward the door. Maybe we can slip past them. If not, I'll give them a taste of the Kreutzer. Hopefully, that'll scare them into backing out of the garage."

"But, Doc, I've never —"

"Shut up and get ready. Here it comes again." And to all of them, "Roll the windows up." He was doing something with the Kreutzer.

The door held against the next blow but bulged inward. The vehicle's headlights glowed through the cracks around and between the doors.

Con forced his nerves to steady while he tried to figure out how to turn the steering wheel.

Doc hollered, "They're coming again, Con! Whip around there before they break through. Now!"

So Con whipped around there. But the cart didn't turn as Doc had directed and Con had intended. Doc cursed.

"Con!" yelled Beulah. "You drive like old people fuck!"

Lois said, "Don't rattle him, Beulah!"

Another crash sent the double doors sailing into the garage as a single unit in a cloud of dust and splinters. The steel bar had held them together, but the hinges had given way. Blinding light limned its flying ruins. It skittered across the garage floor into the parked vehicles. Pieces of it scattered in every direction. Some small ones struck the buggy and cart.

The vehicle, a giant van, stopped in the dust cloud that had followed it into the garage. It had a shield of steel bars with protruding spikes welded to its front and blazing headlights. Its driver's side now roughly paralleled the buggy's passenger side about forty feet away. Both vehicles faced the washroom. Shadowy figures approaching the garage from outside.

The driver stepped out of the van and its side door slid open. Armed men began to emerge from it. The driver was a big guy with a red, pockmarked face. He wore a black shirt and black jeans, a pistol belt strapped around his waist and a rifle slung over his left shoulder. A tall woman with spikey white hair and a hard face, also dressed in black and armed, came around from the van's passenger side to join him.

"That's him," breathed Lois. "The red-faced one is the guy who left the others when Skinner kidnapped me."

The men who had exited the van started toward the washroom. The driver held up a hand to stop them and pointed to the buggy. "We gotta take care of them first." He called to the buggy, "You thinking of going somewhere?"

Doc rolled down his window an inch. "Yeah," he said. "It's time for us to move along."

The man started to draw his pistol. "Not just yet. Why don't you step out –"

The woman with spikey hair grasped his arm. "Hersch, look who's joining us." She pointed at the washroom door.

Hersch. The red-faced man was Herschel Bennet.

Con looked toward the doorway. Rick Skinner stood there.

"Herschel," he called. "These bastards attacked me. I didn't have a chance."

Bennet said, "How do we know you didn't sell us out, Rick? Dante can be a pretty persuasive fellow."

"You know I wouldn't do that."

Bennet looked at the woman. "What do you think, Stella?"

"I think we don't need the little rat any longer."

Skinner held his hands palm out in front of him. "No, no –"

Bennet shot him in the forehead.

Con thought, too bad Skinner hadn't ducked inside the washroom. Now Earl could indeed dance on his grave.

"Okay, guys," said Bennet. "If our busting the door in didn't, that shot blew our cover. Let's head inside. Except for you three." He waved three men to him and pointed at the buggy. "Kill them before you come in."

"Bennet!" came Dante's deep baritone from the washroom doorway. He stood straddling Skinner's body. "What the hell are you doing here?" Men stood behind him in the washroom.

"The game has changed, LaFarge. Drop your weapon if you want to live." The men who had followed the van had begun filling the garage. They moved toward the washroom with weapons raised. Except for the three who approached the buggy with drawn weapons.

Doc whipped open the buggy door, stood to rest the Kreutzer across the top and fired.

The shoulder and upper arm of the centermost of the three disappeared in a spray of gore. The one misfortunate enough to stand behind him fell back through the van's door, his legs protruding. Blood splattered the garage floor and the side of the van.

The rifle's recoil had knocked Doc back into the buggy. "Help me up!" Doc shouted to Con, who helped him return to stand behind the door. The remaining would-be assassin was too stunned by their companion's remains to move. Bennet's other men stopped their assault on the washroom, backed away from Doc or ducked behind the van. Dante and his group also halted in surprise.

Bennet said something about "…fucking cowards…" and shot the buggy door at about the level of Doc's chest. The bullet ricocheted harmlessly away.

To reinforce the invaders' terror, Doc blew a massive hole in the van's motor's side. This time he had braced himself solidly against the buggy.

Bennet turned to face the washroom too late. His brains exploded from the back of his head. Dante, who had stepped over Skinner's corpse, stood with legs spread apart, holding a smoking pistol with both hands. His soldiers poured out of the door around him. Con saw Emerson's blond head and Manny's angry visage. Bennet's little army, Stella among the first, melted away. Dante glared at the buggy and Doc holding the Kreutzer.

"It's time to leave," said Doc.

Con said, "But how…?"

"We change places."

Somehow, Doc pulled Con into the passenger seat while taking the driver's. He started the buggy as Dante stalked angrily toward them. Con knew Doc couldn't possibly turn the buggy around before Dante reached them.

Doc didn't even try turning the buggy. He backed it toward the space between the doorjamb and the van's rear end. It looked too narrow to Con, especially the way the cart wriggled back and forth.

"You're gonna get us killed, Doc!" Beulah wailed from the back.

"Don't distract him!" ordered Lois.

But Doc steadied the cart as they neared the opening. Now, if there was enough room…

Dante's yell, "Get back here, Doc, you son-of-a-bitch!" drew Con's attention to the front again. Dante ran toward them, holding his pistol up, not aimed at them. And he was gaining! Doc's face, clenched in concentration, faced the rear. Con looked behind at the opening, made dark by the night beyond it. Lois also watched it. Beulah sat hunkered down with her eyes closed and her fists clenched. The cart appeared to have less than a half-foot clearance on either side. If the cart wavered even a bit….

"Stop, you bastard!"

Con whipped around to face the front. Dante leaped for the buggy, his outspread arms slamming down on its hood.

But the smooth hood afforded him nothing to grasp. When Doc put on a burst of speed, Dante slipped off.

A surprisingly cool breeze told Con they had passed outside. He looked up to see a sky full of stars. He expelled a whoosh of air, unaware that he had been holding his breath. Doc wheeled the buggy and cart around and started buggy-first down a street perpendicular to the compound. Con looked back to see Dante's silhouette, dimly limned by the garage's lone candle, standing in its doorway with his hands on his hips. His armed men poured out of the garage in pursuit of Bennet's outnumbered followers.

Con mentally wished Dante goodbye.

Sixteen – New Hope, Utah

Con awoke chilled, despite the two sleeping bags fastened together that enwrapped Lois andvhim. She lay with her cheek on his chest, his shirt wadded in her fist. The concrete underside of the bridge loomed high above them.

They had traveled in the dark to hide their heavily loaded cart from as greedy eyes. Last night, Doc had driven them north under a dome of stars dominated by a brilliant waxing gibbous moon. They had closed the buggy windows against the chilly breeze. Con sat in the passenger's seat. Like the others, he spoke little but enjoyed the exhilaration he felt from escaping from Dante's little empire and Bennet's thugs.

Though he recognized the elation as spurious, since he had no idea of where they were going or what would come next, he clung to it. Let tomorrow bring whatever it would bring.

Or, as Doc would have it: Make the most of that night and the least of its passing.

The interstate had risen higher in elevation and the excess baggage slowed the buggy on the uphill slopes. Its usually quiet motor hummed in complaint on the steep grades. That and the gentle rocking had felt so pleasant…

…until a sudden stop and silence jarred Con awake. He hadn't realized he had fallen asleep. To the east, he saw the faint, diffuse milky glow of the false dawn.

"Time to call it a night," said Doc through a yawn. "Let's spend the day under this underpass."

Doc drove the buggy across the shoulder and down a slope. Though he took the least precipitous angle, the jarring awakened Lois and Beulah. Where the land flattened, Doc bounced the vehicle across a ditch to a narrow, paved road and followed it under the overpass. They got out, stretching and groaning but grinning at each other in relief at their escape.

They sat on the concrete apron sloping up from the road, eating beanie weenies from cans, too tired to prepare a real meal.

Con asked Doc, "What if someone comes up this little road?"

Doc shrugged. "Doesn't seem likely – I haven't seen signs of anyone living out here – but we'll take turns standing watch just in case."

"I'll take the first one," said Con. "You must be wiped out from driving."

Doc gave him a one-sided grin and head shake that told Con he didn't trust him to stay awake. "No, I can't sleep; too wired from driving."

"Okay," Con said, "then wake me when you get unwired."

That had been last night.

Now he gently unclenched Lois' hand, rolled her over on her back and pulled the double sleeping bag over her. He sat up. The setting sun cast long shadows of the underpass columns and a chill had replaced the warmth he had felt during his morning watch. Beulah, leaning against one of the concrete pillars that supported the overpass, wore her vest over a long-sleeved shirt.

She said, "'Bout time you're getting up. I'm starvin, ready for breakfast."

Con realized he was too. "Where's Doc?"

She nodded toward the interstate above them. "Went up to get the lay of the land, whatever that means."

The sound of footfalls slipping down the slope announced Doc's return. Lois awakened, and rubbing her eyes, she asked, "What time is it?"

"'Bout dusk, sweetie," said Beulah. "Breakfast time."

Doc's boots skidded down the sandy slope into view and stopped. Then his head appeared as he leaned over to peer at them under the bridge.

"I see you're all awake," he said. "That's good."

"I'm not awake yet," said Lois.

"Come up with me," said Doc. "There's something you gotta see." He took Beulah's hand.

"Got something else to do first," said Con. He stood, lifted Lois to her feet. They put on the vests Beulah had given them against the chill and went across the road to the pile of brush and boulders they had chosen for a latrine the previous evening – ladies to the left, gentlemen to the right. When she joined him, he noticed she looked wan.

"You okay?" he asked. "You look kinda pale."

She frowned. "Just tired. In case you've forgotten, we had a helluva night last night." Then she smiled up at him and took his hand. "Sorry, Hon, I didn't mean to be grouchy. Like I said, I'm just tired."

"Me too. Let's go up and join Doc and Beulah."

Once up there they saw the distant low western mountains crouching darkly under a magnificent orange/salmon/purple sunset.

But instead of admiring the sunset, Doc and Beulah looked south. Curious to see what had attracted them, Con and Lois turned to see a column of dense gray smoke laced with black and orange.

"Is that Vegas?" said Con. "Did one of those gangs blow the city up?"

"Yes, to the first question," said Doc. "Probably not to the second. It should've struck me as little short of miraculous that Vegas hadn't already burned. At least part of it. San Diego was burning down around me when I left."

Lois said. "Los Angeles and its suburbs had fires all over, too. I'll bet it's still burning."

"What started the fires?" asked Con.

"In my case," said Beulah, "lightning hit a transformer down the street from us. Set the trees afire, then the whole neighborhood."

Doc said, "Could've been lightning, squatters, exploding high-pressure gas lines, chemical fires in factories – other things I don't even know about. They do a lot of damage before they burn out. Especially in deserts with high winds like California and all the country we've come through since."

Lois said, "I wonder about Dante's people, Claire and her daughters and their candle shop. I hope the fire didn't reach them. Or if it did, they got away."

"Yeah," said Con. "Dante too. He wasn't a bad guy. For a dictator."

"We'll never know what caused the fire or who it harmed," said Doc. "Let's go have some breakfast and get on the road." As he talked, he started skidding down the slope.

Because of their skimpy meal the evening before, they awakened hungry and enthusiastically devoured the large omelet Beulah prepared from pressure-sealed, self-heating packets. Though Con thought it would have tasted bland without the dried chilis she found in their larder.

With Lois beside him, Con drove when they left into the gathering dusk. She looked back over the seat and said, "You're a man of many talents, Doc. I couldn't believe how straight you backed the cart through that doorway last night. What other skills do you have up your sleeve?"

He chuckled. "We old guys aren't as smart as you kids think. You've only been here long enough to make the mistakes. We've just been around longer. We've made all the mistakes and learned how to correct them. You'll learn how to fix em too."

"So," Lois persisted, "what kind of mistake helped you learn to back that trailer?"

"By the time I got out of college, technology had taken away a lot of people's jobs. Some lived on the dole but I wanted to make my own money. I was lucky enough to find a job with Fish and Wildlife. One of my tasks was backing our boat down into the water. That slip was so narrow, and my boss's cussing made me so nervous I thought I'd never learn to back it, but I did. Now I can back any cart or boat anywhere you want it. And thanks to that boss I do it best under pressure. He had been a drill instructor in the Army and said the only way to train a recruit – that's what he thought of me – was to keep on his ass till he got a thing right.

"Eventually, I got the job college had prepared me for and turned it into a career. But I can still back a trailer. It's like riding a bicycle or having sex. You never forget how."

The desert gradually grew cooler and more fruitful. The bright moon and stars starkly illuminated the features surrounding them. Willows and cottonwoods lined creeks and arroyos. Southern and western slopes remained mostly dry and barren except for patches of pale grass. Drought-resistant trees like junipers, pinyons, scrub oaks and maples grew on northern and eastern slopes. Patches of white lay in the shadows: snow. Great irrigation circles watered whole sections of land for fields. The small groups of buildings they occasionally saw in the distance probably belonged to farms or ranches. The interstate passed through the outskirts of a small town and then another. The few distant lights in the last town indicated survivors. Once, they saw an RV park with a few abandoned vehicles.

After a time, Beulah asked, "Where do you think we are, Doc?"

"Some place in Utah, I'd guess. We must've passed the state line last night. Let's watch for I-70. It branches off to the east somewhere up ahead."

"Does it take us to this Tin Cup?" she asked.

"I have no idea. I never heard of Tin Cup until Con told me about it. I only know that I-70 leads to Colorado."

"How 'bout it, Con?" Beulah insisted. "Where's Tin Cup from here?"

"I don't have a clue. I only know it's in Colorado."

"What in the –?"

Lois came to Con's rescue. "Once we get to Colorado, we'll find someone who knows where it is."

"But what if –?"

"Quit your squabbling," said Doc. "There's a sign saying I-70's up ahead. I think I see the interchange. We've come further than I thought."

A tangle of freeway lanes and ramps lay ahead, surrounded by decorative trees and shrubs painted different shades of gray by the moonlight. The squarish forms in their midst resolved themselves into small buildings. As they drew closer, a few tents and vehicles became discernable among them. Con said, "There's people living there."

Lois said, "I'm glad they're already asleep."

"And I'm glad the buggy's electric motor don't hardly make no noise," said Beulah, "so it won't wake them folks up when we go by."

Doc said, "What's that white board standing in the median in front of the shacks?"

"It's a sign," said Con. As they drew closer he made out the words. "It says 'Medicine Creek Bridge out ahead.' But we don't know if it's on I-15 or I-70." He stopped the buggy. "What do you think, Doc?"

"Maybe we oughta wait till they wake up and ask them. It might save us a lot of time later. We're still too far away for them to hear us. See that stand of pinyons on that little hill to the right? Let's head over there where they can't see us and discuss it."

Con pulled off the road, crossed to the hill and parked with it and its trees between them and the settlement. When they got out of the buggy, the air felt much cooler. A light skiff of snow lay on the north side of the hill and the trees.

"It's after midnight," said Beulah. "Past time for lunch." She and Lois began to root around in their larder to put together a meal.

"Let's have a look at this place," Doc said to Con. With his binoculars, he walked uphill into the pinyons, kicking through the snow. Con followed. Doc stood at the hill's top, raised the binoculars to his eyes, and moved from side to side until he could see between the tree limbs. After he looked for a while, he handed them to Con. "Tell me what you see."

Con found an open spot through the trees and focused the binoculars. The hillock rose a couple of yards higher than the settlement and the moon and stars illuminated it enough for him to make out a few details. It consisted of over a score of small huts made of boards or plywood sheets – a few had corrugated metal roofs – four or five RVs, and a few tents. They formed a U-shape around a bare space, with the opening facing them.

A figure emerged from behind the buildings on the left, walked across the U's opening and sat on a stump by the house on the right, hidden in the shadow of a tree.

Con handed the binoculars to Doc. "There's a guard making rounds. Carrying a rifle. Looks like he's taking a break on a stump under that tree on the right."

Doc took the binoculars and looked through them for a time. Then, "I don't see… There, he just stood up and went behind the house on the right. Continuing his rounds, I guess. Let's go see what the women have rustled up."

As they ate, they discussed how they should deal with the settlement.

"I'm for giving them a visit," said Doc. "We need to find out about that bridge that's out."

"Not me," said Beulah. "That open space betwixt the houses looks too much like the spider's parlor…."

Lois said, "As in, 'Welcome to my parlor said the spider to the fly'?"

"You got it, Angel. After Dante's parlor, I ain't for trustin no other'n."

Lois said, "Beulah's got a point. When we get to that bridge that's out, surely we can find our way across another one."

Con said, "We could if it was just an overpass like the one we slept under last night, but what if it's over a raging river?"

Beulah said, "I ain't seen enough water in these little creeks to get in a decent rage."

"See those mountains over there." Doc pointed to the dark landforms looming to the east. "I-70 goes right through them. I'm sure it crosses fast rivers and deep gorges and we don't know what-all. And I'll bet roads with bridges apart from the freeway are rare and hard for strangers to find."

"I agree with Doc," said Con. "And that open space between the houses looks like a place for a market to me. Peaceful people run markets. Ornery ones would drive off customers."

"Sugar," said Beulah, "didn't you get enough of markets at Dante's?"

"Even though I'm nervous about meeting new people," said Lois, "whether it's a market or not we could see if they'd like to trade real food for kitchen utensils. I'm sick of canned and freeze-dried food already and we've got a ways to go. We don't even know how far Tin Cup is."

"Yeah, there is that," said Beulah. "And Doc has his cannon to keep them in line."

Doc grinned. "Yep. We've got more firepower than anybody for hundreds of miles in any direction."

They agreed to visit the settlement in the morning, lay their sleeping bags by the Moveable Feast, and went to sleep.

* * *

They slept until late the next day, after being so used to being awake driving at night. After they awakened, they sipped tea while Lois took her turn preparing breakfast.

Con asked Doc, "So, do we visit the spider's parlor right after breakfast?"

"Sure. But while the ladies fix it, you and I have a job to do." He rummaged around in the cart until he found a gunny sack, then nodded toward the pinyon trees. Con followed him. "This," he told Con, "is a fortuitous find." He picked up a tiny nut from the ground. "A pine nut. See, you peel off this outer hard covering, roast and salt the tasty bit you find inside. You can eat them plain or put them in pastries or cookies."

"Or in salads," said Con. "I've had them that way."

They gathered the pine nuts until Beulah called them to breakfast. After eating and repacking the cart, they left with Doc driving and Con beside him. They rounded the hillock and bumped across the rough desert to the settlement. To Con's surprise, dozens of people, mostly adults, gathered to watch them the minute they rounded the hillock.

"How the hell did they know…?" began Con, then continued, "Oh yeah. Their sentry must've seen us last night and warned them."

"That's what I'd guess," said Doc. "I don't see many guns. That's a good sign."

They crossed the interstate's northbound lane, flat median and southbound lane. When they drew within about thirty yards of the settlement, a tall man stepped out from the others and held his hand up for them to stop. So Doc did. To Con, the man looked like some ancient prophet. His erect posture, white beard reaching the center of his chest (but no mustache) and stern gaze gave him an aura of authority. His severe dress accented that persona: black suit coat; white shirt; black trousers with suspenders; a black flat-brimmed, flat-crowned hat. He bore no weapons but carried a black-covered, much-riffled Bible.

That's all we need, thought Con, thinking of Spero, another nut-case preacher.

The man approached the buggy and stopped. Doc got out and faced him, also unarmed, though the Kreutzer rested conveniently alongside the driver's seat. Con joined him.

The man said, "Welcome to you and your friends to New Hope, Utah. I'm Reverend Ephraim Folsom, spiritual leader of our little camp. I am a Fundamentalist pastor. I won't say to which denomination because all Christians are brothers and sisters in this time of the Last Days."

"Thank you, Reverend. I'm Donald Drennan, better known as Doc. These are my friends…." He introduced Con, then nodded for Lois and Beulah to exit the buggy and introduced them.

Folsom said, "This used to be a camp our parishioners used to restore their spirituality. The cabins date from those days. The tents and RVs belong to pilgrims who have joined us since the pandemic. Please rest with us for a while and exchange goods if you have something to trade. We're the only bartering place we know of in these parts. Unfortunately, we don't have enough resources for you to stay with us for very long."

"That's very kind of you," said Doc. He indicated the overfilled cart. "As you can see, we have supplies of our own as well as goods to trade."

"Then drive right into the center of our habitation and park. You and your goods will be safe there. We guard our village with a shotgun in one hand and Bible in the other, day and night." Though he obviously trusted others to bear the shotguns.

Thinking of Spero Peace, Con thought, Oh Shit! Not another religious crackpot! but said, "We'd also like to know about that bridge that's out."

"Oh, that's the Medicine Creek Bridge up I-15 about ten miles. After you get settled in, come over to my place and we'll talk about routes around it." He pointed to one of the little houses.

Lois said, "But we're not going up –"

Doc interrupted her, said to Folsom, "I will. Thanks." and, turning to the others, "Climb back aboard our carriage and let's park the thing."

The crowd parted to allow Doc to drive into the open space and park. Lois whispered to him, "Why did you hide which way we're traveling, Doc?"

"I'd like to keep our route between us. And away from a guy who rules with a Bible and a gun."

After a moment's thought, she said, "Maybe that's a wise precaution."

"Yeah," said Beulah. "Ain't we glad Doc made all them mistakes and learned how to fix em?"

Lois reached from the back seat to grasp Con's shoulder and said, "Do you hear those chickens clucking? Know what that means?"

"I do," said Beulah. "Eggs and fried chicken."

Doc and the preacher's conversation had distracted Con. Suddenly hearing a rooster crow, he looked around for the chickens. Lois pointed to a large flock in a pen between two RVs. A chicken coop stood at its rear and behind it, a tall wall to shield it from predators, human or animal, from outside the settlement.

The crowd had only moved far enough away from the buggy to allow it to enter the open space and park. After the four got out, the crowd gathered closer to ask questions about where they had come from, the conditions there, what towns they had passed through and their destination. With the sadness he always felt about the scarcity of children, Con noticed few of them and no babies that could have been born during or since the pandemic.

The preacher had disappeared, but an old woman Con had seen in the crowd passed through its ranks toward them, chiding her neighbors. "Where's your manners? These folks've been traveling for weeks or maybe months and need some rest. Now beat it." And after the crowd had broken up, she said to Doc and the others, "I'm Marjory Winkler. I apologize for these folks. Haven't been any travelers through here since Thanksgiving and they're starving for news about the outside world. They elected me to be our Mayor, but Reverend Folsom's the official greeter. We depend on him a lot. Did you folks say you had some stuff to barter? And what would you like to trade for?"

Doc said, "We've got kitchen utensils, blankets, clothes, stuff like that. And we'd like to trade for food. We've got a lot of canned goods but we'd sure like some fresh vegetables and meat that's never seen the inside of a can or pressure-sealed pouch."

"We might have some food like that to spare," she said, "especially for some warm blankets and clothes. We're a bit short of them. Some of our neighbors drop by to trade sometimes too. They may be interested in some of your stuff."

"We could use some water too," said Lois, "for baths and to wash clothes."

"There's a creek down that-a-way," Marjory pointed to a space between two of the rear houses. "I'll make sure the kids don't invade your privacy. There's pots down there to heat water in and rooms to bathe in. The water's cold when it comes down out of those mountains.

"One more thing: The whole community cooks and eats together, twice a day, at daybreak and dusk. We cook and take our meals back in

those far two houses. We would accept a little help with the cooking too."
She looked at Lois and Beulah and then left.

Seventeen – All Travelers Are Nuts.

Con and the others gathered blankets and clothes and followed Marjory's directions to a trail leading downhill through densely growing juniper bushes. At the bottom of the hill lay a large bowl-shaped depression, hidden from above by the junipers. A creek entered it from the northeast and ran through it to disappear into a culvert on the other side. On the way, they found trails branching off, some identified by signs as leading to men's or to women's latrines. Con went down an unmarked one. The emerging smell led him to hog pens and sheds.

An hour later, having bathed and the men shaved and after hanging their laundry on lines to dry, the four returned to the Moveable Feast. They spread their trade goods out on a tarp beside the dune buggy. The residents and visiting neighbors spent the afternoon trading and gossiping with them. They all lusted after news of the outside world. Doc left them for a while to go to Reverend Folsom's house to discuss a detour around the I-15 bridge. As the afternoon waned, the residents returned to their homes and the neighbors left for theirs.

Doc found his three companions alone at the dune buggy when he rejoined them. He complimented them on the food they had acquired: salted meat, dried fruit, tubers and other vegetables.

Beulah said, "So what did you learn from the preacher-man?"

"I pretended we were going north up Interstate 15 instead of east on I-70. He told me about a couple of detours we could take around the Medicine Creek Bridge. And said it was too bad we weren't going east along I-70."

"Why's that?" asked Lois.

"A trader named Clive McCullough and his folks passed through here a couple days ago on their way to Fishlake National Forest and beyond. Folsom said he could've guided us through it so we'd miss the interstate. He goes through Fishlake by way of County Road 20. Even though the road's been abandoned for years, he says it's still passable."

"Why would we do that?" asked Con. "A minor road like that'd slow us down. The buggy'll get us past any bad guys on the freeway. It's bulletproof and you've got the Cracker."

"Kreutzer," corrected Doc. "Folsom says they've heard that some people in those towns along I-70 are pretty dangerous. And hardly anyone lives in the national forest."

"How much longer would the County road take than the freeway?" asked Con.

"He claims only a few days."

"Does he know where Tin Cup is?"

"He's heard of it. Thinks it's in western Colorado south of Grand Junction which is a major Colorado town on I-70. He also extended an offer to us. He suggested we stay here another day to rest up. What do you think?"

"I could certainly use a day of rest," said Lois.

"Definitely," said Con. He remembered how pale she had looked that morning. A day of rest would be good for her.

When the New Hope women started gathering in the cooking hut, Lois and Beulah joined them.

"One thing hasn't changed," said Con. "Women still do the cooking."

"Works for me," said Doc. "I'm a lousy cook."

"I've noticed. You have trouble even heating up stuff out of cans. And that stinky fish you eat…." Con made a face.

"Ah, yes. Kippered herring. Too bad we're out of it. And what I wouldn't give for a bottle of Kusaya or some lutefisk."

"I don't even want to know what that is."

Lois and Beulah ate with the women with whom they had prepared dinner. Afterward, they joined Con and Doc, who sat around an outdoor fire with a group of men, regaling them about their adventures along the road.

Finally, one grizzled older man said, "Ain't you guys tired of traveling? I mean, you just go here and there and yon. You're wasting your lives."

Doc said, "You've never heard of the Buddha's quote, 'Happiness is a journey, not a destination?'"

"Or," said Con, glad he could contribute, "think of life as a journey, not a destination.'"

"Nah," said the grizzled man. "Them's dumb sayings."

Lois said, "Our journey is like the Odyssey. The pandemic was the Troy we fled. We're on our way to Ithaca."

"But," said Beulah, "we ain't come to that goddess bitch's island yet —"

"Circe, the witch," said Doc. "She turned Odysseus' men into pigs."

"Was she the one who kept Odysseus there with her so long?"

"That was Calypso," said Doc. "He stayed with her for seven years and then just up and left. He was having too much fun to leave before that."

Lois shook her head, "Odysseus couldn't leave till Zeus made Calypso let him go."

"But he didn't ask to be let go," said Doc. "For seven years, he had the finest wine and food, not to mention sex with a goddess. He wasn't in any hurry."

Beulah said, "Dante was the guy who wrote about hell, wasn't he? So we been to Hades."

"You're right, Beulah," said Con. "But we haven't found Calypso yet."

Lois playfully swatted him. "And you are not going to."

The grizzled man got up and walked off, muttering something about all travelers being nuts.

Con's beer-drinking buddy, Henry, had been a daydreamer. He remembered Henry's father chastising him for letting his mind wander and Henry's retort by way of a bumper sticker.

Con stood and called to the grizzled man, "Hey, man," and quoted the bumper sticker, "'All who wander are not lost.'"

Without turning, the man made obscene gestures with both raised hands.

∗ ∗ ∗

Reverend Folsom invited Con and Lois to spend the night in his living room on pallets by its fireplace, saying the nights had gotten too cold to sleep outdoors. Marjory and her man Jeff made Doc and Beulah a similar offer.

Con awakened alone the next morning. He hoped that Lois rising earlier than he did meant she felt better. He got up, wrapped a blanket around his shoulders and went outside, shivering in the cold, his breath misting the air. He headed for the trail down to the creek and the branch leading to the men's latrine. On his way back he passed close by the women's latrine. He heard someone crying inside. Please, he begged, don't let it be Lois. In the settlement he went up to Doc and Beulah who stood by the buggy.

"Have you seen Lois?" he asked.

"No," said Beulah, "but we just got out here." Con thought she looked concerned.

"Nature probably called," said Doc. "Some trips to the john take longer than others."

Then Lois emerged from the trailhead. Con went to meet her. She looked pale and, had crying caused her red eyes? He put his arm around her as they walked toward the buggy.

"Are you okay, Babe?" he asked.

"Sure," she said. "I'm just worn out is all. After today's rest I'll be back to normal." But her smile looked forced to Con.

Doc said, "Breakfast will be ready pretty soon. I smell bacon cooking." And to Lois, "That'll bring you around."

Con said, "It's been so long I've forgotten what real bacon tastes like."

"Me too," said Beulah. "There should be eggs to go with it."

Just then, one of the women called, "Chow's on!" from the little house they used for a kitchen/dining room. Breakfast included fried potatoes as well as eggs and bacon.

As they ate Lois said, "This is the first place I've been that hasn't been run by lunatics, thugs or dictators. I hope Tin Cup will be like this."

"If it isn't we'll move on to the next place," said Con. "Doc'll get us away with his cracker."

"Kreutzer," said Doc with a frown, annoyed by Con's baiting about the rifle's name.

"Doc, why are the guys who run these towns such assholes?" asked Beulah.

"Just like nature abhors a vacuum," said Doc, "government hates anarchy. When societies crumble, somebody takes over. Lots of times it's a strongman but they're not all bad. Dante wanted to build an empire, but he had compassion for his people. Sometimes they don't, like Bennet and his girlfriend. Hopefully, Tin Cup will be a classic small democracy.

"But if not, like Con says, we'll keep looking. Eventually, we'll find a place."

"Or create one of our own," said Beulah. "I vote for Doc as our boss."

Only Doc failed to raise his teacup to clink theirs in agreement until Beulah grabbed his wrist and forced his cup to join theirs. Then all but Doc cheered. He grinned, shook his head and said, "I'm too cranky to be a boss."

After they finished eating Doc said, "Let's go see if we can help them with something to pay for our meals." But their hosts had few chores in winter and none that day. After they packed the cart and buggy – Doc wanted to leave right after breakfast the following day – they loafed with the residents. In late afternoon Doc and Beulah joined card players in a drafty, one-room shack jokingly called the recreation room. Con and Lois visited with Marjory, her man Jeff and Reverend Folsom in Marjory's house.

During the conversation, Jeff said, "You wouldn't believe that I was once the most hard-core capitalist conservative. Now I live in a socialist commune."

Marjory hugged him. "The times they are a-changing, dear. I'm sure there aren't as many capitalists now that the money's gone but they'll find a way to invent a new kind of money."

Finally, Lois yawned and said she would like to take a nap.

"Go back to my place," said Folsom. "Your pallet's still on the floor in front of the fireplace." He started to get up. "I'll stoke up the fire for you."

"No, I'll take her," said Con.

She said, "Thanks, Reverend."

Con walked her to Folsom's house. On the way, he said, "You should have another day of rest. I'll ask the preacher…"

She said, "Don't be silly. I'm fine. In fact, after I wake up let's take the buggy over to that little hill we stayed at the first night and set up the tent. You'll see." She took his hand and gave him a suggestive smile.

That sounded fine to Con but he still wasn't sure she was up to travel the next day. "Okay, but we'll see how you feel when you wake up."

After the fire had warmed the preacher's living room and Lois had fallen asleep Con went out. A wan sun had warmed the open area some. Seeing Beulah standing by the dune buggy he joined her.

"Got tired of the card game?" he asked.

"Yeah. Couldn't get em to play for money so I got bored."

"Hasn't anybody told you the value of money has dropped?"

"Yeah, like all the way to nothin, but it's a way to keep track. Where's Lois?"

"Taking a nap. She said it'd make her feel better. Hope so. I'm worried about her."

Beulah looked at him cynically. "You don't know much about women do you, Con?"

He said a little hotly, "I know enough about Lois to care for her."

"You don't know any more about women than I do cars. In a car, I poke the starter button. If she goes, fine. If she don't, I don't have no idea what to do. All you guys know about women is how to poke –"

"Wait a minute, Beulah. What the hell're you talking about?"

"Even Doc hasn't noticed it. And his wife even had children."

"Wait a minute… You mean she's – is it morning sickness? Is she pregnant, Beulah? Is that it?" Con's heart leaped joyfully.

"She's had morning sickness for almost three weeks. She's just good at hiding it. I figured it out and confronted her about it. She didn't want me to tell you, but you need to know."

"Wow, Beulah! I'm gonna be a daddy! And the woman I love's the mother! But wait. Why doesn't she want me to know?"

"Think about it. How many newborn babies have you seen since the pandemic? Or any babies for that matter. The only kids here were at least a year or two old when people started getting sick last summer. Same way with the children at Dante's Market."

"You mean –"

"And there are fewer women than men here. Just like at Dante's Market."

"What are you saying, Beulah?"

"That giving birth can be a death sentence for the baby and mother both. Lois can see that. Making babies in this kinda world is worse than irresponsible. You shoulda thought this out."

"We thought we were being careful. But you don't see any pharmacies around to go to for anti-baby drugs, do you. We thought we counted the days between her periods and –"

"Y' know that joke about what you call people who use the rhythm method? The answer is parents. Well, it ain't a joke. You shoulda added a coupla days to be sure."

But there had been a few babies at Orlando's. He wished he remembered how many. "I know a nurse at Tin Cup, Beulah. She'll deliver the baby. She'll make sure that both Lois and the new little Colby make it just fine."

"If you can find this mysterious lost city of Tin Cup."

"Oh, we'll find it. We'll find it. I've got to talk this pregnancy over with Lois. Reassure her."

"Yes, you need to have that talk with her, Con. Just do me a favor."

"Sure."

"Act like you're not as dense about women as you really are. Pretend you figured her pregnancy out your own self so she won't know I ratted her out."

"Why, uh, sure."

Beulah wandered away to join some women sitting by a crude standing hand loom they had set up in the sun, one weaving and the others gossiping.

Con sat in the buggy's passenger seat thinking of the new child, boy or girl, he didn't care which, suckling at its mother's breast, giggling as it rode its father's knee.

His elbow rested on the windowsill. He jumped when someone touched it. He looked out to see Lois' smiling face. She looked rested and happy. He reached out to cradle her face in both hands and kissed her, a gentle but long-lasting kiss. He would find Tin Cup. And Chloë would be there to safely deliver their baby and keep Lois safe.

As they drew apart, she said, "Wow! You sure are ready for our private hill."

"Oh, you don't know how ready." He opened the door for her and moved over into the driver's seat. He noticed that the sun had sunk farther behind the western mountains than he had realized. The smells of dinner wafted toward them.

She asked, "How far away do you think Tin Cup is?"

"If we had a car, we'd be there tomorrow evening. The buggy'll take a couple of days."

They both pretended Con knew what he was talking about. They prattled on about the next stage of their trip starting the next morning.

The dinner bell rang. They feasted on ham, squash, corn and a salad featuring pine nuts and watercress. Afterward, Doc and Beulah started to follow the men who had sat around last night's fire. Doc said to Con and Lois, who stood holding hands, "You gonna join us?"

"We'd kind of like to visit that hill we slept near the night before last," said Con.

"Sure," said Doc with a knowing grin. "Just be back in time for breakfast. We leave early."

"You bet." Con dreaded having that important conversation with Lois. Since her nap though, color had returned to her cheeks. Maybe she wasn't pregnant after all. He could wait and see. No, he couldn't count on that.

Con and Lois walked hand in hand to the dune buggy. He unhooked the cart to make it more maneuverable. They moved the tent and sleeping bags from the cart into the buggy and got in. Con drove out of New Hope with the lights off. The waxing moon made driving easy and, even though the solar panels had bathed in sunlight all day, they wanted them as fully charged as possible for the next day.

They reached the hill, stopped behind it and got out of the buggy. She reached for a sleeping bag and he the tent.

"No," she said. "Let's only take the sleeping bags. We'll zip them together like before. We can see the stars through the trees."

"Good idea."

He'd talk to her about the pregnancy first and, as Beulah had advised, would pretend to have recognized it himself. He would reassure her about Chloé, Yet his passion had grown as they neared the hill. He sensed hers had too. He grabbed the other sleeping bag and, fighting the lower tree limbs in the dark, they dragged them up the hill. They lay them on the snow and began fastening them together awkwardly because of working so quickly in the dark, giggling at their clumsiness.

To hell with it, he thought. The conversation could wait.

A small light in the south caught his eye. Lois, who faced north, hadn't seen it but, apparently noticing his intense look and frown, asked, "What is it?"

"A light on the interstate. Looks like it's not moving. I need to check it out." He went back to the buggy through the trees and got Doc's binoculars. Then back to Lois.

"It couldn't be someone chasing us," she said. "Even though Dante was angry at us he didn't come after us. And his men wiped out Bennet's gang. Besides, the city burned down."

"We don't know that he got all of Bennet's gang. Or if the whole city burned down. For that matter, we don't know if Dante still runs his Market. Maybe someone took over who thinks we helped with Bennet's invasion. Still, you're probably right but I need to check."

While he talked, he held the binoculars to his eyes and adjusted them. Then he said, "You gotta be shitting me."

"What?"

"They're setting up camp in the median. The light comes from an everlight on a pole. And there's two trucks, a big sand-colored military-looking one and some kind of farm truck."

"How many of them are there."

"Kinda hard to tell," he said. "At least twenty."

"Could that be Bennet's gang?"

"One item guarantees it. The military truck sprouts a rack of spikes from its snout. Just like they had on that big van in Dante's garage."

She shivered, and not necessarily from the cold. "So how do we make the least of this?"

"We get back to New Hope and wake up Doc. Then we leave a little early. Like right now."

Eighteen – "...you will die a slow, painful death."

"Come on, Doc," whispered Con, shaking his friend's shoulder. Doc and Beulah had bathed before dinner and gone to sleep early, in preparation to leave right after breakfast.

Doc pushed his hand away, turned over and said, "Mumphl."

"Wake up. We gotta get out of here."

Doc rolled onto his back and looked up at Con blearily. "Is it breakfast time already?"

"Shh. Don't wake Marjory and Jeff. We're leaving. The Bennets are on our tail."

"Are you nuts? What the –"

"No time to explain." Con started to move over to awaken Beulah but she had already risen far enough to prop herself on an elbow. She stood up and wrapped her blanket around her. Doc followed suit and they went outside with Con.

They shivered in the cold. As they crossed to the buggy, Con explained how the everlight in the median had attracted his attention and how the armored truck, armed with spikes much like the van that Doc had destroyed with his Kreutzer, convinced him that it belonged to the Bennets.

"Yes," said Doc, "they must surely be the remnants of Bennet's gang."

"How do you know they're after us in particular?" asked Beulah.

"I don't," said Con, "but I don't want to be here to ask them if they are. I already woke Ephraim, told him why we're leaving and warned him about his new visitors."

They had reached Lois at the cart. She said, "I agree with Con." She had stayed there to transfer the parkas Doc had stored in the cart to the buggy. Then she tried vainly, because of its weight, to attach the cart's shaft to the buggy. Con helped her finish the task.

"Me too," said Doc as he locked the emergency cart chain. "At least they won't follow our actual route. These folks'll tell them we went on up I-15." Then, "See how those parkas fit." And to Lois, "I'm afraid they'll all be too big on you, little girl." While the others pulled on parkas and took their seats, he rooted around in the cart to find a small heater and it brought up when he joined them.

Lois had covered the mandrake plants in their buckets behind the back seat with their tablecloth to protect them from the cold. When Con checked them, he thought their leaves looked shriveled and desiccated but the soil around them wasn't frozen.

Con drove, with Doc beside him, up I-15's northbound lane and then along the offramp to I-70. The trees and topography kept them out of sight of New Hope in case anyone remained awake there to see what direction they went. Doc fiddled with the heater and plugged it into a socket in the dash. "I shoulda equipped the Feast with its own heater," he said, "but I never figured on it leaving southern California. I almost didn't bring the parkas."

"Good thing you did," said Lois.

Con smiled at the way her small body looked lost in her parka, though it was the smallest of the four.

When they reached I-70, the freeway gradually began to rise. More patches of snow appeared on the north side of things and in the hollows and capped the high mountains farther to the east. The sky remained clear and the moon, which had grown larger every night, allowed Con to drive without the headlights as Doc suggested. Con thought it unlikely that a Bennet sentry in the median so far away could see their lights but said nothing. The buggy labored heavily, seldom surpassing 35 miles per hour on the steeper inclines. The little heater gurgled but produced little heat to the front seat and none to the back. Seeing Lois and Beulah huddling coldly, Doc placed the heater between the front bucket seats and pointed it at them as close as its cord allowed.

Clouds began to drift over the stars and moon, reducing visibility and hiding icy patches on the road. Con's nerves, strung tightly by the need to go as fast as possible and worry about losing control on the ice, said to Doc, "I think it's safe to turn the headlights on now."

"I agree. And let me take over for a while. Just riding's getting boring."

"Gladly."

Con stopped at the top of the next hill so Doc wouldn't have to buck grade starting up and traded places with him. Gradually, he felt the muscles in his back and arms, knotted by tension, begin to relax.

Doc said, "That County Road 20 Folsom told me about?"

"Yes?" said Con.

"That's its turnoff up ahead. And it looks like it disappears behind a stand of fir trees. They oughta hide us from the interstate so we can sleep for a while. Though I'm sure all this caution is overkill since the Bennets'll be chasing us up I-15."

"Go for it," said Con.

To Con, worn out from lack of sleep, the tension of driving and the flight from potential enemies, reaching the exit seemed to take forever, though it probably took no more than a quarter of an hour. Doc finally reached and drove down the exit ramp. He turned right at County Road

20 and went east. A skiff of snow covered the road which curved to the right around the side of a hill covered with fir trees. The land dropped off a few feet on their left. As Folsom had warned them, the road appeared to have been abandoned. Potholes, often hidden by the snow, pitted its rough surface and made him reduce speed. Sometimes the buggy slipped on ice or snow. As the road rose the drop-off to the left deepened. He slowed down to make it through narrow places caused by erosion sluffing off the road on that side. The hill on their right rose to form a ridge. The road curved to the right and left until the ridge and trees hid them from the interstate.

At last, Doc stopped and asked, "How's this for a place to sleep?"

"Perfect," said Con. "Though it'll be a little hard to turn the buggy and cart around here in the morning."

Beulah said, "Don't you remember how this dude backed this thing?"

"Yes," said Lois. "I wouldn't want to take this road any farther. Look how narrow it is up ahead. And the snow looks deeper."

Doc turned off the headlights and the motor.

"So tell me, lover," Beulah said to Doc, "what kind of 'mistake' taught you how to drive through snow and ice so well?"

Doc chuckled. "To tell the truth, I've never driven on it before. I'm from San Diego, remember? The closest I've ever been to snow is seeing it on a calendar. My ass was snapping at this seat all the way up here."

"I'm sure glad we didn't know that," said Con. "Let's get some sleep. Can we keep the heater going somehow?"

Doc said, "Sorry. Not without running the battery down. Girls, grab those blankets out of the compartment behind you and pass a couple up to us."

Con wrapped up in his blanket and ignored Doc and Beulah's bickering about the crowded conditions in the buggy and the cold while he drifted off to sleep.

* * *

A full bladder woke Con. He opened the door and stumbled out into the snow, wrapped in his blanket. Though the sun had been up for some time, the road lay in the shadow of the ridge. Clumps of clouds passed overhead. After he finished, he heard what sounded like the diesel engine of a large truck from the direction of I-70. He stomped through the snow around several twists of the road and looked down toward the freeway.

The sound came from the truck bristling with the steel fangs. It had started a slow ascent of their road. The farm truck remained at the bottom of the offramp.

What the hell are they doing here? jumped to his mind as he raced back along the road's curves to the buggy. He yanked the driver's door open and jarred Doc awake.

"Listen to that, Doc."

Doc blinked fully awake, then listened for a moment. "Tell me that's not what it sounds like."

"Wish I could, Doc. It's the one with the spikes."

"Get in!"

But Con was already racing around the vehicle to do just that.

Doc started the motor. Their voices and the buggy's jostling awakened the women. Doc answered their querulous questions with, "Listen to that truck engine. It's our friends from the median."

"The Bennet gang?" said Lois. "They're supposed to be on I-15."

"Why are they coming up here?" asked Beulah.

"They're either after us for some reason," said Doc, "or they're mistaking us for someone else. They saw our tire tracks in the snow coming off the interstate. Now let's be quiet and let me concentrate on driving."

The road narrowed but the snow remained only one or two inches deep except for drifts. When they came to one a half foot deep, Doc floored the accelerator and blasted through.

Then the motor hiccupped and died. But only for a moment before it coughed and started again.

"What the hell was that?" demanded Con.

"Our worst nightmare," said Doc grimly. "The solar panels are giving out. They need a big dose of sunlight. Turn that fucking heater off. It's sucking the power out."

Con figured the larger truck couldn't go any faster than they did on this deteriorating road but that wouldn't matter if the solar panels failed. The buggy rounded another bend in the road before it died again. But, as it had last time, it restarted a few seconds later.

Con said, "What the hell we gonna do, Doc?"

"That might be our salvation up ahead."

Con saw a snow drift blocking the road, sloping from the hill down to the edge of the road. "We can't get through that. And it looks like the road ends on the other side of it."

"I hope it will end for that big honkin truck."

The drift sloped across the road at nearly forty-five degrees. Con didn't see how the dune buggy could force its way through it, especially pulling the cart. If the buggy even had room. The road looked too narrow. When they got closer, Con realized that what looked like a drift was the road itself. He saw part of its rugged surface showing through the inch or two of snow that covered it. It looked as if material sluffing off the cliff had created it. This close, it looked wide enough for the buggy and cart, but just barely and only if they didn't slide across the snowy plane and over the cliff.

Doc continued toward the "hump," as Con now thought of it, slowing when the buggy's front wheels started up its slope. Con held his breath as the buggy began leaning to the left. Please, God, he prayed, don't let the motor crap out now.

At the top of the mound, it did. Just as the buggy's rear started slipping slowly to the left, pulled, Con realized, by the weight of the cart. It all happened in slow motion. There's trees down there, thought Con in panic. They'll catch us. I hope. Con heard gasps from the back seat.

The motor hummed to life. The front wheels, finding traction, tried to pull them forward. But the rear wheels spun on the snow. The cart continued to gently pull them toward the cliff. The buggy's rear wheels helplessly spun. The buggy suddenly shuddered as one of the cart's wheels spun off the road and hung over the cliff.

Then the back wheels spun their way through the light cover of snow to the road's surface. The four wheels together could not pull the cart's wheel back onto the road but they moved buggy and cart over the hump with the buggy's right front fender sliding along the hill's face while one cart wheel hung uselessly over the cliff. In that manner, the buggy started down the other side of the hump. At its far side the road turned abruptly to the right and leveled out. The buggy, almost facing that direction, shot forward. Buggy and cart suddenly sat on the road. Doc stopped, turned off the motor and leaned back in his seat, breathing heavily.

"Damn, Doc," said Beulah, "how'd you manage that?"

"Damned if I know. Be quiet till my ass quits snapping. We're not out of this yet."

After a time, he started the buggy and went on. The road continued its curvilinear, gently rising route. Doc still slowed for potholes and eroded roadsides. The motor died more frequently. Finally, it gasped and died for good. As always, after a short wait for a little energy to build in the motor, Doc tried to start it again in vain. He waited a longer time before trying again. Still nothing.

After two more attempts, he said, "Not even a click."

They had only gotten a couple miles or so from the hump.

"So this is as far as we'll get," said Lois.

Doc said, "Till those solar panels spend some time in the sun."

Con didn't point out that the stretch of road as far as he could see ahead lay shrouded in shadow.

"We oughta be safe here for now," said Beulah, "that big-assed truck can't get around that slanted curve."

Con said, "No, but the men on that truck can walk across it."

"Let's go greet em, Con," said Doc, grabbing the Kreutzer.

"Okay." Yet Con wondered what two could do against twenty or more, even with Doc's big gun.

"Let me go too," said Lois. "Doc, you said yourself I'm a better shot than Con."

"No," said Con. You're staying here."

"But –" she protested.

"Con's right," said Doc. "If you came, he'd be watching out for you instead of doing what he should be doing. In the meantime, you gals find a place to hide up in those trees." He pointed up the hill. "Find a way up that has the least snow, across some rocks maybe. Brush out whatever footprints you leave with a leafy tree branch."

"I think we should all go face em," protested Beulah. "I ain't never shot a gun but I got to be pretty handy with a knife in east LA."

Doc said, "Absolutely not. This conversation's over." He checked the Kreutzer and jacked a shell into the chamber. Con came around the buggy to join him.

"We'll walk in the buggy's tire tracks," said Doc. "That'll blur our footsteps at least a little."

The perfidious clouds alternately hid and revealed the sunlight, though the road remained in the ridge's shadow. They rounded the bend the buggy had just passed under a cloudy sky. On the other side of it the clouds parted and sunlight streamed from a notch in the ridge straight across the road. Con hadn't noticed the notch when they had passed it in the buggy. Then, fleeing their enemies had claimed his full attention. A small waterfall, frozen now, had formed the gully. Its water disappeared into a culvert under the road.

His examination of the gully had let Doc get ahead of him. Doc glanced back with some annoyance. Con hurried to catch up. They rounded another curve. The road disappeared around the next one a short distance ahead.

Doc stopped them and said, "We could run into those guys around any of these curves. I suggest we find a hiding place and wait for them."

Con said nothing for a moment, thinking of the large number of men the truck could carry. They could never win a shootout with them. All he could think of was that he didn't want to die.

"Well?" said Doc a little impatiently.

He wouldn't let Doc see his terror. He said, "I think I know how it feels when your ass snaps."

Doc grinned and slapped his shoulder. He pointed to a high rugged boulder near the road surrounded by juniper bushes. He said, "Can you jump from the tire track into those juniper bushes, so no one can see your footprints?" Con nodded. "And climb that boulder?"

"Piece of cake."

Doc slung the Kreutzer over his shoulder, jumped into the bushes and started climbing. Con followed. Once on top, they lay prone on the snow covering the rough but more or less flat surface. Doc aimed the Kreutzer and Con his rifle at the next curve in the road.

In a few minutes, their enemies began to appear. They came three or four at a time, their weapons ready. Con counted twenty-three. Their leader stopped them with a raised hand. She pushed back her fur-lined parka hood to reveal white spiked hair – Bennet's woman, Stella.

She cupped her hands about her mouth and shouted, "Listen, you assholes, if you're still within hearing, which you're probably not. You know our truck can't follow you over that cussed hump, and that on foot we can't catch you in your silly little vehicle pulling your childish cart. But know this. I promise to find you for betraying us to that scumbag, Dante LaFarge. Because of you, my Herschel lays dead and LaFarge ran us out of town. That little rat, Rick Skinner, probably helped you. Then you left Dante like the cowards you are. And for that, you will die a slow, painful death."

Then she turned, pushed her way through her people and stalked around the curve, followed by the others. She didn't know their dune buggy lay immobile less than a mile away.

Relief flooded Con. He and Doc waited a long time until they heard the distant sound of the big truck's engine start. Doc said, "I'd hate to back that big hummer all the way down that road." No part of that narrow track would allow them to turn around.

Doc began to clamber back down from the rock. Con followed. Lying prone on the cold rock had made him stiff. He stamped his feet to make the feeling return to them and then followed Doc back to the buggy. A stiff breeze began to follow them.

The women had disobeyed Doc. They stood hidden just behind the rocks at the curve waiting for them. Lois had a rifle ready and Beulah her knife.

"We worried when we heard that woman hollering," Lois said as she grabbed and held Con. "We couldn't hear what she said though."

"But not hearing any shots was a good thing," said Beulah, pulling Doc into a hug. "You must've hid from that bitch and her men. Who was she?"

"We'll tell you all," said Doc, "but first we gotta get out of this wind."

They got back into the buggy and pulled blankets around them.

Doc said, "She's their leader, Bennet's woman." He described her diatribe and her assumption that they had gotten away in the buggy.

"But she said they'd keep looking," said Con.

"Let her look," said Doc. She can't know we're headed to Tin Cup. Which she's probably never heard of. Though I wonder why she took I-70. I'm sure Folsom's people would have told them we took I-15."

"Now that you guys failed to get yourselves killed," said Beulah, "How do we get sunlight to these solar panels?"

"Yeah," said Lois. "The sun goes south this time of year. It can't shine over that ridge."

Doc said, "On the other side of this bend a gulch makes a break in the ridge. It's deep enough to let a little light through."

"Yeah," said Con, "a little creek gnawed a notch in the ridge."

Doc looked at him in surprise. "You're becoming a very perceptive young man."

Con shrugged. "You're rubbing off on me, Doc."

"But that crack's back down there," Beulah pointed out, "and we're up here."

Lois said, "I'll bet Doc has some buggy-pushing in mind for us."

"You're a smart girl, Lois," said Doc. "But I think we have time for lunch first."

Nineteen – "It's about time you got here."

The solar panels fully charged the batteries that afternoon. They left the next morning with Doc driving. Because of the ridge to their right shading the road, Con knew they still faced the problem of inadequate sunlight. Doc's grim expression showed that he shared the same worry.

But fate decided to smile on them. As the road climbed, the land opened before them into a valley. Narrow at first, it increasingly widened into an old-growth forest covering a rolling terrain. Mountains walled the valley at too great a distance to shade the road. Though the air remained chill, the sun shone from an intensely blue sky. It's rays melted the snow on every surface they touched. In places, the trees fell back, allowing them to pass over long stretches of unshaded roadway. Larger pines, lodgepole and ponderosa, and spruce and fir trees replaced the pinyon pines and junipers of the lower elevations. Copses of white, bare-armed aspens invaded the dark conifers here and there. The sun cheered them, even Lois who had not felt well earlier in the morning.

"Just twenty years ago," said Doc, "you couldn't've driven this road in winter for the snow, it was so much colder then. After a few more years of this warming climate, it'll be the potholes." The deteriorating road forced him to drive slowly.

Late in the morning, Doc let Con drive. Con stretched and walked a little before taking the wheel. The back seat cramped his five-foot-eleven frame. It better accommodated Doc's smaller body. Con drove with Lois at his side.

After he had driven for a short time, the coniferous trees abruptly give way to a sea of white: aspen trunks, bare for the winter, rising from snow-covered earth. Only black scars where deer had eaten the trees' bark after the snow hid the grass relieved the monochrome background.

"Look at that," he said. "It's like the aspens are taking over the world." Then, "Oh, oh. We're not alone." He pointed to something far down the road.

They all strained to see.

"Looks like a wagon," said Doc, "with riders on each side of it."

As they drew closer, they saw a man holding a rifle sitting in the back of the wagon watching them. The riders turned to look at them. The wagon pulled far enough off the road to give them space to pass and stopped. Con slowed the buggy, and Doc checked the Kreutzer without letting the man in the wagon or the horsemen see him. The shell from their near-confrontation with the Bennets remained in the chamber. Outriders, some of them women, rode ahead of the wagon and moved through the aspens, all armed, rugged-looking people. Most wore Western style clothing and hats. Only when Con passed the wagon could he appreciate its huge size. Its sides rose above the buggy's top. Rawhide laces tied through grommets on the tough-looking canvas covering its top to rings on the wagon's sides held it in place. Three teams of horses pulled it.

When they pulled abreast of the driver's seat, Doc said suddenly, "Stop here, Con."

So Con, thinking, What in the world? stopped the Feast wagon.

Doc clambered out of the back seat. He said to the two men on the front seat, "Are one of you Mr. Clive McCollough by any chance?"

The driver, bearded like the rest of the men, jumped down. "Guilty as charged. How did you –?" He grinned. "Oh, yeah. I'll bet you stopped by New Hope and old Ephraim told you about us." He held out a hand.

Doc shook it. "Doc Drennan. Ephraim told us you were a merchant that got around quite a bit."

"Yeah, we decided to try this after the epidemic. My brother and his wife didn't survive it. He had a horse ranch here in Utah, so we had to figure out what to do with all these horses. We started at a salt flat west of here. We'll go through Utah and almost halfway through Colorado. Trade mostly in salt, a valuable commodity to cure meat since there's no refrigeration."

"I don't suppose you know where Tin Cup in Colorado is."

"I sure do. We'll end up there in the spring and then start back along the same road."

"Well, sir, you can help us out. That's where we're headed. But we don't know how to get there."

McCullough grinned. "What's the odds of that? Most people never heard of it."

"So we're finding out."

"We're about to take a lunch break. Why don't you join us, and I'll show you how to get there. Stop up ahead at what used to be a forest rangers' station and go into the visitors' center. You'll get there faster than us, but we'll be along directly."

"See you there." Doc got in the buggy.

Con said, "Good thinking, Doc. But I guess there wouldn't be many other traders along this road."

They came to the rangers' station a short distance ahead and went into what had been a visitors' center, furnished with a fireplace, a counter with racks long bare of brochures, chairs and tables that had once held exhibits. Not as dusty as they had expected, which meant that someone maintained it. The enclosed space felt colder than the outdoors.

"They's wood right by the fireplace," said Beulah, hugging herself against the cold, "but I spose we oughta leave that for them who fetched it and get our own."

"Tell you what," said Doc. "Why don't you ladies start a fire while Con and I gather some wood to replace it."

"There's horses coming up outside," said Lois.

Looking out a window, "Doc said, "Some of McCollough's guys. With axes. Looks like they intend to cut some wood too. C'mon, Con. We got hatchets someplace in the cart."

By the time the men reached the station Doc and Con had their hatchets in hand. The horsemen dismounted and tied their horses' reins to the porch railing. The foremost of them was a big man with white teeth grinning through a black beard. He wore a cap made of some kind of animal fur.

"Hey, fellers," he said, "looks like we got some help cutting wood." And to Con and Doc, "I'm Jock."

"Jock the Rock," laughed one of his fellows. They made introductions all around, though Con immediately forgot most of the names.

As Jock led them around the station and back into the white forest, Con looked curiously at the haystack beside the building.

Jock said, "While the phones were still working Clive called some hunters he knew up in the mountains, asked them to leave us hay for the horses and we'd leave salt for them to cure their meat."

"Hunters living in a national forest?" said Doc.

Jock showed his white teeth in a grin. "Folks that got tired of living on the dole. And there wasn't many forest rangers around to hide from any more after the sickness."

They saw the huge wagon and its teams outside when they returned to the visitors' center, and inside, a welcome fire had blunted the worst of its chill. McCullough and the rest of his band had crowded into the room. Con counted fifteen men and women ranging in age from teenagers to middle age.

McCullough motioned Doc and his group to a table. He tore a piece of paper from a tablet and placed it on the table. "I'll pencil in the route. It won't be to scale but I'll label the road numbers. Stay away from the interstate and main highways. Decent people probably run some of the towns, but cutthroats hang out in the others. You won't know which is which. This route will keep you away from all of them and take you right to Tin Cup." While he talked he drew a crude map, commenting about the routes as he sketched.

"How long will it take us to get there?" asked Con.

McCullough scratched his cinnamon-colored beard thoughtfully. "If you had a car, I'd say less than a day. With your contraption, pulling that cart, a good two days. We'll be a lot slower than you. Not just because of the wagon. We plan to stop and trade along the way."

Con asked, "Is there a nurse there named Chloë?" He realized he had never known her last name.

"There's doctor by that name. Chloë Hempstead."

So Chloë had given herself a promotion, thought Con. Of course, she probably fit that position better than anyone else in Tin Cup.

Lois and Beulah laid out a cold lunch. Clive and a woman he introduced as Josie brought their lunches over to join them.

Beulah asked Clive, "What's this Tin Cup like?"

"Nice little town. Only a couple dozen people live there. Pleasant folks but pretty libertarian. They get together to party or for projects that need a bunch of people but otherwise leave each other alone. Its elevation is around 12,000 feet so it's cold in the winter but not as bad as it used to be. Was a ghost town in the winter then. Now people live there all year round."

"Sounds like my kinda folks," said Beulah.

Con thought so too.

"What do you know about this huge aspen grove?" asked Lois. "How big is it?"

"That's Josie's bailiwick," said McCullough. "She's the forester."

Josie said, "Yes, I was in charge of conservation and resource management here in Fishlake National Forest. This 'grove' covers over 106 acres. It's a single organism, the biggest, densest living thing in the world. It's estimated to weigh almost thirteen million pounds."

"Whoa," said Beulah. "You're losing me."

Her explanation had the tone of a lecture she had given many times.

Josie grinned. "An aspen grows from a single seed and sends out roots. Clones of itself grow up from the roots. There are over 40,000 individual trees in the Pando, all part of one living thing."

"Pando?" said Con.

"Latin for 'I spread.' The scientists that discovered it gave it that name."

They ate in silence for a while.

Then Doc asked, "Isn't this a pretty harsh life? It's a dangerous world nowadays."

Clive said, "Back in the day, I made my living bartering. In the underground bartering markets. There had always been such things as flea markets and garage sales where people bought and sold personal goods. Companies and small peddlers like me used the modern bartering markets to trade manufactured products. They got to be so widespread the government declared them illegal 'cause they couldn't find a way to tax em. It's easier now. In those days, I had to watch out for thieves, cops and tax collectors. Now there ain't none of the last two kinds of thugs. A few months ago, I gathered up these roughnecks and somehow attracted this wonderful woman." He enclosed Josie's hand, which lay on the table, in his. "We like trading and living off the land. And we're tough enough that others let us be.

"My granddad lived to be a hundred and twelve, which wasn't so unusual before the Disease. He told me I wouldn't have a job when I grew up unless I had a college education. My folks couldn't afford to send me to college, and I didn't care to go anyhow. They died in an auto accident when I was eighteen anyway. My granddad figured that out as a kid in the nineteen-eighties. That's when machines called automatic teller machines, known as ATMs, became popular. People still used paper money then. They could get cash and do all their banking through these machines. He said a few months after they got popular, he'd walk into a bank and see all the teller's windows except one or two closed up. Each closed one meant a lost job. He remembered reading about all the jobs lost to mass production during the Industrial Revolution two hundred years before. He knew technology would take a lot more away then. Maybe he was one of the first to recognize it. And that his days as an over-the-road trucker were numbered. Sure enough, smart machines took over task after task. In a few decades, self-driving trucks took his job, though he was ready to retire anyhow."

He finished the last of his sandwich and stood up. His people had also begun to rise. He turned to Jock who, along with some others, had been listening to their conversation and said, "We don't let nobody push us around no more, huh Jock?"

The big man grinned. "No, sir." Then he placed a hand over his chest, looked upward with a most reverential expression and said, "Yea, though I walk through the valley of the shadow of death, I will fear no evil…"

The rest of the gang loudly quoted, "For I am the biggest son-of-a-bitch in the valley!"

The whole group roared in laughter at what must have been a well-worn performance. Several of the men beat each other and Jock on the back.

Clive told Con and the others, "I need to get my gang back on the road. Maybe we'll see you in Tin Cup next spring." He shooed his people out the door and followed them with Con's group. While some of his men pitched the hay the horses hadn't eaten onto the back of the wagon he told Doc, "It'll take you a while to get through the Pando but about a mile beyond it you'll come to my favorite part of the park, the lake the park's named after."

"That'd be Fishlake," said Doc. "I look forward to seeing it."

They got in the buggy, followed by goodbyes and good lucks from McCullough's people and started off, Con again driving.

As McCullough had warned, it took almost an hour to pass through the aspen clone.

Lois said, "I've only seen pictures of aspens, but I bet this would look beautiful in the spring or fall."

"I have seen em," said Doc, "and pictures don't give them justice. Some call them quaking aspens. The leaves are a bright, glossy green on top and dull green beneath. The lightest breeze makes the leaves flutter, bright to dull, dull to bright, so fast the whole tree looks like it's shaking. In the fall the leaves turn shades from yellow to golden. They accent the hillsides where they grow among dark coniferous trees. Seeing these thousands of aspens quaking together certainly looks stunning."

The road took them northeasterly. The sunlight persisted, the snow retreated except where it stubbornly lurked in the shadows. They soon came to McCullough's favorite long, beautiful lake, bookended by mountain ranges on both sides. At about the halfway point they passed a large building with a sign over the entrance stating, "FISHLAKE LODGE AND MARINA." They passed other lodges and resorts and a deserted RV park. None seemed in a bad state of repair. Con could imagine them opening for business in the spring.

They pressed on. As the sun slid over the western mountains, Doc said they should stop and make camp.

"We can use the headlights," said Con, still driving, wanting to get to Tin Cup as soon as possible for Lois' sake.

"We've been lucky so far," said Doc. "We haven't even damaged a wheel, but I don't want to press our luck. Driving in the dark is too big a risk on this crappy road."

Lois agreed with Doc. "If Mr. McCullough's right we're only a day and a half away from Tin Cup."

And so did Beulah. "We don't want to walk the last day to get there."

Con relaxed. They were right.

They found a clearing some distance off the road. Since it grew dark early at that time of year and the nights were cold, they took time to pitch their tent, build a fire and have a hot dinner. They considered the risk of attack low but kept their firearms near and took turns standing guard.

* * *

The next day resembled the previous one: uncomfortably cold in the early morning when they struck camp and started out, sunny later and pleasantly cool as long as they wore their coats. They soon exited the national park and took a county road east. Then, following McCullough's map, they took a more or less easterly state route that took them down out of the mountains. About noon the highway became a Colorado State highway.

Later that afternoon, they came to a junction with US Highway 50. Clive had said, and Doc agreed, that the most dangerous part of their trip could lay ahead. They would find more more large towns along Highway 50. Higher populations potentially meant more desperate people. McCullough's group looked so tough and well-armed they wouldn't have as much trouble as four people in a dune buggy. And the bulging cart would look like a tempting prize.

They encountered no one on the highway to the southeast nor the detour around a large town named Montrose. They camped for the night on the other side of Montrose.

Tomorrow, they would reach Tin Cup.

* * *

The next morning, they took US Highway 50 easterly to the college town of Gunnison, Doc driving, Con beside him. The sign directing them to Tin Cup led them through Gunnison. They found signs of looting and burnt buildings but no inhabitants. Beyond the town, the road soon began to rise. It remained in good repair until they reached an abandoned resort. There, they changed to a road that hadn't been maintained recently. As the road continued to rise it grew colder under an overcast sky. More snow covered the road; no one had driven it since the last snowfall. Noon came and went but no one suggested stopping for lunch.

Doc slowed when they saw the sign so they could read it: "WELCOME TO HISTORIC TIN CUP – TWO MILES AHEAD." Under that, they read the crudely lettered: "STOP AT THE KIOSK."

"Well," Con said. "Looks like they're careful about who gets in."

"That could be a good thing," said Lois.

"Or an unfriendly thing," said Beulah.

"I vote for Beulah's interpretation," said Doc. "Because of the lettering."

The snowy and rougher road slowed them, so the last two miles took an excruciatingly long time. At last, they saw a crudely built structure set among fir trees ahead of them on the left side of the road. Doc drove to within twenty yards of the leaning "kiosk" and stopped. To their left, a meadow sloped down to the forest and a boulder field rose on their right. He said, "Their so-called kiosk could only hold a couple of people."

"Three if they're real good friends," said Beulah.

Nothing happened for a moment. Then, they saw a golf cart speed away from the back of the kiosk and up the road toward a collection of old, weathered houses in the distance. Tin Cup. A man wearing a parka and a pistol belt around his waist came from behind the kiosk, holding his revolver down at his side. He walked down the edge of the road and stopped beside a tree across from the buggy at the edge of the meadow, regarding them coolly but saying nothing.

Doc rolled down the window and said to the man, "I take it that that's Tin Cup ahead of us. We're here to see a friend. Is it okay to go on?"

"Not till the boss lady takes a look at you." He gestured toward the receding golf cart with his chin. "Hammy went to fetch her."

They watched "Hammy" stop before one of the distant houses and enter it.

"I ain't likin this," said Beulah.

Neither did Con, especially the way the man looked at their loaded cart.

Doc rubbed the Kreutzer. Con loosened his target pistol in its holster.

Hammy and someone else came out of the house and got in the golf cart. They started back toward the kiosk.

"We'll soon know," said Doc.

They waited.

The golf cart stopped behind the kiosk. They hadn't been able to see who rode in it. When the two riders appeared from behind the kiosk, One was a woman. She wore a strangely familiar hooded fur parka. A scarf covered her lower face.

But Con knew Stella's voice the moment she spoke.

She said, "It's about time you got here."

"Bennet's woman!' said Doc. He grabbed the Kreutzer and pushed the door open…just as Stella said, "Kill them."

The man at the side of the road raised his revolver and shot Doc in the chest.

Twenty – "We'll see if Spero's little sorcerer root really works."

Con started to reach for him where he had fallen outside the open buggy door. No, it couldn't happen to Doc. He couldn't be out there.

He shook himself and sat back. The guy who had shot him was still there. He didn't remember drawing his pistol but found it in his hand. But when looked for the killer, he saw only his revolver and a little of his hand and face extending from behind a tree in its shadow. The face moved out a ways and the revolver pointed directly at him. In panic, Con tried to aim.

He jumped at the sound of a shot from the back seat. The man fell from behind the tree onto his side in the snow and didn't move. Looking at the back seat, he saw Lois withdrawing her pistol from the window, which she had rolled down just far enough to extend her pistol. Sure. She was a crack shot.

He flinched again at the sound of bullets striking the windows on the buggy's other side, fired from the boulder field. Automatic gunfire from the kiosk sprayed the windshield.

"Close that door!" Lois shouted at him, peremptorily but in terror.

He slammed the driver's door shut, leaving Doc bleeding on the ground outside.

Pistol fire answered the boulder field from the back seat, three shots. Lois again. No return fire came from the boulders.

Con couldn't get out to succor Doc or retrieve the Kreutzer where he had dropped it. Stella stood partially behind the kiosk. Only one arm, enough of her face to see the buggy and a tuft of white spiked hair showed. The golf cart driver lay prone beside her, aiming the automatic pistol at the windshield. He, not Stella, had fired at it. Neither they nor the firers from the boulders had known the dune buggy's windows were bulletproof. They did now. Its windows were so pitted from gunfire that some were difficult to see through.

Hearing Lois' breath catch, he said, "Are you all right?"

In a small voice, she answered, "Yes."

He reached back and took her hand. "You don't sound like it, sweetheart."

"I – I never killed anybody before, Con." She had been crying.

"But you saved my life."

"And I'd do it again." She sounded tearfully resolute.

He squeezed her hand. Then he realized only Lois was in the backseat. "Where's Beulah?"

"She slipped out the back when those guys shot at us from the boulders. I thought she was scared and maybe we should all run, but I think she had something to do with ridding the boulders of the gunmen. I don't know how many there were, but I hit two of them. I don't know how badly they're hurt but they haven't made a sound."

"Yeah, she said she was good with a knife."

He squeezed her hand again, turned and opened the passenger's side door.

"What're you doing?" she said in panic.

"They can't see me so well from the kiosk at this angle. I need to get rid of the guy with that automatic pistol first." Then Spikey Hair, he thought. They didn't hear the door open from the kiosk. He crawled under the buggy and aimed the pistol oh-so-carefully, holding it with both hands like Doc had shown him. He fired. The gunman jerked and the pistol fell from his hand. Con had no doubt he was dead. Stella appeared and grabbed his automatic. He fired instinctively. She screamed and fell behind the kiosk. Unbelievably, he had hit her without even aiming.

He got back in the buggy. "I gotta get Doc, Lois. Cover me, okay? Stella's behind the kiosk, maybe only wounded."

"Okay," she said. "We can get Doc into the back seat."

Con slipped out of the buggy, keeping an eye on the kiosk.

Doc sprawled on his back. Con gently picked him up by the shoulders while Lois stood over them, pistol trained on the kiosk. Blood stained Doc's shirt on one side of his chest. Con felt for and found a pulse, a very faint one. Doc breathed with difficulty. Con tried to ignore the horrible sucking sound from Doc's chest every time he breathed.

Lois asked, "Is he…?"

"He's alive," said Con.

She took him by his ankles, and they laid him in the back seat. His eyes briefly flickered open, while he strained to breathe. Con and Lois got in the front, Con behind the wheel with the Kreutzer at his side. He started the motor and –

Stella stumbled out from behind the kiosk. One hand held a blood-soaked scarf, the one she had worn about her face, over her left ear. The other held the golf cart driver's automatic pistol. She aimed it at them, though by now she must have known their vehicle's windows were bulletproof.

"Don't think you're going anywhere!" she shouted.

His shot had only hit her ear. Because of her, Doc lay dying. He would run her and the flimsy kiosk down with the buggy. But first, he had to know. He rolled the window down an inch so he could hear her.

"Before I kill you," he called to her, "tell me how you knew we'd be here."

She laughed. "That was easy. Lots of people in Dante's Market knew you were coming here. Skinner found out and told us. We came not only to kill you for revenge, but because this'd make a good hideout while we got reorganized. I was so mad I wanted to capture and torture you. But I'm tired of fucking with you. Now I just want you dead."

"I guess you've forgotten that it was Dante who actually shot 'your Herschel.'"

"But your bunch warned Dante's people about our raid. If not for you, everything would've gone the way we planned and we'd be running Las Vegas now."

Con started the motor. He had to get Doc to Chloë.

She shouted, "It's too late for you to run away. I told reinforcements to come if we looked like we needed them."

The sound of a diesel engine starting attracted their attention. The armored, spike-nosed truck appeared from behind one of Tin Cup's buildings and roared toward them.

"You can't outrun it or fight it," Stella called. "I'll be rid of you in five minutes."

Con shut off the engine and took up the Kreutzer. "Let's get out your side," he said to Lois. "I'll fire on that monster from behind the buggy."

"But that thing'll crush it like an eggshell." But she got out.

"It won't get anywhere near the buggy. Remember what the Kreutzer did to their van?" He got out and followed her. "And I don't have to be a good shot to hit that big thing." He patted the Kreuzer and looked the high-powered weapon over. Its knobs and dials made it look more complicated than any gun he had ever seen. But he remembered that the shell Doc had chambered was already in place. Then, along with Lois, he watched the truck's approach.

When it had almost reached the kiosk, coming fast, he saw that Bennet's toughs filled its open bed. Many stood, glaring eagerly at their prey. Remembering how the Kreutzer's kick had knocked Doc down, he braced himself, rested his elbows on the buggy's roof, planted the butt of the Kreutzer's stock in his shoulder and set his feet solidly apart on the buggy's rear bumper.

As the truck cab drew near the kiosk, the driver noticed Con pointing the Kreutzer at him. His eyes and mouth opened wide. Perhaps he remembered the Kreutzer from Dante's garage. He frantically whipped the steering wheel to the right just as Con fired. And the Kreutzer pitched Con backward into the snowy ditch.

Unable to see what happened, Con nevertheless heard a loud cacophony of sounds, mainly crashes and screams. A tremendous explosion shook the dune buggy. Objects struck it and flew over his head.

"Are you okay?" he asked in a shaken voice.

"Yes. I jumped in the ditch."

"What the hell happened? Did the shot hit the gas tank?"

"I didn't see," she said. "I was down here beside you. But bullets don't really blow up fuel tanks. That's just in movies."

"I saw what blew them suckers up from up in the rocks," said Beulah.

They whipped around. She was calmly wiping her knife blade with a bandanna.

"Beulah!" They said in unison and Lois demanded, "Where have you been?"

"Making sure that wounded asshole you shot won't never sneak up on nobody again. And a third one you might not've known about won't neither. He was aiming at the Feast-wagon when I slipped up on him."

Con and Lois scrambled to their feet. The truck lay on its side at the edge of the meadow, warped from the explosion, its underside toward them, a wheel spinning. Twisted and burned bodies lay around it. Acrid-smelling smoke rose from it. Its bed had bashed the kiosk into kindling.

"Good work, Beulah," said Con. "But c'mon. We gotta get Doc up to Tin Cup and look for Chloë."

They got in the buggy and Con started it. He barely got it between the boulders on the right side of the road and the wreckage of the truck and kiosk on the left. They saw a farm truck racing through Tin Cup in the opposite direction.

"That's the rest of the Bennet gang," said Lois. "The commotion scared them off."

They saw a score or more of Tin Cup's residents running toward them. One man carried a rifle and another a shotgun. Con pulled to a halt as they met. Spotting a big, attractive black woman in the crowd, he leaped out of the buggy and hollered, "Chloé! Over here. We've got somebody who's hurt bad."

Chloé looked at him in surprise but came over to him. She said, "Young man, do I know you?" but went to the back door of the buggy as Con opened it.

He looked down at himself. Thinner than when she knew him, more muscular, bearded and filthy, wearing dirty, ragged clothes.

"I'm Con Colby. From the warehouse clinic in Tres Robles. You saved my life."

She frowned at him, but after a moment, she smiled and said, "Yes, I remember you." She glanced at him with a look that said, What the hell are you doing here? as she reached into the back seat and gently opened the front of Doc's shirt. She grew serious. Without turning, she said, "Clarence, quick. Give me the baggy you keep your pot in."

A big black guy near her said, "Sure, but what –?" as he pulled a plastic bag out of a rear pocket.

"Hurry, before his lung collapses. He's got a sucking chest wound." He handed the plastic bag to her. She continued giving orders. "Cheryl, get to the community house kitchen and start boiling water. Sissy, get the operating table ready. Roger, get my sterile surgical equipment out and bring the stretcher." As she talked, she started to dump the marijuana out of the plastic bag onto the ground.

"Wait!" said Clarence, holding his hands together, palms up, under the bag.

Chloë frowned impatiently but shook the bag's contents into his hands. Then he ran toward the community building. She placed the empty bag over the wound. She told Lois, "Sweetheart, sit beside him and hold the bag like this, with three sides tight enough to keep outside air from entering the chest. Leave one side open to let any intrapleural air escape when he breathes out." And to Con, "Drive this contraption up to the community house. That's it over there. I'll ride along with you. Then Clarence and Roger will carry your friend in. I'll have to start a thoracostomy immediately. That'll drain the air from the pleural cavity and allow the lung to inflate. Then look for the bullet that made the hole. Unfortunately, I don't have any anesthesia."

"I do," said Con. And silently to Doc as he started driving toward the house, Now we'll see if Spero's little sorcerer root really works, Doc. Sorry it has to be tested on you, buddy.

Chloë said, "What do you mean? You do what?"

"Have an anesthetic. A pharmacologist gave it to us. It's in the cart." He didn't tell her the pharmacologist was crazy.

"What kind is it?"

Con hesitated.

"I won't use it unless I know what it is."

"It's powder made from mandrake root." And quickly, when he saw her shake her head, he explained what Spero Peace had told him about it. "Please give it a chance, Chloë. Without it, even the pain of the surgery can kill him."

"Have you seen it used before?"

"Yes, this guy that's been shot and our friend Lois used it before for minor injuries."

She thought it over. She shook her head and said, almost to herself, "Mandrake root's some dangerous shit."

"He'd want you to use it. Lois will measure the dosage for you and explain how to prepare it."

She hesitated, then sighed resignedly. "You tell me the dosage and how to make the preparation. I don't want any more people in there than necessary. You three can wait out here during the procedure."

"Okay." He stopped before the community building, ran to the cart to find the vial of powder and Lois' spoon and returned to give it to Chloë. After he explained how to prepare it and gave her the measuring spoon, she went inside. Clarence and Roger emerged with a stretcher, placed Doc on it and carried him into the building. Con sat on the edge of the porch with Lois and Beulah. They watched people go down toward the truck's wreckage.

"Now, Beulah," said Con. "Tell us what blew the truck up."

"Okay. After I killed the motherfuckers, I came down through the boulders to the buggy. You two was hunkered down behind it so you couldn't see the truck, but I did. This dude stood up in the bed. He held something with his arm reared back like he was gonna throw it. Had to've been an explosive of some kind. Then the truck turned to the right real quick. The front wheel hit the ditch and the truck started to keel over into the meadow. The dumb bastard lost his balance and dropped what he was gonna throw. They musta had a stash of that explosive in the truck. Kablooie!"

"Good for him," Con said softly.

Clarence and Roger came out of the house and started down toward the wrecked truck. All the townspeople who had gone down there earlier, except for the two women assisting Chloë, had remained. Some of them had looked at Con suspiciously earlier as if he and his companions had had something to do with the Bennets' arrival. Which, of course, they had.

Con stood up. "I've got to go down there. Help with the clean-up." He nodded toward the smoking, demolished truck.

"I'm sorry, love, but I can't," said Lois. "I've seen too much killing."

"Me too," said Beulah, putting her arm around Lois. "We've had enough."

"That's fine. Holler at me when the surgery is over."

As Con neared the site, the stench grew worse, a complex smell, putrid like cooking spoiled meat. When he reached the first of the corpses, it became so intense and rich that it almost resembled a taste. The smoke arising from the truck produced an acrid, burnt smell like motor oil spilled on a hot exhaust manifold. The explosion had tossed the corpses at various distances from the truck bed, except for the two in the truck's cab. Many of them had been eviscerated or blown apart. Body parts lay about. A reddish-black stain discolored the snow. From blood, he wondered?

He saw Stella's remains tangled in the wreckage of the kiosk. The truck had mashed her into its structure before it blew up.

Clarence stood among a dozen or so men deep in conversation, most of whom held handkerchiefs over their noses and mouths. Some looked at Con rather coldly, as if they blamed him for the Bennets' arrival.

One of the men told Clarence, "We decided to pile this human trash at the bottom of the meadow and burn it."

Clarence nodded. "Sounds good to me. Let's get started."

Con said, "I'm here to help."

"Come on then," said Clarence.

Like most of the others, Con tied his handkerchief around the lower part of his face, though it did little good. He doubted if he would ever completely get the smell of burnt flesh out of his nose. He helped with the gruesome job for a little over an hour. At last, Chloé appeared on the porch. Lois and Beulah stood to talk to her.

Con told Clarence, "I have to go see how the surgery came out on my friend."

"I'll go with you," said Clarence. On the way, he said, "I see you and Chloé know each other, so I guess you know she came here to find her boyfriend, Carl."

"Yes."

"Well, Chou's Disease got Carl. No surprise there, of course, And just so you know, I'm trying to take his place."

"Good luck there. I think she's a great gal."

"Me too."

At the community house, Chloé's frown worried Con. When he reached the porch though, she gave him a small smile.

"Everything's fine, Con. The anesthetic worked perfectly. He's breathing normally, his heartbeat's steady."

"But you still look worried."

"I've never done anything like this. Inserting the chest drain for the pneumothorax was simple enough, but I'm not qualified for more complex surgery and we didn't work in the most antiseptic of conditions. The surgery took longer than I liked but I had to find the bullet."

"Even though you ain't qualified," asked Beulah, "You did find the bullet, huh?"

"And did you get it out?" asked Con.

"Yes, to Beulah, no to Con."

Before the three could assail her with questions she held both hands up and swept them with a stern look.

"Fortunately, we found a former doctor's books, the paper kind, and I study them when I have the time. From them, I knew I didn't have to remove the bullet if I found it some place where it wouldn't cause any more trouble. I found it firmly stuck in a bone, far enough away from flesh or nerves that it won't do any harm. Trying to remove it would mean enlarging the wound and leaving it open longer. That would increase the risk of infection."

"But you still look worried," insisted Con.

"Any opening in the body can allow the admittance of sepsis, especially since we live in a world without antibiotics. But he's stable now. You can go see him any time you like."

Beulah said, "Doc's too tough to give in to infection."

"He sure is," said Lois.

Con thought of Doc thwarting the bikers, blasting the Bennets' van in Dante's garage with the Kreutzer and driving the dune buggy on a snow-covered four-wheel-drive mountain road for the first time in his life. Always with a puckish sense of humor.

He said, "Yeah, he'll make it."

✳ ✳ ✳

The community house had facilities for travelers that the three badly needed. They took breaks from watching over Doc to bathe, Con to shave and Lois and Beulah to prepare a properly cooked meal.

Chlo⊠ or her assistant Cheryl came to check Doc frequently. When Con went to see Doc after dinner, he found Chlo⊠ and Clarence sitting in the meeting hall outside his room. She told him Doc was sleeping and he could join them until he awakened if he liked.

Con took a chair.

Chlo⊠ said, "Without the beard, you look more like my young helper in the warehouse. But leaner, more muscled and certainly more traveled."

"But no wiser," he said.

"I told Clarence about you stumbling into the warehouse clinic, sick with your second onset of Chou's. And how you recovered and helped me feed the patients and clean bedpans."

"But," said Clarence, "she told me she didn't know how you came to show up in this little town that nobody outside of Colorado even knows it exists."

"Well, it happened like this," said Con. "They moved the few patients in the warehouse to a hospital so Chlo⊠ had nothing to do. She had told us she was going to this little town nobody ever heard of to look for her boyfriend. She left early one morning while I was asleep. I had wanted to wish her goodbye, but one of the guys who brought us food and did other stuff there, Tony, said she didn't like goodbyes.

"Then this Chou's Disease came along. I lost everyone I knew and loved. I couldn't stay in that neighborhood, or even the town, anymore. Too many ghosts. When I told Tony that, he said, 'Where you gonna go?' The only person I knew and respected was you, Chlo⊠, how you had cared for all those sick and dying people and cheered them up and fed them and cleaned their asses when you were dead tired. So, I told him I thought I'd head for Tin Cup. I was determined. And it still surprises me that I made it. Another thing I was afraid of was that you'd get here and find everybody dead."

Clarence said, "Fewer people got the Disease here than other places. Thirty-six out of a hundred and ten lived. Only to come near getting wiped out by a bunch of thugs."

"They had us outnumbered and outgunned," said Chloë. "Some of the old ones here have trouble getting around. And there's only four firearms in the whole town. We think those crooks planned to kick us out or kill us and take over the town."

Con looked away, feeling guilty for inadvertently leading Bennet's people there. "I suppose we were partially responsible," said Con. He told them how it had happened.

"No one can blame you for that," said Clarence, "after we explain the full story."

Con said, "We can provide a few more guns. While Doc scrounged for goods after the pandemic, he collected guns and ammunition whenever he found any. I'm sure he wouldn't mind distributing them among your folks. By the way, I saw the last of Bennet's people head out of town in a truck."

"Yeah," said Clarence. "They lit out toward Tin Cup Pass. They'll have trouble getting over it this time of year."

"I've been determined to come to Tin Cup ever since I left Tres Robles," said Con. "But even if I had changed my mind, something later happened that drove Lois and me to come."

"And that was…?" said Chloë.

"Lois got pregnant. There's so few babies being born and mothers dying in childbirth. You're the only person I knew that could give Lois and our baby a chance."

Chloë said, "I don't know what to attribute the low birthrate to. Usually during times of disaster, it increases. Maybe we'll see a crop of new births during this new year." Then she smiled. "One thing I do know is that little Maxwell Garrett was born to Lisa Garrett two months ago. And mother and baby are healthy and doing fine."

That buoyed Con's spirits.

Chloë said, "I know Lois is tired tonight, but would you tell her I'd like to have a little chat with her tomorrow? None of you need to stay up with Doc tonight. Cheryl's my nursing aid-in-training. She'll keep tabs on him."

"Thanks a lot," said Con. "But I think I'll take one last peek in his room."

He did and saw that Doc was still sleeping. Though exhausted, he hoped Doc would wake up long enough to tell Con how he felt. He wanted to hear it in his own words. In the meantime, he couldn't help but doze a little....

He started awake about midnight. Doc lay in the same position, still unconscious.

Twenty-One – "So here we are at journey's end…."

Con drank his morning tea sitting on the bench behind his house overlooking the southern slope, his favorite spot in Tin Cup. Below him spread a broad meadow bedecked with high-altitude flowers. The rising sun enhanced the explosion of their colors: white, yellow, orange, blue and purple, while the town still lay asleep in the mountain's shadow. Thanks to the locals, he now knew the names of most of the flowers: heart-leaf, Indian paintbrush, Caltha, arrowleaf balsamroot, harebell and his favorite, the Colorado blue columbine. No wonder Colorado adopted it as its state flower.

He saw Chloë coming down the path from the east. An early riser like him, she often stopped by to see him on her morning walk around the town. She stopped and wished him a good morning.

"Same to yo. Will you sit for a while?"

"For just a bit." She sat down beside him. "I've got a patient to see as soon as I finish my walk. The Franklins' six-year-old has the croup. But I had to stop by to admire your little man-plants." She leaned over to look at the four mandrake plants spreading their wrinkled leaves over the ground across the path from them. "I see the blossoms have opened, right in the middle of the plant, beautiful blue and white flowers."

He asked, "How are your own plants doing?" He had given her offsets from his mandrakes.

She frowned and shook her head. "I planted them in pots like you said but they're growing so slowly."

"Same with those I planted. That's probably natural. The guy I got the plants from said to keep the offsets in the containers for two years and then transplant them outside in a sunny spot. He was right about the plants blossoming in the spring. Here it is the middle of May. He also said the berries come out in late summer but wait till they're overripe in the fall to get the seeds to plant. I'll give you some then. They survive the cold pretty well. They made it through our hellacious drive up here in January."

"Of course, we had a mild winter this year."

"Seemed plenty cold and slippery to me."

"That's because you came from a land with no winter. If you stay, you'll get used to it after a year or two. This is the second wonderful thing you've done for us, Con, bringing this source of anesthetic to us."

"And the first was…?"

"Saving us from those Bennet gangsters. At first some blamed you for their coming. But they finally realized you couldn't have known about it. And you whipped them by yourself. I didn't think that the Con I knew in Tres Robles could have done that."

"You're right. He couldn't have. From last August in Tres Robles to January, I changed a lot." Con shook his head in wonder at his transformation. "I was fortunate to have traveled with Doc."

"I hear you'll be gone most of the day. Clarence tells me you and him and several others are going out to select trees for logs for your real house."

"Yes. I told them we could leave right after Clive does. I want to say good-by to his people."

She laughed. "Well, as much as they drank last night it'll be a while before they're up." She waved a hand at the little house behind him. "Sorry you got stuck in this little shack for so long, Con. It's the only vacant house we had."

"After our camp sites along the road, this was a mansion. And its fireplace kept those two rooms toasty warm."

"Good." She stood up. "Well, I'm off to the Franklins now. Good luck finding the trees."

"Tell Mark and Harriett hi, and little Willy he'll be well soon. And I'm not leaving the trees to luck. I'm letting Roger pick them out. He used to be a rough-in carpenter and he'll supervise the house's construction."

"Good move. He built a couple of the log cabins you see here."

After Chloë left he noticed that the sun had peered far enough over the mountain to light the roofs on the far side of town. The community building, which set next to Con's house still lay in the mountain's shadow. He saw its back door open, and Clive McCullough step out, carrying his own cup of tea. He waved. Con returned it and scooted over to give Clive a place to sit.

"Morning," said Clive when he sat beside Con. "This sure is good tea. I started drinking herbal teas after we couldn't get coffee anymore, but this beats them by far."

"That's because it's real tea. A lady named Crystal Moon Darlington loved Taiwan High Mountain Oolong Tea so much that after she moved up here thirty-some years ago she ordered some seeds and planted them in a field behind her house. She has expanded it over the years, so we now have all we want."

Clive said, "She has an interesting name."

"Her parents gave her her first name. They were what people used to call free thinkers. She married a Darlington."

"I see. So, Tin Cup's a kind of commune like New Hope, huh? I've been here a few times over the years but never could tell."

Con finished his tea. "Not at all. We're very libertarian. If we want some of Crystal's tea, we pay for it with food or candles or labor or whatever. These people value their own space and privacy, but they help each other when needed and work together on joint projects."

"Like they're going to help you build your house."

"Exactly. But hey, what's this 'early leaving' Jock bragged about last night? I don't see any of your people up and around."

Clive chuckled. "Some of the women are up fixing breakfast and a couple of guys are feeding the horses. I knew those young'ns'd drink too heavy to leave early so we packed the wagon yesterday. I'm gonna rouse em when breakfast is ready. Where in the world did you get such good whiskey? The beer was okay too."

"Jesse Ames brews the beer here. He's got another batch lagering in a cave up on the mountain. As to the whiskey, Clarence Hartwell and Roger Young trade with a town called Buena Vista on the other side of Tin Cup Pass. Among other things they have a distillery and a cannabis greenhouse. When Clarence and Roger go a-trading the people here give them things they want to trade at Buena Vista. I went with them on the last trip in April. We talked to them about meeting here this summer for dinner and a trading day so we can get to know each other."

"If you feed them as good as you did us last night, they'll be friends for life. I was surprised you came up with such a good feed. Here it is springtime, and you won't have any fresh vegetables for a while."

Con said, "Beulah knows where greens grow wild, even in the winter, and now that it's May there's more variety. She learned that after she left east LA. And Doc taught us about pinyon nuts. Wild greens and pinyon nuts, with some onions thrown in, made a fine salad. And these folks' root cellars still had potatoes and squash and carrots left. Of course, the potatoes looked pretty ugly before they got peeled and cooked."

"Yeah," said Clive. "By spring potatoes' eyes grow so long they look like aliens' tentacles."

Con said, "We used the last of our salt on the elk that favored us with last night's roast. You got here just in time."

"You got plenty of salt now. And charcoal for your blacksmith."

"Yeah, Clarence Higgins," said Con. "He hasn't been able to do much smithing."

"But we got the best of the deal," said Clive. "Candles, soap, butter, cheese, good heavy rope and twine. And this tea is bound to be a hit every place. Wish we had room to take more of it."

"But remember, Clive, don't tell anyone where you got all this stuff."

Clive shook his head. "Yeah, I promise, though I think you worry too much about bad guys finding out where you live. And I wish you'd let us pay you something for the anesthetic powder. It's a wonderful thing."

Con shrugged. "We don't have much and didn't cost anything. But next year we'll have enough to sell. Then you can trade us something for it and make a profit from it yourself. This little dab we're giving you now might come in handy in one of the hassles you run into. Even if Jock is the biggest son-of-a-bitch in the valley."

Clive laughed. "But for just thirty-six people you do produce quite a variety of goods."

They turned at the squeak of the door opening behind them.

"Thirty-seven," said Lois, standing in the house's back doorway, rocking little Menda Suzanne in her arms.

Clive stood up. "Come on out here and sit down. Young mothers shouldn't have to stand holding their precious little'ns."

"No thanks, Clive. I've got to feed this 'little'un.' I just wanted to say hi and ask when you're pulling out so Menda and I can say a proper goodbye."

"I'm not sure when we're leaving, but you'll hear the wagon, horses and my rowdy guys in plenty of time to come out to see us off."

As they talked, Josie approached them from the community house. When she reached them, she slipped an arm around Clive. He bent to kiss her cheek. Then she greeted Con and Lois and went over to her. "Can I see your little sweetheart?"

Lois pulled back the blanket that partially covered Menda's face. Josie's wistful smile, Con thought, must mean she was thinking of her own little girl. Clive had told him the pandemic claimed her at less than a year old, as well as Josie's husband.

Josie asked, "How old is she now?"

"She'll be a month old in a couple of days."

"May I hold her one last time?" Josie asked. She had played with the baby several times over the last two days.

"Of course." Lois handed Menda Suzanne to Josie.

"Next time you come," Con said to Clive, "try to stay a little longer. We've enjoyed your company, and I can tell your people are still pretty worn out."

Clive said, "Three days were all we could manage this time. We should have been on the road back two weeks ago. We had to sit out two blizzards on the way here. And I told you about the little problem with another gang. But we'll do our damnedest to get here earlier next year and stay longer. We like your little town."

Clive had mentioned the conflict with the other gang but left out the details. Con respected his secrecy. All his people had survived the conflict, but several wore bandages or bruises. Which reminded Con of his hassles on the trip to Orlando's with Doc, and especially the journey to Tin Cup. He looked forward to life in this pleasant little town, despite the cold winters. Though the invasion of the Bennet gang had shown how vulnerable its small population made Tin Cup.

They talked a little longer. Then Josie handed Menda Suzanne back to Lois and said to Clive, "We had breakfast almost ready when I left, dear, and our guys are all awake enough to bitch about their hangovers so we'd best head back."

Lois said, "And we should have our breakfast too, Con." Then to Josie and Clive, "We'll see you off after breakfast."

An hour later Con and Lois heard the grating of wagon wheels on gravel and snorting horses pawing the road in front of the community building. When they went out, they saw activity surrounding the McCollough wagon. The members had opened the rear of the tarp covering it to stash personal belongings that wouldn't fit in their saddlebags. Others harnessed the three teams of draft horses and hitched them to the wagon.

Clive and Josie stood apart from the wagon. Several of the townspeople visited with them, including Chloé, Clarence and Beulah. Con and Lois joined them.

Beulah said to Lois, "I need to borrow your husband for a minute." She took Con's hand and led him out of hearing by the others. She said quietly, "I need to apologize to you, sugar. Last night Lois told me about you two messing around while you was blasted on that mandrake powder."

"Well, yeah, but what are you apologizing for? We didn't even know you then."

"Lois said that was when you made little Menda Suzanne."

"So?"

"So I chewed you both out for being so immature about having the baby. But don't you see? It wasn't your fault. It was the mandrake that done it. You can't be responsible when you're stoned. My first baby boy came to Virgil and me on account a some really fine weed.

"So anyhow, accept my apology."

He grinned. "Consider yourself forgiven."

But when he started to turn away Beulah grabbed his sleeve. "Wait. I ain't through yet."

He looked at her questioningly.

"I know you and Lois and Chloé still got some of that powder. When we all gonna get together and try it out?"

He laughed. "I wondered when you'd think of that. You and Lois and Chloé pick a time and we'll do it."

She winked and raised her fist. He tapped it with his. They rejoined the group around Clive and Josie.

Lois said, "Here comes the mayor."

"Yeah," said Beulah, "with his usual shit-eatin grin."

They all looked up to see Doc approaching. When he reached them, he kissed Beulah's cheek, told her to behave and greeted the others.

"Hey, Con," said Clive with a grin, "You're telling me these folks are libertarians. Yet they elected Doc as mayor. I thought libertarians didn't believe in government."

"Doc's special," said Chloë. "He brought us a wonderful gift, a new kind of battery. We put it in a vacant room in the community building. It stores energy from the solar panels on the roof. After we build Lois and Con's house, we're going to build a special building for it and cover the whole roof with solar panels. It'll give us more energy than we need."

"What kinda battery's that?" asked Josie.

Doc said, "A compressed air energy storage battery. They're not exactly new though. The small ones like this one've been around for decades. I worked on these things for a guy in Las Vegas for a while. While I was at it, I built one to bring along and gave it to these folks. It's enough to power their electric generators with energy left over.",

"That sounds interesting," said Clive. "I don't spose you'd be interested in making these to export."

Doc shook his head. "Not at all. That's too much work and I'm gonna take it easy from now on."

Taking Clive's hand, Josie said, "You're always thinking of sales."

Clive said, "That's how we make our living." And to Doc, "We'll talk about it when we come back next spring. By then you'll be king of this whole mountain, and you can hire people to do the work."

"We probably made a mistake with Doc," said Clarence facetiously. "Politics is full of sneaky guys like him. Now that we elected him Mayor, he's trying to make us more political. Wants to set up a town council. I don't know if we can go that far."

Doc said, "I'll talk you into that eventually, Clarence. See, just like nature abhors a vacuum —"

"…society abhors anarchy," Clarence completed. The rest of the Tin Cuppers laughed. "We've heard enough of that one from you."

The crowd had grown larger until virtually the whole Tin Cup population surrounded them and the wagon.

Jock had joined them. "Clive, we got our stuff stashed in the wagon. And the teams hitched to the wagon and the riding horses saddled."

"Reckon it's time to go then."

Clive's people and the townspeople mixed to shake hands and say their goodbyes. Clive soon broke free and went around the wagon to check the tarp fastenings and the horses' harnesses. At last, he stopped by Con.

"Several of these folks told me how you whupped that Las Vegas gang. We could use someone like you in the gang. After your daughter gets a little older if you wanna join us for a season once in a while, let me know. I'll be here every spring."

"I'm honored at the offer, Clive, but my wandering days are over."

"I think that after you've traveled a bit it gets in your blood. By next spring you'll be hankerin to get on the road again. After a few days' rest at one end of the trip I can hardly wait to start back the other way." Most of the rest of the gang had saddled up. Josie sat in the wagon's driver's seat. As he turned away, Clive said, "See y' next spring."

Con watched Clive's caravan move out, heard the creak of wagon and harness, the crunch of wheels and hoofs on gravel, people urging their horses on.

Lois said, "Menda's getting fussy, Con. I think she's ready for an early nap."

He grinned. "Too much partying for her today."

Lois turned back to the house. Beulah accompanied her. The rest of the crowd gradually dispersed. Only Doc remained by Con's side.

Con said, "I'm glad you didn't want to make any more of those batteries to sell. I know you're not too lazy to make them. I'll bet you just didn't want to attract the wrong kind of people."

"You guessed it. I'm too old to keep fighting. And I'm sure as hell not gonna do any more wandering."

Con said, "Clive loves wandering. He thinks we should too."

"Yeah. To him, and I quote a statement you made to that asshole in New Hope, 'Life is a journey, not a destination.'"

Con said, "But not for me. My goal was the destination, Tin Cup." He thought of something he had never asked Doc. "But Tin Cup wasn't yours, Doc. Why did you come along?" He realized he didn't really know anything about Doc.

Doc grinned ruefully. "I had failed at my goals. I left San Diego after the pandemic to outrun my ghosts. Haven't lost them yet. Then I found a soulmate with Lucille. She was trying to lose her own ghosts. After I lost her, I decided, fuck goals. Until Spero's theft of my Moveable Feast gave me a new one: to retrieve it and kill the son-of-a-bitch. First person I'd ever wanted to kill. That shows what a thin veneer of civilization covers us.

"When I saw how intent you were on reaching Tin Cup, I decided to help you. Glad I did. You've helped Tin Cup, and it's made you grow up. So here we are at journey's end, neither of us wanting to chase down another road, fight another battle and we're stuck with each other."

Con shrugged. "I guess we'll just have to make the most of it."

Book Reviews are important to authors. They can make a difference whether or not our novels sell. They're useful to other readers as well by helping them decide whether the book is for them. Reviews don't have to be long and wordy. Just put down a few thoughts about what you liked or disliked about the book. If you'd like to leave a review, please click "Search Amazon" and enter "Making the Most of It by Jim LeMay."

About the Author

Jim "Thunder Lizard" LeMay spent most of his working life gathering material for his novels. In the process, his vocations and avocations included waiter, copywriter, editor, commercial artist, homebrewer, bartender, bar owner, land surveyor, civil engineer, land developer and others best forgotten. A few years ago, he decided he was finally ready to create characters and the worlds they live in. He has written a few short stories and five novels, including *Armageddon's Shadow, A Shadow over the Afterworld, Shadow Jack, Shadowspawn and Making the Most of It.* He has lived in many places but now lives and writes character-driven adventure tales in Denver, Colorado.